100

SKEIN OF THE CRIME

SKEIN OF THE CRIME

MAGGIE SEFTON

WHEELER
CHIVERS

This Large Print edition is published by Wheeler Publishing, Waterville, Maine, USA and by AudioGO Ltd, Bath, England.

Wheeler Publishing, a part of Gale, Cengage Learning.

A Knitting Mystery.

The text of this Large Print edition is unabridged.

Other aspects of the book may vary from the original edition.

Set in 16 pt. Plantin.

LIBRARY OF CONGRESS CATALOGING-IN-PUBLICATION DATA

Sefton, Maggie.
  Skein of the crime / by Maggie Sefton. — Large print ed.
    p. cm. — (Wheeler Publishing large print cozy mystery)
  Originally published: New York : Berkley Prime Crime, 2010.
  ISBN-13: 978-1-4104-2951-3 (pbk.)
  ISBN-10: 1-4104-2951-2 (pbk.)
    1. Flynn, Kelly (Fictitious character)—Fiction. 2. Knitters (Persons)—Fiction. 3. Fort Collins (Colo.)—Fiction. 4. Large type books. I. Title.
PS3619.E37S57 2010b
813'.6—dc22   2010021328

BRITISH LIBRARY CATALOGUING-IN-PUBLICATION DATA AVAILABLE

Published in 2010 in the U.S. by arrangement with The Berkley Publishing Group, a member of Penguin Group (USA) Inc.
Published in 2011 in the U.K. by arrangement with The Berkley Publishing Group, a division of Penguin Group (USA) Inc.

U.K. Hardcover: 978 1 408 49291 8 (Chivers Large Print)
U.K. Softcover: 978 1 408 49292 5 (Camden Large Print)

Printed and bound in Great Britain by the MPG Books Group £ 15.47

1 2 3 4 5 6 7 14 13 12 11 10

ACKNOWLEDGMENTS

Once again, I would like to thank my friend Natasha York for her advice and consultation. Natasha is a fellow knitter and an officer with the Larimer County Police Department here in Fort Collins, Colorado. She was very helpful in explaining how illegally obtained prescription drugs wind up on the recreational drug scene.

And a special "thank-you" to my daughter, Serena, a Doctor of Internal Medicine, who explained the various opiate narcotic prescription painkillers and the dangers of abuse. Serena and I have had "Killer Consults" for as long as I've been writing mysteries.

Last, I must point out that the "Golden Lake" resort mentioned in the novel is based on the real Colorado resort Gold Lake, which is every bit as beautiful and peaceful as I've described.

CAST OF CHARACTERS

Kelly Flynn — financial accountant and part-time sleuth, refugee from East Coast corporate CPA firm

Steve Townsend — architect and builder in Fort Connor, Colorado, and Kelly's boyfriend

Kelly's Friends:

Jennifer Stroud — real estate agent, part-time waitress

Lisa Gerrard — physical therapist

Megan Smith — IT consultant, another corporate refugee

Marty Harrington — lawyer, Megan's boyfriend

Greg Carruthers — university instructor, Lisa's boyfriend

Pete Wainwright — owner of Pete's café in the back of Kelly's favorite knitting shop, House of Lambspun

Lambspun Family and Regulars:

Mimi Shafer — Lambspun shop owner and knitting expert, known to Kelly and her friends as "Mother Mimi"

Burt Parker — retired Fort Connor police detective, Lambspun spinner-in-residence

Hilda and Lizzie von Steuben — spinster sisters, retired school teachers, and exquisite knitters

Curt Stackhouse — Colorado rancher, Kelly's mentor and advisor

Jayleen Swinson — Alpaca rancher and Colorado Cowgirl

Connie and Rosa — Lambspun shop personnel

PROLOGUE

Early August

Kelly Flynn navigated her car out of the shopping center parking lot and merged into Fort Connor's thinning late-night traffic. Only a total lack of coffee would force her to stop by the grocery store on the way home from a post-game celebration at her softball team's favorite Old Town café. It was nearly midnight, but some things were too important to worry about inconvenience. Coffee was at the top of that short list.

Her cell phone sounded from the seat beside her where she'd tossed it. Kelly pulled to the right lane and slowed down before answering. Her friend Jennifer's voice came over the line.

"Good, you're still up. Did the game run long tonight?"

"Not really, but we went to our favorite café afterwards. I'm driving home now.

What's up? Why're you calling so late?"

"I'm doing Mimi a favor. She tried calling you guys but forgot you and Megan and Lisa were all playing ball tonight, so she called me. Mimi needs help with one of those beginner knitting classes at Lambspun tomorrow morning. You know, the summer ones with guest teachers. Mimi will be out of the shop in the morning, and Rosa can't spare time away from customers to help, so Mimi asked if one of you guys might be able to. What's your schedule like? The class is at nine and runs an hour, so it doesn't take long."

Kelly ran through her mental day planner. No outside appointments tomorrow, just regular client work. A former corporate CPA, Kelly could now arrange her schedule at will. Her new consulting business was thriving. "Sure, I can manage that, as long as I'll be a helper. I'm not qualified to teach classes."

"Don't worry. Barbara Macenroe is teaching. She's really experienced, too. Have you met her? She's a nurse over at one of the doctor's clinics near the hospital. Tall, big-boned gal."

"That doesn't sound familiar, so I don't think I've met her yet. Does she come to the shop often?"

"I've only seen her late in the afternoons when I've dropped by after the office, so you may have missed her. But she's started teaching classes at the shop, helping take the load off Mimi. Anyway, she's a real 'take charge' sort, so you won't have to worry. You'll be her assistant, that's all. I'd do it, but it's a morning class and I'm working in the café, so I can't."

"Sure. Tell Mimi I'll be glad to help," Kelly said as she turned onto another large avenue. A Big Box store and its sprawling shopping center shone neon bright ahead. "How come you're still up? Don't tell me you and Pete were working a catering job this late."

"Okay, then I won't tell you," Jennifer joked. "Yeah, we were both beat by the time we finished. I just got out of relaxing in the tub. Now I'm heading to bed."

Kelly angled into the left-turn lane. "Me, too, as soon as I get home."

"Steve still in Denver?"

"Yeah. He's starting to stay down there a couple of nights a week. He's gotten some part-time work for another company."

"After working all day for the architect firm? That's rough."

"Yeah, it is. He barely has time to talk, let alone sleep," Kelly said, remembering the brief conversation she'd had with her boy-friend earlier that evening. "At least he'll avoid that morning commute from Fort Connor to Denver. It's beyond awful. I had to get into that rush-hour mess last week when I was heading out to meet my new client near Brighton. Man, it took me nearly two hours to get there."

"I know. I went to a regional real estate meeting a month ago in Denver and allowed over two hours so I wouldn't be late. But I still got there with only ten minutes to spare."

Kelly turned onto the street that bordered her favorite knitting shop, Lambspun. "I hear you. I don't know how Steve stands it." She waited for cars to pass, then turned onto the gravel driveway that ran between the shop and her cottage beside the golf course. Ablaze with lights, the little cottage was the only bright light in the dark. Kelly didn't like coming home to a dark house, especially an empty dark house.

"Steve doesn't have a choice, Kelly. He's only doing what he has to to get through this terrible housing market. I hope things start to improve in a few months. It's brutal out there."

"Yeah, I know, and it doesn't look like it's getting any better."

"Listen, I'm gonna go to sleep. See you tomorrow."

"Bye, Jen." Kelly clicked off her cell phone, then nosed her car into its space in front of the cottage she had inherited three years ago after her aunt Helen's murder. The car's high beams bathed the front of the beige stucco and red-tiled roof cottage in bright light. Kelly heard her Rottweiler Carl barking his "welcome home" bark in the backyard. Carl could always tell the sound of her engine and knew when she returned.

Grabbing her bag, she exited the car and headed down the walk to the steps of her snug cottage. Once inside, Kelly opened the patio door where Carl stood, not so patiently, barking to come in and join her.

"Hey, Carl, how're you doing?" she said as Carl bounded inside, barely pausing for a head pat before heading toward the kitchen. Maybe forgotten food crumbs lingered.

Glancing outside to the concrete patio, Kelly searched for Carl's water dish. "Carl, did you drag your water dish into the bushes again? I swear, you must be dying of thirst by now."

She stepped out onto the patio and scanned the ground for the blue dish when a slight movement to the left caught the periphery of her eye. Turning quickly, Kelly was startled to see a young woman standing only six feet away from her on the patio.

Kelly instinctively jumped back, her heart racing double time. "What the hell?" she cried, staring at the young woman standing in the dark. "Who are *you?*"

The young woman didn't answer. She simply stared back at Kelly, smiling. Kelly could see her features from the lights shining inside the house.

"Who *are* you, and where did you come from?" Kelly demanded, peering at the girl. The young woman appeared college-aged and was slightly built with medium-length blonde hair, a pretty face, and a snub nose. She was wearing a print dress that came to the tops of her knees, and she was barefoot.

Again, the girl made no answer, but her smile grew wider. She clasped her hands together in front of her and began to rock gently side to side.

Suddenly, Kelly knew. *Drugs.* The girl was stoned. Totally. That vacant, not-really-there look in her eyes, that big pumpkin grin, and the rocking. Gently rocking back and forth, as if to some inner music. *Ohhhh, yeah,* Kelly thought to herself.

She'd seen this before. Years ago in college at parties where drugs were freely available. Some chose to partake and temporarily "leave the planet behind" so to speak, and others stayed, feet firmly planted on terra firma. Kelly always stayed planted.

Kelly studied the girl again and lowered her voice, trying once more to get a response. "Where did you come from? What's your name?"

But there was no response. The girl continued to grin and rock back and forth. Kelly backed away toward the patio door and stepped inside the house, sliding the door shut. Then she flipped the lock, just in case. Even though the girl appeared harmless, Kelly wasn't about to take a chance. Especially given that the girl was clearly not in possession of her faculties at the moment.

The girl needed medical help. No telling what drugs she'd taken or how many. There were several apartment complexes across the intersection with the Big Box shopping center. And there were also older neighborhoods housing students bordering the Old Town area. Maybe she wandered down the river trail from one of the parties.

Early September still brought late summer's warmth with it, so nights were extremely pleasant. Perfect for outside parties and gatherings like Kelly had enjoyed with her teammates tonight. On such a nice night, the girl could have wandered from anywhere in the vicinity.

Carl came up beside Kelly and stared through the glass but didn't make a sound. No barking, nothing. That surprised Kelly. Her extremely loving, sweet dog had always lived up to his Rottweiler reputation as a vigilant watchdog. Evildoers usually left Kelly's cottage alone. Whenever she heard his "intruder alert" bark in the middle of the night, she was glad he was on patrol.

"What's up with this, Carl?" she interrogated, as she went for her phone. "How come you weren't barking your head off when I came home? And you never even let on there was a stranger out there."

Carl looked up at Kelly, clearly perplexed by her concern.

"I'll bet you already knew she was spaced-out. Doggy sixth sense, huh?" Kelly punched in the numerals 9-1-1 and felt an anxious twist to her gut. The last time she'd called 911 was years ago when her father was dying of lung cancer and she needed an ambulance.

The police department's dispatcher came on the line and asked Kelly to give her name and her location.

"My name's Kelly Flynn, and I'm here in my home at 1111-A Lemay Avenue. I came home a few minutes ago and found a college-aged girl, a stranger, standing outside on my backyard patio. She appears to be stoned because she doesn't talk or answer questions. Clearly, she doesn't know where or who she is right now. I think she needs medical help."

"Officers will be there shortly, ma'am."

Kelly stood on her front stoop outside with Carl on his leash, watching the activity unfolding between her cottage and the knitting shop. The gravel driveway was crowded with a police car, an ambulance, and a regular-length fire engine. Kelly didn't understand why both an ambulance and a fire engine responded to the dispatcher's call, each with their own EMT or paramedic team. Maybe it was a slow night in Fort Connor. There must be ten people standing about, all surrounding one young girl.

Every now and then, Carl would emit a low bark or "ruff," as if he should be patrolling the entire situation.

"Easy, Carl. They don't need you there. It's crowded enough already."

Two police officers, a man and a woman, had first responded to her call. Their huge black flashlights sent bright arcs of light shining around her cottage as they circled it, then entered the backyard. They found the girl still standing on the edge of the patio, gazing up at the sky. Kelly watched from inside the house as they repeatedly asked her questions. The girl didn't respond to the police, either. She simply continued to smile broadly and rock back and forth as the wail of emergency sirens cut through the night air.

The police officers led the young girl from the backyard to the front of the cottage just as the fire engine had rolled down the gravel driveway, brushing the overhanging cottonwood branches as it did. Kelly grabbed a cola from the fridge and put Carl on his leash in order to watch the proceedings from her front step. Maybe the paramedics would have better luck communicating with the girl.

They didn't. Kelly had watched a team of four encircle the girl. Then one paramedic tried to elicit a response from her while the others checked her eyes, her heartbeat, her skin, all the while asking the girl her name, where she lived, and how she got to this location. To no avail. Kelly was actually surprised all that talking and probing didn't stimulate some kind of response.

Only once did the girl respond. But not to the paramedics. She raised both arms slowly skyward, gazed up into the heavens, and began to sing. Kelly couldn't understand a word and decided she was probably communicating with the "Mothership." She watched the professionals respond to the girl's song by asking more questions. No answers came.

Five minutes later, an ambulance had arrived, and Kelly watched the entire procedure repeated with another team of paramedics. This time the girl stopped singing and simply rocked back and forth the entire time the ambulance team examined her. Finally, those paramedics placed the girl onto a gurney and loaded her into the ambulance.

Kelly drained her cola as the ambulance backed up, yellow lights flashing and the insistent warning sound beeping shrilly before it headed out the driveway. She noticed the two police officers were headed her way. At last. She had a lot of questions. Carl also noticed them and had broken his "down," standing in front of her, on the defensive.

"Easy, Carl. It's okay, it's okay," Kelly reassured him, rubbing Carl's smooth black head as the two officers paused at the end of the sidewalk.

"He okay?" the young man asked, pointing toward Carl.

"Yeah, he'll be okay. Carl, *sit,*" Kelly commanded. "It's okay." Carl needed a slight jerk of the collar to comply, but he sat. "Stay," Kelly ordered, palm up, adding the visual command. "Good boy."

"Nice dog," the female officer said as she and her colleague slowly approached.

"Thanks, he's a sweet boy, but he's also a good watchdog. Good dog, Carl," she said again and rubbed Carl's head.

"Did you check the yard as soon as you came home, Ms. Flynn?" the guy asked.

"No, sir. I came inside and did my usual routine. I let Carl in from the backyard. He came in and didn't let on there was anyone out there, so I was really surprised to see her."

"We realize this must have been pretty frightening," the guy said.

"Well, it certainly gave me a start, I'll say that. To turn around and see the girl standing there so close in the dark . . ." Kelly shook her head. "That was definitely spooky."

"And you said your dog wasn't barking or acting unusual."

"Nope. He acted normal. I have a feeling Carl had already decided she was stoned out of her head and consequently wasn't a threat. Because, believe me, Carl goes ballistic if anybody suspicious-looking shows up, any stranger at all. Even golfers who wander too close, looking for stray balls, set him off."

"I think you may be right. Carl figured it out first, didn't you, boy?" the woman said, smiling.

"Tell me, officers, what do you think she was taking? Any idea? She was totally spaced. I watched you guys try to get something out of her, but nothing. Except the singing."

"The paramedics said she'd probably used either Ecstasy or LSD, judging from how fast her heart rate was," the man replied.

"Will they keep her overnight at the hospital?"

"They'll keep her until she sobers up and comes to her senses. When the drug wears off, they'll try to find the name and number of someone who could come pick her up. Then they'll release her."

Kelly stared off toward the golf course, shrouded in night. "I wonder where she came from. I know there are parties going on regularly in those houses bordering Old Town. Do you think she wandered from over there? I mean, that's a ways to walk, and she was barefoot."

21

"We figured she probably took the river trail," the man said, pointing. "That would bring her beside the golf course where she was bound to see your cottage all lit up. She must have headed straight for it."

"Heading toward the lights, that makes sense," Kelly mused out loud. "Once the university is back in session this fall, there'll be even more parties going on. I sure hope others don't start wandering across the golf course."

The fire truck's big engine revved up then, bright lights flashing.

"I don't think you have to worry, Ms. Flynn," the man called over the sound as he turned to leave. "Odds of something like this happening once is pretty low. The chance of it happening again would be almost impossible. Good night."

"Good night, officers, and thank you very much," Kelly called out, returning the policewoman's wave as she watched the fire engine lumber down the driveway toward the street.

Kelly had always been suspicious of statistics.

ONE

Early September

Kelly hastened across the gravel driveway and up to the front door of the knitting shop, House of Lambspun. Bright annuals bloomed in the pots that dotted the sidewalk and steps. Red, white, and purple petunias, yellow marigolds, blue lobelia, scarlet, white, lavender, and peach impatiens. Summer's temperatures were still holding forth, so flowers were usually safe until later in the month. However, September sometimes brought early snows to Fort Connor and an early end to summer blooms.

Pushing the heavy wooden door open, Kelly paused in the foyer to let her senses drink in the fall colors that had appeared the first days of the month. Right on schedule, Mimi and her shop elves had removed the brighter and lighter summer yarns and repositioned them to other rooms. The foyer and central yarn room were now adorned with autumn's palette of lush, rich, earthy colors.

Browns, the color of rich garden soil and fallen, crushed leaves. Deep forest greens, mushroom grays, gourd yellows, and pumpkin orange. And cranberry, both vibrant and dusky soft.

Kelly wandered into the room, fingers touching fibers as she passed. Wooden bins and shelves lined the walls, and all were filled with the fall colors. She sank her hand into a pile of tweed alpaca and squeezed. Soft, soft. Next she caressed a bin of sage-colored mohair and silk. Luscious. Then another bin of multicolor bulky wools beckoned and another and another.

The shop assistant Rosa walked by, two bundles of yarn in her hands. "Hey, Kelly. Thanks for helping out again. I'm taking care of a customer, but Barbara is setting up in the classroom right now."

Kelly pulled her empty coffee mug from her shoulder bag and headed for the classroom. She'd need a ration of strong coffee before she could face eager students. She walked through the classroom doorway and spotted the tall, big-boned, middle-aged woman she'd worked with before. "Hey, Barbara. You've got me as your helper again. Mimi called this morning and said she was shorthanded. Rosa is busy up front as usual."

Barbara's strong features softened into a smile. "Thanks for coming in again, Kelly. I'll definitely need some help with these new students. Six have signed up for the class, and appearances to the contrary, there's only so much of me to go around." She gave a hearty laugh.

Kelly joined in. "Glad to help, Barbara. As you know, I'm reasonably knowledgeable if it's simple knitting. The complicated stuff you'll have to explain." She glanced around the table, saw the copies of patterns spread out. "What will they be knitting?"

"This is supposed to be an advanced beginner class, so I thought I'd teach them how to make a hat. Starting now, they'll have it finished and ready to wear by winter."

"That's great," Kelly enthused. "Hats are my specialty. Simple hats, you understand. Not the complicated ones. I'm used to doing mine on the circular needles."

Barbara smiled reassuringly. "That's exactly what they'll be doing. I wanted them to start simple and gain even more confidence. They've been making scarves and a couple said they made a pair of mittens."

"That kind of sounds like my path," Kelly

admitted, dropping her shoulder bag onto a nearby chair. "All except the mittens. Those tiny little needles would give me a headache."

Barbara smiled broadly, her dark eyes lighting up. "Oh, you should give it a try, Kelly. If you can knit a hat, you can knit mittens."

"That's what everyone says, but I'm not so sure," Kelly said, grabbing her mug. "Working in such a small space, there's no telling what kind of mistakes I could make. I have enough trouble with bigger projects."

Barbara laughed loudly. "We'll have to see what we can do about that, Kelly."

"Right now I need more caffeine, or I'll be fading soon. Be back in a minute." Kelly noticed two women enter the classroom. "Come on in, you're in the right place," she said as she headed toward the doorway. "This is Barbara. I'm Kelly, and I'm helping, but I'm seriously caffeine-deprived, so I'll be back after a fill-up."

Rounding the corner into the main knitting room, Kelly spied Mimi Shafer, owner of Lambspun, standing beside the long library table where knitters and fiber artists regularly gathered.

Mimi looked up at Kelly's approach. "Thanks so much for riding to the rescue again, Kelly. I've been amazed at the response we've had to these new fall classes. I never thought we'd need to teach two levels of beginners."

"I'm glad I can help, Mimi." She noticed several patterns spread out on the table. "Are you picking out a project for this new class?"

"These patterns are for an advanced class. I'll start off my beginning students with a simple scarf. That's how you started, remember?"

"Wow, that was over three years ago, Mimi. It seems like such a long time." Kelly glanced into the adjoining yarn room and noticed a familiar young woman examining the yarn bins. "Is Holly taking another one of your classes?" she asked, pointing.

A warm smile spread across Mimi's kind face. "Yes, she is. You remember when she started her first class with me last month? Well, she enjoyed it so much she wants to take it again and knit another scarf. She'll certainly be all set for chilly weather later this fall."

Kelly observed the slender blonde dressed in cropped pants and a summery shirt. There was barely any resemblance to the waiflike, drugged-out, barefoot girl who had shown up on Kelly's patio only a month ago.

"What a difference a month makes. Maybe that experience of wandering down the river trail and into my yard was Holly's wake-up call."

Mimi nodded. "Holly has really turned herself around. Now she reminds me of the bright-eyed young girl I remember. She was always tagging along after Barbara's son, Tommy. It broke my heart and Barbara's to see her slip into that college drug scene a few years ago when they both went to college."

"You deserve a lot of the credit for helping Holly make that turnaround, Mimi. You took her under your wing. Brought her here to Lambspun every day after she left the hospital. Watched over her."

"Well, Holly's never really had much mothering since her mom passed away years ago and her dad moved out of town. So I just filled in the gap, I guess." A cloud passed over Mimi's face. "I didn't want to watch another young person be destroyed by drugs."

Kelly remembered that Mimi's only child, her son, had died years ago after taking some unknown drugs at a college party. Now "Mother Mimi," as Kelly and her friends called her, watched over all of them with a maternal eye. Kelly was about to change the subject when she noticed Holly approaching.

"Hey, Holly. How's that class you signed up for at the university going?" Kelly asked.

"It's going good, Kelly," Holly said, a bright smile lighting up her pretty face. She reached over and gave Mimi a big hug. "Hey, Mimi."

Mimi returned her hug and added a parting squeeze. "Is that the yarn you picked out for the class? It's beautiful."

Holly fondled the blue-and-green variegated wool. "Can I still use my size eight needles?"

"Absolutely," Mimi reassured her, giving Holly a pat on the arm.

"I hear you're taking another of Mimi's classes. You'll be passing me before you know it," Kelly teased.

"Are you kidding?" Holly retorted. "I'm just hoping I don't screw up as badly as I did on the first scarf."

"Don't worry. It'll turn out wonderfully," Mimi said, giving Holly another squeeze. "Come on, let's head to class."

"Oops, thanks for reminding me. I've got to get coffee before my class starts. Barbara will think I bailed on her." Kelly gave a wave, then raced down the hallway to the café at the rear of the shop.

"Okay, your head measures twenty-one inches," Kelly said, examining the tape measure. "So look at the pattern and tell me which size hat you'd be knitting. Do you know how to figure out how many stitches to cast on?"

The young woman stared at the pattern and replied, "That would be medium-sized, so I'd cast on sixty-three stitches. Three times the measurement."

"That's right. Now get your circular needles and settle back and start casting on. There are some stitch markers on the table. I'd advise putting one every twenty stitches as a guide. It'll help later when you're finishing the hat."

The young woman, who appeared to be in her early thirties, like Kelly, peered at the metal needles attached to each other by a round piece of plastic approximately the same size as the needles. "I'm trying to remember how I cast on for the scarf. That was several weeks ago."

Instead of jumping in right away and casting on for the woman, Kelly held back. She remembered how well-meaning friends often "helped" her out when she was starting by casting on stitches for her. But that actually slowed down her learning. Sometimes it was better to struggle along for a bit and see if the stitch "memory" came back. If not, she'd gladly show the woman how to cast on again.

"Well, take a few minutes and see if it comes back. If not, just give a yell."

Kelly glanced over at the other five students seated around the table, all in various early stages. One older woman was slowly casting on with methodical, neat stitches. Another younger woman, college-aged, sat on the other side of Kelly. She'd cast on her first row and was busily knitting away on the next row. There was always a "star" in every class, Kelly noted. The other three were middle-aged and were still casting on their first row of stitches. Barbara was helping the last woman learn how to cast on.

Kelly noticed that each one used a different method. She'd been told early that there were scores of ways to cast on stitches, and whatever worked for an individual knitter was fine. As long as the stitches got onto the needle and stayed, you were good to go.

She glanced back to the young woman she'd been helping and saw several stitches appear on her needle. *Success.* "Hey, you remembered. Good job," Kelly praised as she pulled up a chair beside the girl.

"Patty reminded me how to wrap the yarn around my fingers," she said with a nod to the college-aged girl on the other side of Kelly. "So, I kept fiddling with it until it came back." Her fingers slowly formed the twisting motion, needle going over and under to form a stitch.

"Thanks for stepping in, Patty," Kelly said to the other girl.

"No problem," Patty replied, her needles forming more stitches.

Kelly watched the first girl cast on several more stitches, then leaned back and took a big drink of the dark, rich coffee. Having a café at the rear of the knitting shop was too convenient. Plus the grill cook, Eduardo, made his coffee as black and strong as Kelly liked it. She couldn't do better herself. Consequently, Kelly had a running tab at Pete's Porch Café.

Kelly took another sip, then spoke. "I saw Holly a few minutes ago. She's taking Mimi's beginner class again. I'm amazed at the way Holly has turned herself around, Barbara. She's even taking a class at the university."

Barbara looked up with a worried expression. "Frankly, I'm amazed, too. I just hope

32

it lasts. I've watched Holly try to change her dangerous habits before. Unfortunately, she always falls back into those old ways after a while."

That wasn't the response Kelly had expected. "Well, let's hope this last experience scared her enough into changing for good. She's such a nice kid."

Barbara wagged her head. "That's the problem. She's still a 'kid.' Holly's never really grown up, despite all our help. She still expects other people to solve her problems."

One of the knitters looked up from her needles. "Who's Holly?"

"Someone Kelly and I tried to help," Barbara replied in a clipped tone. "Now, let's get back to these hats. Who hasn't finished casting on yet? I can help you if you need it."

The older woman held up her hand. "I've been going slowly. I didn't want to make a mistake."

"We all make mistakes, so don't worry about it," Barbara reassured. "Here, let me see what you've got so far." She picked up the woman's needles and examined the stitches.

Patty leaned over to Kelly and whispered, "Barbara has known Holly for a long time.

We all kind of grew up together and went to the same school. Plus, her son has been dating Holly ever since college. Believe me, Barbara isn't happy that Tommy is still together with Holly."

Kelly glanced up at Barbara, who was immersed in instructing the older woman how to cast on in a more efficient manner. Every family had a drama, Kelly thought to herself. If you look beneath the surface, you'll find it.

"Oops, something's wrong," the girl on the other side of Kelly said, staring balefully at her needles. "There's a stitch missing. Right there. See, it's just a loop. How'd I do that?"

Kelly leaned next to the girl, examining the stitches. "It's easy. You simply dropped a stitch, that's all. I can still do it if I'm not careful. Don't worry." She repeated Barbara's advice. "Let me show you how to pick up the stitch."

"Hey, I'm glad to see you," Jennifer said as she walked into the main knitting room. She dropped her large knitting bag onto the table beside Kelly. "How'd the class go this morning?"

"Very well, actually," Kelly said, continuing the hat she was knitting. "Barbara has them all knitting hats so I was in my element."

"All right," Jennifer said as she settled into the chair beside Kelly. "Who's this hat for?"

"Steve. I thought I'd knit him one to go with that scarf I made for him a couple of years ago." She fingered the soft gray tweed yarn. "I hope he likes it."

"I'm sure he will," Jennifer said, pulling out a scarlet red sweater. Nearly finished already, Kelly noticed.

"He's not out on the building sites anymore, but I figured he could wear it skiing," Kelly added. "If he can find time to ski this winter."

"Ooo, don't talk about winter when it's so pretty outside," Megan scolded as she walked into the room. "I'm hoping for a long fall like last year."

"You know Colorado," Jennifer said, looking up from her sweater. "There's no guarantee from one year to the next what the weather will be. It's always a gamble."

"Don't I know it," Megan said, plopping her bag on the table. Settling into a chair across the table from Kelly and Jennifer, she withdrew a shamrock green wool.

"Your color, Megan," Kelly observed. "No one can wear that green as well as you can with your fair skin and dark hair. Are you doing a sweater?"

"Yeah, but it's for Marty, not me this time," Megan said, picking up the stitches she'd begun. Only five rows appeared on her needles. "So, I hope this green looks just as good with bright red hair. It's against knitting rules to mess up your boyfriend's sweater."

"Not to worry. I saw Marty wear a bright green scarf once last winter and it looked great," Jennifer said.

Megan glanced over to Kelly. "Another hat? Don't you have enough hats, Kelly? I swear, you've gone overboard in the hat department."

"This one is for Steve. I'm hoping he can wear it skiing this winter. Assuming he has time to ski." Her voice couldn't conceal her concern.

Time was something Steve didn't have enough of. Ever since he'd started working with the architectural firm in Denver in July, spare time had evaporated. Kelly had envisioned summer would be a repeat of the year before — hiking and camping in the mountains, sleeping under the stars with Carl by their sides. Plenty of baseball and softball games, plus summer nights in Old Town with friends Megan and Marty, Lisa and Greg, and Jennifer and café owner Pete.

But it didn't happen. Steve had thrown himself into his new job in Denver, hoping to make enough money to keep his business going. Kelly got to play ball and go out with her friends, but Steve was rarely there. When he did get home, they'd grab a pizza on the way to a game. Kelly would stay, and Steve would go to his Old Town office instead, trying to keep his own construction business afloat. By the time he returned to the cottage, he'd fall asleep beside Kelly, exhausted.

Megan glanced over at Kelly. "Maybe the housing market will get better this winter. What do you think, Jen?"

Jennifer gave a deep sigh before answering. "I wish I could say that will happen, but I really don't think so. There are still too many houses for sale now, and buyers are looking for bargains. That's why they're scooping up those foreclosure homes."

"Let me guess what you guys are talking about," Lisa said as she strode into the room. She pulled out a chair beside Megan. Long blonde tendrils had escaped the scrunchy hair band holding back Lisa's hair. She pulled out a multicolored shawl and picked up her stitches. "How's Steve holding up?"

"As well as you can expect, considering

Steve," Kelly observed wryly. "He can't control any of this, and it's driving him crazy. He's holding on, but if Jennifer's right, I don't know what will happen. If he loses Baker Street Lofts . . ." Kelly's voice trailed off.

Baker Street was the project nearest Steve's heart. The one he'd dreamed of doing ever since he was in college. Remodeling an old warehouse in Old Town into a distinctively designed building with offices below and trendy loft apartments above. With their great view of the Cache La Poudre River meandering nearby, the lofts had sold out quickly as had the retail space. But now . . . the constantly deteriorating real estate market was causing chaos all over northern Colorado, including Steve's last building site in Wellesley.

Lisa's pretty face puckered into a worried frown. "Darn it, I hadn't planned to mention this, but I guess I have to." She looked over at Kelly with concern. "Another foreclosure sign appeared at Steve's Wellesley site. I saw it this morning when I drove into work. I'm sorry, Kelly."

Kelly winced. "Damn," she said softly, so as not to disturb customers who were browsing the yarn bins lining two walls of the knitting room. Bookshelves stuffed with books and magazines on every fiber subject imaginable lined the other two walls. "I can't tell him, I just can't."

"Don't worry. The mortgage company will tell him," Jennifer said gently. "I saw that sign today when I took a buyer out to look for foreclosed homes."

"Damn, damn, *damn*," Kelly repeated in frustration, her stitches getting tighter. The emotions ran straight through her all the way into the yarn. "Now Steve will have to work even harder. He's just started to work a second job at night to earn extra money. This builder-developer guy, Fred, hires extra architectural help whenever he needs it. It was only a couple of nights a week. Now he'll have to work more, which means he'll be staying in Denver more."

"It'll get better, Kelly, it's got to," Megan said, her face revealing her concern.

"Will Steve be coming back this weekend?" Lisa dropped her knitting on her lap. "We'll all get together at our place and have one of those crazy games. That always seems to relax him."

"I don't know if that will work this time," Kelly said. "We'd better take him out to the batting cages instead. Let him take it all out on the baseball."

Jennifer placed her hand on Kelly's arm.

"Steve will get through this, Kelly. We'll all help him. There are only three foreclosures over at the Wellesley site —"

"Don't forget the one at Baker Street," Kelly remarked bitterly. "That was the cruelest blow. I mean, he's watching everything he's built up over ten years as an architect and builder crumble right in front of him. And no matter how hard or how much he works, he can't stop it. It . . . it just breaks my heart to watch."

Kelly's friends sat in silence, not saying a word. Finally, Lisa spoke again. "Has Steve ever thought about taking on a partner? I mean, an investor, maybe. Someone who'd like to have an interest in prime Old Town property? I know how Steve feels about Baker Street, but desperate times call for desperate measures."

Kelly let Lisa's words play through her mind. It was not the first time she'd heard them. "I actually suggested that to Steve once, but he didn't want to talk about it."

"He may have to, Kelly," Jennifer added. "Every builder in town is in the same boat. Some have folded already. If Steve wants to pull through this hard time, he may have to take on an investor."

"I agree with you, Jen, but Steve won't even discuss it. He just shuts down —" A woman's loud voice cut into their conversation suddenly.

"That sounds like Barbara. I wonder who she's talking to?" Jennifer said.

Kelly glimpsed Barbara through the classroom doorway, standing next to the loom, cell phone pressed to her ear.

"Tommy, you have to stay in Denver and study. You *can't* keep coming down to Fort Connor to babysit Holly. She has to learn to take care of herself," Barbara said, a distinct note of pleading in her tone. "Holly will be fine. She doesn't need you here —"

"Uh-oh," Kelly said. "I think I know what that conversation is about. Someone in this morning's class said Barbara's son is the boyfriend of the same girl who showed up in my backyard last month. You've probably seen her here at the shop. Cute little blonde named Holly."

"Oh, yeah, I've seen her a few times," Megan said. "Looks like she's doing okay now."

"She's really turned herself around since August," Kelly continued. "She's even taking a class at the university."

"That's because Mimi practically adopted her. She had Holly over here at the shop every day, keeping her busy," Jennifer added.

"Mother Mimi," Lisa said, fingers working the colorful yarn.

"You know, I still can't believe she wandered from Old Town down that river trail and wound up on your patio," Megan said. "That would have freaked me out."

"Well, it did give me a start."

"A start!" Megan snorted. "I would have screamed so loud it would have woken the dead."

"How'd she get there, again?" Lisa asked.

"She probably looked across the golf course and saw the cottage all lit up across the greens. I always leave the lights on when I'm coming back late. I don't like walking into a dark house."

Megan shook her head vigorously. "Me, either. I even leave the music on. Marty's been working late several nights lately."

"You know, Megan, if you're that spooked, you ought to get a dog," Kelly said. "I never worry about my safety as long as Carl is there. He scares away anybody who's up to no good."

"Well, I wouldn't be so spooked if there hadn't been six women assaulted this past summer." Megan shuddered as she knitted.

"Megan, those women were all walking alone in the wooded areas of town or on the trails late at night," Kelly said. "You're safe in your apartment."

"That girl, Holly, is darn lucky someone didn't grab *her* on the river trail that night," Megan added, knitting at warp speed.

"You better believe it," Lisa chimed in. "Six attacks in three months. It's enough to make me want to get a dog."

"You can borrow Carl if you have an urge to walk at night," Kelly said with a smile.

"I couldn't imagine walking down that dark trail at night. All the drunks go there to sleep it off. Scary."

"Well, it was clear that all of Holly's brain cells weren't working that night, so decision-making was definitely impaired," Kelly said.

She glanced up to see Barbara talking with the shop owner, Mimi, in the central yarn room. They were obviously having an animated conversation. Barbara was gesturing, clearly agitated.

"Actually, most of those drunks are rolled up sound asleep under the trees," Jennifer observed as she brushed her auburn hair behind her ear. "I know, because I helped with the last census. Our group had to count the homeless who were on the streets in Old Town. The ones sleeping outside and all."

Lisa looked up. "Really? What'd you guys do?"

"We were assigned to small groups to

survey different areas. My group was assigned the river trail section down from Old Town. We had to walk the trail in the middle of the night and shine our flashlights along the ground and under the trees all along the river. That's where these guys usually roll up and go to sleep. It was cold as hell as I recall, especially at three o'clock in the morning in February."

"Whoa, that must have been scary down there." Megan's blue eyes were huge.

"Well, we were together in our little clusters, so we were okay. And they gave us doughnuts and coffee afterwards."

Kelly chuckled. "Is that all they paid you?"

"Oh, no, we got a paycheck. That year was a downturn, too, so I was scrambling for money."

"Did you find many homeless sleeping outside?"

"Several, as a matter of fact. Not everybody can get into the Mission. Especially on a cold winter night. It fills up quickly."

"Well, hello, girls," Mimi said, greeting them as she entered the knitting room. "It's so good to see all of you at once." She scanned the yarns each of them was working. "Megan, that's your color," she added with a grin.

"It's for Marty, so make sure you tell him

it looks good when he wears it," Megan said.

"How's Barbara doing, Mimi? We couldn't help but overhear some of her phone conversation," Jennifer said. "She really sounded upset."

Mimi's smile disappeared. "Oh, she is. With good reason. Her son, Tommy, is making some very poor decisions right now."

"It sounds like you know the families well," Megan said.

Mimi settled into the chair at the end of the large library table where they all sat working their yarns. "Yes, I do. I've known Barbara for years from church. And I watched both Tommy and Holly grow up. Holly was over at Barbara's house as much as her own. Holly's mother died several years ago, so she lived with her father. But he worked long hours and was out of town a lot and didn't really supervise Holly. So she kind of grew up without much direction. She and Tommy were friends from childhood in school together, and they just gradually became boyfriend and girlfriend. That was okay with Barbara, except Holly got addicted to the party scene and drugs when she and Tommy went to the university a few years ago." Mimi sighed and glanced across the room toward the paned windows. "Tommy concentrated on his studies, but

Holly stopped studying and dropped out."

"It sounds like Tommy made the right choice," Kelly offered.

"Yes, he did. Tommy went on to become an honor student. He got his degree in premed and worked as a paramedic for three years, trying to get a scholarship to medical school. And this year he landed a plum." Mimi's eyes lit up in maternal delight. "A full scholarship to the University of Colorado School of Medicine in Denver. Barbara is so proud. She's raised him all by herself. She and her husband were divorced when Tommy was a baby."

"That's great, Mimi. Tommy deserves congratulations," Kelly said. "But Barbara didn't sound happy on the phone a few minutes ago. What did she mean 'babysit Holly'? This girl in class, Patty, grew up with Tommy and Holly, and she says Barbara's not happy Tommy's still dating her."

"That's Patty Warren, and she's right. Barbara's worried that Tommy's attachment to Holly will jeopardize his medical studies. He moved down to Denver in August, right before Holly's last drug escapade. Med school started in August, but he's come back to Fort Connor every weekend to make sure Holly's okay. He tries to study, but it's hard when Holly keeps calling him."

Mimi's worried frown pinched her pretty face. "I worry about Holly, too, but we can't babysit her. Holly has to learn to be strong on her own and not lean on Tommy. Apparently Holly calls Tommy every day in Denver and several times a day when he's here trying to study on the weekends."

"Uh-oh, not good," Lisa commented, glancing up. "Holly sounds like a manipulative personality to me."

"Spoken like a psychology major," Megan said with a grin.

"It sounds to me like Tommy needs to make better decisions," Kelly interjected. "I've had friends in med school, and that's a whole lot of homework. He can't run back and forth to Fort Connor and still do his work. What's the guy thinking?"

"I know, Kelly," Mimi nodded. "And you're right. But Tommy's always felt responsible for Holly, so whenever she needs him, he drops everything and rides to the rescue."

Kelly shook her head. "He's going to lose that scholarship if he's not careful," she warned.

Mimi flinched. "Oh, please don't even say that."

"As intriguing as this little drama is, I have to leave," Jennifer said, shoving the red sweater back into her bag. "Pete has a catering job and I have to meet him over there at five thirty. So, I'll see you guys."

Kelly checked her watch and saw it was nearly five o'clock. "Oops, me too. See you tomorrow, Mimi. I've gotta go back and feed Carl and myself before practice tonight." She pushed Steve's hat into her bag. "Where are we practicing, Megan?"

"At the ball fields near Rolland Moore Park."

"Oooo, wasn't that where the last woman was attacked? She was walking through the trees bordering the fields," Lisa said, pushing back her chair.

Megan looked at Lisa, aghast. "Thank you *so* much for reminding me. Now that's all I'll think about on the way to practice tonight."

"You gotta get a dog, Megan," Kelly said as she headed for the front door.

TWO

Kelly examined the drilling company documents Curt had handed her. "So it looks like all the wells are producing. They're all online and up and running, right?"

"Yep. Gas is flowing smooth and easy. You've got a good patch up there in Wyoming, Kelly girl." Curt leaned back in the booth at the coffee shop. "Those royalty checks are pretty substantial, too," he added with a grin. His suntanned, weather-lined face revealed a life spent outdoors watching cattle and open land. Denim shirt and jeans. Stetson hat resting on the booth seat. Curt was the picture of a Colorado rancher. He was also Kelly's trusted mentor and advisor.

"Yes, they are, Curt, and they're certainly nice. That's the only way I could let go of the alpaca accounting clients. The income from those royalty checks allowed me to make that change." She took a sip of coffee.

Strong coffee, just the way she liked it. "Of course, when I took on those two new consulting clients you introduced me to, that made all the difference. I could let every one of the alpaca clients go except Jayleen." She smiled at him over her cup.

"Jayleen's real grateful you're keeping her on. She's gotten used to having a CPA do her work." Curt grinned. "Kinda like once you taste sirloin steak, you can't go back to hamburger."

Kelly had to laugh. "Those bookkeepers are hardly hamburger, Curt. They're good, experienced accountants and they'll take care of the rest of my old clients." She looked out over her favorite Old Town coffee shop. Non-corporate and non-chrome, the walls were covered with paintings from local artists. There was even a large rendition of Van Gogh's *Starry Night* taking up half of one wall, giving the coffee shop its name. "I'd gotten really fond of several of them, but . . ."

"But the work just wasn't challenging enough, right?" Curt sipped his coffee. "I wondered how long it would take before you got bored. Every time I asked about your job, your answers got shorter and shorter. Face it, Kelly. Alpaca ranching doesn't provide the same challenge as Bob Houseman's company, right?"

"You're right about that. Houseman's got properties all over northern Colorado."

"And now that you've taken on Werner Development, I guarantee you won't lack for challenge."

Kelly took another sip of coffee and watched the customers line up for lattes and other specialty drinks. "I can't thank you enough for recommending me to those companies, Curt. That was perfect timing."

"Well, I was watching you and kind of figured out when was a good time, judging from your restlessness. Plus, the Wyoming wells were settling in and producing at a steady rate, so I figured you'd be receptive to my suggestion." He grinned over his cup. "It's nice to be successful, isn't it?"

"Ohhhh, yeah," Kelly said with a laugh. "In fact, I think now would be a good time for me to refinance the cottage and get out of that awful loan Aunt Helen made three years ago. It's been over two years, so those penalty clauses have run out."

"That sounds like a good idea, Kelly girl. You're a successful businesswoman now with significant assets in your name. So, you'll be able to get a loan when a lot of folks can't."

Kelly ran her finger around the rim of her

coffee cup as the word "successful" shimmered in her head. Curt was right. She had created a successful business in the years since she'd come back to Fort Connor for her aunt's funeral.

"I wish I could spread some of that success around, Curt. Steve's in such a bad place right now. It's really heartbreaking to watch him work so hard, and things keep getting worse, not better."

Curt shook his head in the manner of someone who'd endured his share of economic hard times. "I know, Kelly. This is the roughest construction downturn I've seen. I know he's barely hanging on. I've seen those foreclosure signs at his sites. And I heard about the apartment in Baker Street."

"Maybe you could talk to him," Kelly suggested, leaning over her cup. "Suggest that he take on an investor. That would take off the pressure of losing those properties. He's taking on extra work in Denver so he can earn more to keep those bank loans current."

"I'd be glad to suggest it, Kelly, if there were any investors out there to talk to. But they're scarcer than hen's teeth right now. They've gone to ground, just like the buyers."

"Damn," Kelly said softly. She lowered her voice, so as not to be overheard by neighboring tables. "I was hoping there was someone out there who'd like a stake in prime Old Town property."

"I'm sure there is, Kelly, but right now they can't get investment loans. The money's not there." His expression turned solicitous. "They'll come back into the market, Kelly. It's just a matter of time."

Kelly gave a snort. "Time is something Steve doesn't have anymore, Curt. He's watching everything he's built up over the last ten years crumble away before his eyes. And Jennifer says it won't be over anytime soon. I don't know how long he can hold on."

Curt leaned over the table. "Believe me, Kelly, I'd loan Steve the money myself, but he wouldn't accept it. I actually offered last month when he started driving down to Denver. He thanked me and said he'd handle it."

"Damn!" Kelly said louder, not caring this time if anyone overheard. "That's stupid. I thought for sure he'd accept help from you. I mean . . . he won't take it from me." She gestured in aggravation. "I offered, but he looked at me with this shocked expression and then said, *'no way.'* "

"Steve's not going to take money from you, Kelly. So don't even ask him," Curt advised sagely.

"But *why?* He'd give me money if I needed it."

"Steve's too proud to accept help from anyone right now, Kelly. And especially not you."

"But if investors can't get loans, I may be the only one who could."

"It doesn't matter, Kelly. Steve's not going to take money from you. You know that," Curt said with a wry smile.

Kelly did know that. When she'd first made a tentative offer to help him get through this rough patch, Steve looked at her as if she'd grown another head. A mixture of shock and horror.

"Arrrrgh," Kelly complained, dropping her head into her hand. "It makes no sense."

Curt chuckled. "Sense isn't the reason a man and a woman get together in the first place, Kelly." Then added, "You know that."

Kelly grabbed her over-the-shoulder briefcase and her coffee mug, then slammed her car door. She had to have some of Eduardo's coffee — extra-strong coffee — before she tackled the Houseman accounts. And she was going to work in the knitting shop instead of her cottage. She was still stewing over her earlier conversation with Curt concerning Steve. The more Kelly thought about Steve and his "pride," the more annoyed she became.

She heaved the heavy wooden door open and sailed through, heading into the foyer toward the main knitting room, drinking in all the colorful yarns. She'd drop her brief-case first, refill her mug, then settle in with her laptop. Maybe all the warm and fuzzy yarns and fall colors would put her in a bet-ter mood. As she turned the corner, she saw retired Fort Connor detective Burt sitting at the library table talking with a young man who looked to be college-aged. They both turned at her approach.

"Don't stop talking, Burt. I'm just drop-ping off my stuff and getting coffee."

"That's okay, Kelly, this young man wants to meet you," Burt said with his genial smile. "Kelly, this is Tommy Macenroe, Barbara's son. Tommy, meet Kelly Flynn; she's the one who lives in the cottage across the driveway."

Tommy leaped out of his chair and ap-proached Kelly, hand outstretched. "Ms. Flynn, I wanted to thank you for helping my girlfriend, Holly, last month. Thanks to you, Holly got the medical help she needed."

Kelly shook his hand, observing the earnestness in his brown eyes. Tommy was tall and slender and had a nice face. "You can call me Kelly, and I'm glad I was there to help. My cottage was the only bright spot along the dark golf course, so I'm sure that's why Holly headed for it."

"Well, I'm glad she found you at home. I don't want to think about what might have happened if she hadn't found someone to help her."

"Tommy's a paramedic, or at least he was until last month when he moved to Denver to attend medical school," Burt said, his smile revealing a paternal pride.

"Yes, I've heard about your accomplishments from Mimi. Congratulations, Tommy. Not many people can snag a med school scholarship," Kelly said, letting her admiration show.

"Thanks . . . thanks both of you," Tommy said, a slight blush creeping up his still youthful face. "I was really fortunate."

Kelly dropped her things on the table. "I've observed that good fortune usually occurs to those who're prepared. Mimi told me she's known your mom for years and watched you grow up. Did you meet Burt at church, too?"

"Actually, Tommy and I met on a traumatic occasion, Kelly. He was one of the paramedics on the ambulance that responded when my wife had her heart attack four years ago." Burt looked over at Tommy. "I've kind of taken a fatherly interest in Tommy since then."

"I always appreciate your advice, Burt," Tommy said, then glanced at his watch. "I'd better get going. I have to find Holly and talk to her before I drive back to Denver."

Kelly couldn't help her reaction. "You drove in from Denver today just to talk to Holly? Why didn't you call her on the phone?"

Tommy gave her a sheepish look. "Well, I need to explain why I can't stay here in town this weekend like I have before. My anatomy professor scheduled a Saturday study session. I just want to make sure Holly understands." He shrugged. "I want to make sure she's okay. Holly doesn't really have anyone else in town, except my mom and me. Her mom's dead, and her dad moved to Florida."

"Holly seems to be doing really well now," Kelly said, settling into a chair beside Burt. "I'm so glad. She was totally out of it the night she showed up on my patio. Couldn't remember her name or anything. She couldn't communicate at all."

"I know, that's what happens when she's taken Ecstasy. I got her to swear to me she wouldn't take it anymore. She promised," Tommy declared.

"I'm glad to hear that. Those hallucinogenic drugs are dangerous. I saw kids in college get pretty messed up with those. Let's hope Holly stays away from them for good."

Tommy nodded. "This last time really scared her. She's sworn to me she's done with them." Moving toward the doorway, he added, "It was great to see you again, Burt. And, Kelly, nice meeting you, and thank you again."

"No problem, Tommy. Good luck with those med courses."

"Keep your nose to the grindstone, okay?" Burt added.

"You bet." Tommy gave a wave and hurried for the front door.

Kelly stared after him for a moment, then leaned back in her chair. "Boy oh boy, let's hope Holly stays on course."

Burt shook his head. "We can only hope, Kelly."

"Mimi was at the table the other day, and she filled us in on the long history between those two. She also said Tommy has come down to Fort Connor every weekend to make sure Holly's okay since her incident. Not good, Burt. His medical studies require his full attention."

"Yeah, I know." Burt sighed. "It's a shame Holly can't seem to get herself together and stand on her own two feet. Tommy's got too many demands on him now to run back and forth from Denver to check on her."

Kelly pondered what Burt said, then decided to speak her mind. "I think you're letting Tommy off the hook way too easily. Holly can't force Tommy to leave his work and drive back to Denver. He chooses to do it."

"Yeah, well, apparently Barbara's told Mimi that Holly whines and cries whenever Tommy tries to say 'no.' So, he caves in."

Kelly shook her head. "You know, I only met Holly a month ago, so I don't have any past history with either of these two kids like you guys do. So I'm just telling you what I see. It appears to me that Holly depends on Tommy to take care of her. Mimi says she calls Tommy every day and even when he's here in town trying to study. That sounds like manipulative behavior to me, Burt. And Tommy is allowing himself to be used, for whatever reasons. He needs to grow a backbone and learn to say no. If he's serious about becoming a doctor, he's going to have to make hard choices, and this is one of them. He doesn't have time to study and pass medical school exams and do the class work *and* be at someone's beck and call. No matter *who* that someone is."

Burt sent Kelly a wry smile. "I have to hand it to you, Kelly. You nailed it. I felt the same way at first, but I've allowed my friendship with Barbara and Tommy to cloud my objectivity in the situation. It's good to have you around, Kelly."

Kelly grabbed her mug and pushed back her chair. "Well, you've done the same for me, Burt, so I thought I'd return the favor."

Steve pulled off his tie and tossed it to the coffee table. His suit jacket was already across a chair. He plopped down on the black leather sofa, leaned his head back, then let out a long sigh.

"Rough commute, huh?" Kelly said, settling beside him, her favorite microbrew in hand. Steve was already upending the bottle with the colorful label.

"Yeah, Friday-night bad." He tipped back the bottle again. "Can we order pizza or something? I don't feel like driving anywhere. I'm beat."

"Well, the gang is already gathered at Lisa and Greg's. Pizza's already delivered," she said, feeling slightly guilty for even suggesting it.

"Awwww, hell . . . I don't feel like seeing anybody tonight, Kelly. I just want to crash."

Kelly put her hand on his arm. "I know, but they're really anxious to see you. It's been nearly a month since we've gotten together. Everyone's there. C'mon," she coaxed. "It'll relax you."

Steve let out a sigh that came from inside. "Okay, let me change clothes." He gave Carl a head rub. "You drive, all right?"

"Deal."

"Smells like pepperoni," Steve said as he sank onto the love seat in Greg and Lisa's living room. Kelly settled beside him.

"Dig in, Steve. These starving beasts have already gone through two boxes," Megan said, gesturing to Marty beside her on a sofa and Greg across the coffee table.

Jennifer placed two bottles of Kelly's and Steve's favorite Colorado microbrew on the coffee table. "There's a sausage and cheese pizza in the kitchen, if you guys would rather have that," she offered as she settled into a chair beside Pete. "And Pete brought two of his raspberry pies."

"Whoa, that's worth driving through all that Friday traffic," Steve said, a crooked smile forming. "Thanks, Pete."

"No problem," Pete said with his genial grin. "It gives me an excuse to indulge. Gotta stay away from the customers' pies in the café."

"We're supposed to stay away from those?" Jennifer looked over in feigned surprise. "Uh-oh."

Kelly watched Steve gobble up two slices of pizza while their friends teased each other about dessert weaknesses. She wasn't sure, but she thought she saw Steve's shoulders relax.

Steve glanced around the living room of Greg and Lisa's rental house — one of his Wellesley houses. "You guys have added more stuff since I was here last. Looks good." He inhaled another pizza slice.

"Thanks. Since we now have more wall space than we did in our condo apartment, Greg and I could bring out those pictures we've been storing in the closets," Lisa said, her hand resting on Greg's shoulder as he sat beside her.

After another two slices, Steve tipped back a beer. "Let me know if you see any action on those foreclosure houses, would you, guys?"

"Sure, Steve, absolutely," Greg answered, his normal teasing grin disappearing.

Kelly watched all her friends' expressions change once Steve mentioned the source of his current economic problems.

"Don't worry, Steve, I'm keeping a close eye on Wellesley. I've taken a couple of foreclosure buyers here already," Jennifer added, sipping from a canned soda.

"Bless you, Jennifer," Steve said. "Were they serious buyers or just looking?"

"They act serious, but there are a lot of foreclosure houses in northern Colorado to look at. So they aren't anywhere near a decision. And even if they were, who knows if they could get a loan," Jennifer said with a worried frown. "The mortgage market is in total chaos. People with good credit, good jobs, and savings in the bank can't get loans. It's ridiculous."

"Tell me about it," Steve said, finishing the last piece of pepperoni pizza.

"This won't last forever, buddy," Marty said, resting his arms on his legs as he leaned over. "Jennifer was telling us the buyer demand for these foreclosures is building. Banks have got to loosen up the credit soon."

"We hope," Kelly said as she went over to the green-and-black granite counter to retrieve the sausage and cheese pizza.

"Any nibbles on the Baker Street condo?"

Megan asked, clearly concerned.

"None yet," Steve said, then drained his beer. "And I just got an e-mail from one of the retail tenants that they're going out of business, so they'll be moving their stuff out this month."

"Whoa . . ." Greg said softly, balancing his beer bottle on his knee.

Silence settled over the group as Kelly watched each of her friends ponder the implications of what Steve said. Another Baker Street tenant moving out meant less rent received, and that would make it even harder for Steve to keep up with the payments on the new loan he'd negotiated, which covered both the Wellesley and the Baker Street Lofts properties. Kelly chewed her lip, wishing she had something reassuring to say, but she had run out of words. The continuing wave of bad real estate news washed away what feeble encouragement she might offer.

After another quiet moment, Pete leaned forward, hands clasped between his knees. "Hang in there, Steve. You're doing everything you can to keep it going," he said in a quiet voice. "Jen said you've taken on some extra work in Denver. Are you consulting or what?"

Steve shook his head. "Naw, consulting is

too risky right now. All the companies have cut back. So I hired on at night with a Denver builder who needed extra help drawing up plans for a Northglenn shopping center he's building."

"Wow, how was he able to get funding?" Marty asked before he grabbed a sausage and cheese slice.

"He had it nailed down before this downturn started."

"What are you doing exactly, Steve? Making architectural drawings?" Lisa asked.

"Yeah, and checking all the specs. Believe me, it was a challenge. I hadn't done much commercial work since I was in grad school in architecture. So, it was a struggle at first. But I've settled in now, so it's coming easier. Plus, all the software programs have improved so much."

"What kind of hours are you working, Steve?" Greg asked, slipping a slice of pizza from the box.

"Hey, save the rest for Steve and Kelly," Lisa scolded. "You and Marty ate nearly two pizzas yourselves."

"Ahhh," Marty said, with a satisfied grin. "And delicious they were, too."

"I'm working as much as I can, actually," Steve said, balling up his paper napkin and dropping it onto his plate. "I've been going over to Fred's office straight from the architectural firm around five thirty a couple nights a week. But I'll have to start working more, now that the other foreclosure has popped up here in Wellesley. And that guy's moving out of Baker Street." He sank back into the sofa and toyed with his empty beer bottle.

Kelly settled beside Steve and placed her hand on his shoulder, touch trying to convey what words could not.

"So, we may not be seeing you much, I guess," Megan offered after a minute of quiet. The ticking of Lisa's grandfather clock was the only sound.

Steve gave her a wry smile. "I'm afraid not, guys. Marty and Greg can have my share of the pizza."

"He's promised he'll come back on Saturday nights if he can, so we can all get together then . . . maybe," Kelly offered, not sure if that would happen or not. *Who knows how much time they'd have together?*

Marty slapped his hands on his knees. "Well, since we don't know when we'll see you next, maybe this is the time to tell you some great news."

"Yeah, please. We can use it," Lisa said, tearing off a piece of pizza.

Marty and Megan looked at each other

and grinned, then turned to the others. "I asked Megan to marry me, and she said yes," Marty announced. Megan grinned beside him, her face flushed.

Kelly stared at Megan, then Marty, mouth open. She hadn't expected this. She glanced around the circle. The rest of her friends looked just as surprised.

"Oh, my God!" Lisa cried, hands to her face. "You're getting *married!*" She leaped from the sofa and raced over to embrace Megan. "That's wonderful!"

Kelly and Jennifer immediately joined Lisa, swallowing Megan in hugs and good wishes. Greg, Steve, and Pete clustered around Marty, slapping him on the back amidst heartfelt congratulations.

"I'd say that announcement calls for raspberry pie," Pete said as he headed for the kitchen.

"I'll make coffee," Lisa said, popping off the sofa again. "Ohhhh, this is so exciting. When's the date, or don't you know yet?"

Marty sank back into the sofa beside Megan and put his arm around her shoulders. "We haven't decided for sure yet, but probably fall of next year."

"You're waiting a whole year?" Jennifer asked.

"Yeah, there's a lot to do. Organizing

everything, guest lists, catering, scheduling the reception. It takes at least a year," Megan said, finishing off her beer.

"Reception, that means food," Greg said, eyes alight.

"Ohhhh, yeah. A lot of it," Marty added. "Pete, I don't know whether to ask you to do the reception or not. I'd rather have you be a guest and have a good time."

Pete looked up from slicing the raspberry pie and smiled. "That's okay, Marty. I don't do weddings anymore. I learned long ago that brides and their mothers can drive you certifiably crazy. But I can recommend some caterers who do an outstanding job."

"Oh, lord, I don't even want to think about the lists Megan will make," Kelly said, settling beside Steve. "They'll be down to the floor."

Megan grinned. "I'm going to start this week."

"Why are we not surprised?"

Greg shook his head. "Megan, are you sure you want to attach yourself to this guy? I always thought you were sensible."

Megan reached over and placed her hand on Marty's knee. "Yeah, I do. He's kind of grown on me over these last two years."

"Sounds like a fungus," Greg said, accepting a plate of pie from Pete. "You can go to the doctor and get cured."

Megan and the others laughed out loud while Pete and Lisa distributed the pie. Kelly took a bite and let the delectable taste of berries melt on her tongue. Then looking over at the flushed happy couple on the sofa, Kelly added, "I'm not sure that would work, Greg. I think Marty may be totally incurable."

THREE

Kelly and Steve slowed to a jog as they reached the golf course. The Sunday-morning sun was creeping over the foothills, sending blinding shafts of early sunshine across the greens. September always brought the scent of fall to the air even though the temperatures were mild, often balmy. Kelly could still smell the difference in the early morning, particularly when she took her run.

"What's your plan for today? Head over to your Old Town office?"

Steve slowed to a walk and stretched his arms over his head. "Yeah. Go over all the bills that have piled up since last weekend. Figure out how I'll pay everyone. Rather, how much I'll pay each one."

They neared the cottage backyard, and Carl spotted them. He started his welcoming bark. "You want me to bring you something for dinner?"

"Why don't you pick up some takeout and a DVD and we'll stay in tonight. I'm hoping I can finish by five or six." Steve stretched his arms behind his back as they walked around to the front of the cottage.

"You look tired already," she observed. "I hope you can finish up earlier and come home and crash."

"So do I. Let's see what's waiting for me. What have you got on tap for today?"

"I've got some account work to do. But first, I promised Mimi I'd help out with some of her classes. She scheduled a special kids' knitting class today, and she's a little short-handed since Rosa's had to cut back her hours."

"What's up with Rosa?"

"Same thing as with everyone else," Kelly said, scooping up the rolled newspaper from the sidewalk. "Her husband's construction job was cut so Rosa's had to start working another part-time job in addition to working here at Lambspun."

Steve wagged his head. "Brother . . ."

Kelly unrolled the paper as she followed Steve up the steps to the front door. "You go ahead and jump in the shower while I make coffee . . . *Whoa!*"

"What?"

"Oh, no! A girl was killed on the river trail

71

night before last."

Steve leaned over Kelly's shoulder as they stood in the front doorway. "You're kidding? That's right in our backyard."

"Maybe it was that guy who's been attacking women on the trails. That's awful! They gotta catch him."

"It could be more than one guy. Meanwhile, swear to me you'll stay off the river trail after dark when I'm out of town, okay?"

Kelly looked up to see Steve's worried face. "Absolutely. No way am I going on that trail alone."

"Any information about the victim?" Steve asked as he headed toward the bedroom.

Kelly skimmed the article as she walked into the kitchen. "No, they usually don't give out much when they first report something. They have to contact next of kin. *Damn.* No one's ever been killed before. Why did that happen?"

No answer from Steve this time, only the sound of the bathroom shower starting to run. She retrieved coffee from the fridge and started the coffeemaker brewing, then leaned back against the counter to finish the article.

Only the barest of details were mentioned. *A young woman was found dead on the river trail early Saturday morning.* Kelly and Steve usually ran along that same stretch of trail every morning but decided to go the opposite direction that day, following the trail into Old Town instead. She hadn't heard any sirens blaring late Friday night, nor seen any flashing lights sweeping the darkness of the golf course when she and Steve returned from Greg and Lisa's around midnight. Carl had barked a few times. But then, he usually heard something to bark about in the middle of the night.

Who would be foolish enough to walk at night along the river trail? The newspapers and media had been reporting every one of the assaults for the past few months. All of the victims were women walking alone at night. Maybe this woman was a new university student from out of town who didn't know about the attacks.

The ding of the coffeepot sounded, and Kelly sniffed the delectable aroma of fresh-brewed coffee. Checking the clock on the microwave, Kelly dropped the newspaper on the counter and returned to her morning routine. A hungry dog, a hot shower, and a busy schedule were waiting — in that order.

"Okay, now slip the tip of the right needle underneath that last stitch on the left needle," Kelly instructed the young girl beside her.

The sixth-grader stared at the rows of stitches Kelly had cast onto the circular needles for her. "Like this?" she asked as she shoved the needle beneath the right side of the stitch.

"That's the right side. Slip it under the *left* side of the stitch." Kelly refrained from moving the needle herself.

She remembered that she learned faster when she was allowed to fumble through the stitches herself. Learning by doing.

The youngster tried again. This time she slid the needle over the left side of the stitch. "Like this?"

"Almost. Make sure the needle you're knitting with goes *underneath* the left-hand needle." She watched the girl slowly move the needle to the correct position. "That's right. Now, you hold both needles by the tips while you use your other hand to wrap the yarn from the back to the front."

"How do I do that?" the youngster asked, clearly perplexed.

"Here, let me show you, then you can do it." Kelly reached over and took both needles from the girl's hands. Placing the fingertips of her left hand near the tips of the two needles, she held them in place.

74

"You can hold the needles tightly but not in a death grip. Like this. Just tight enough to keep the stitch in place so you can wrap the yarn." She took the dangling strand of yarn and slowly wound it from the back of the bottom needle, through the middle where the two needles crossed, and to the front. "Now you do it." She unwrapped the yarn and handed the needles back to the girl.

"I'll try. They're kind of wiggly." She tentatively accepted the needles.

"I remember them feeling like that when I first started. Then before you know it, it starts feeling different. You don't feel as clumsy as you do at first."

"Got that right," another girl down the table said.

Kelly glanced at the eight sixth-grade girls in Mimi's junior hat class. Each one was in a different stage of progress on the beginnings of their first hat.

"Hey, guys. I still feel clumsy, so don't worry about it," Kelly confessed.

"I think I got them," the youngster said, holding the tips of the two needles with her fingertips.

"Okay, make sure you're holding them tightly enough so they won't fall, then start to wrap the yarn." She watched as the girl tentatively picked up the yarn strand with her right hand and brought it forward. "That's right. From the back, between the two needles, and to the front."

"Now what?"

"Now you take the tip of that right needle again and slide the stitch on the left needle, then slide that stitch from the left needle to the right."

"That sounds confusing."

"Well, it makes more sense when you see it happening. Go ahead."

"Okaaaay . . ." the girl said dubiously. She slowly slid the right needle under the stitch and slipped it off the left needle onto the right. She blinked up at Kelly, surprised. "Like that?"

"Exactly like that," Kelly congratulated. "Good job. Now do the next stitch."

"Whoa, I think I forgot how to do it all."

"Just slip that right needle under the stitch on the left needle, and I bet it'll all come back to you," Kelly said, hoping to infuse confidence. "You did a great job. You learned faster than I did when I started."

"No way," the girl countered.

"Yeah, way. I made more mistakes than a dog has fleas." Some of the girls laughed softly, while others stayed focused on their knitting, rows forming on their needles. The little Megans, Jennifers, and Lisas of the world.

Burt walked into the knitting room carrying a large plastic bag filled with creamy white wool fleece. "Hey, Kelly, that's nice of you to come by today and help Mimi with her class."

"Well, I thought it would help relax me before I start my account work this afternoon. Speaking of relaxing, why don't you pull up a chair and sit and spin while we knit away?"

"I was thinking of doing that very thing," Burt said. "Hey, girls, mind if I sit and spin awhile? I'll be glad to answer any questions you might have."

All eight girls nodded their heads, peering at Burt's spinning wheel as he settled into the corner. He set the large bag of fleece on the floor beside him and grabbed a handful of fluff.

Kelly watched Burt gently stretch the handful of wool fleece, drafting the fleece into what spinners called *batten* or *roving*. She glanced around the table at the eleven-year-old beginning knitters. Their attention had obviously shifted from their knitting to Burt's activities. She decided this was an ideal time to stoke their curiosity.

"Do you know what Burt's doing now?"

she asked them as she walked beside the table. She pointed toward Burt. "He's stretching the wool fleece so he can spin it."

"Is all that wool from one sheep?" a girl asked.

Burt looked up with a smile. "Oh, no. This bag contains the fleeces from two sheep."

"Does the wool come off the sheep looking like that?" another asked.

Kelly knew the answer to that one. "Oh, no. The original fleece when it comes off the sheep is pretty dirty. It's filled with dirt and bits of twigs and leaves and stuff. Once the sheep shearer comes with the razor and takes off the fleece, it has to be cleaned and washed."

"Washed? How? In the washing machine?"

Kelly and Burt laughed along with the girls. "Actually, yes. The fleece can be washed in a machine. But first, you have to card it to get the dirt out. They do that with metal brushes that brush through the fleece to get out all the dirt and leaves and stuff."

"Boy, that sounds like a lot of work," a girl at the end of the table said, picking up her knitting again.

"It is, believe me," Burt said with a chuckle. "I've done a lot of it."

"What kind of combs do you use?"

"Well, they're actually brushes," Burt

explained, then motioned to Kelly. "Check in the spinning room, would you, Kelly? I think there are some brushes there."

Kelly went into the small room adjacent to the main knitting room where bags of colorful fleece sat beside luscious wound skeins of hand-dyed wools and mohairs, silks and alpaca, ready to be spun together into custom yarns. Scanning the crowded room, she grabbed two carding brushes on the table and returned to the class.

"Here you go, girls," she said, holding them up. "I'll pass them around. See those metal teeth? They're designed to catch all the dirt and leaves and stuff that gets caught in the sheep's fleece over the winter." She handed it to the first girl at the end of the table.

"Take some of this, Kelly, and show how they brush it," Burt suggested, handing her a chunk of the fleece.

Kelly took the bunch of fleece and placed it on one brush, then used the other brush to brush through it. "See, it's tricky, and it does take a long time."

"Isn't there a machine that does that?" someone asked.

"Matter of fact, there is," Burt answered. "But they're expensive so most spinners do it by hand. But, there are people who do it as a business. Spinners who want to pay to have their fleeces done take it to someone who'll card it, get out all the dirt and stuff, then they'll wash and dry the fleece."

Kelly remembered that Curt Stackhouse's late wife, Ruth, used to provide that service for spinners before she died of a heart attack years ago. "How expensive is it, Burt?" she asked as she watched each of the girls around the table take a turn trying to brush the fluffy fleece.

"Well, it's not cheap, but it's really a matter of whether it's worth it to you or not. Some people don't have much time to spin each day, and they'd rather pay someone to do the time-consuming task of cleaning and preparing the fleece. That way they can spend their time doing what they like best — spinning." Burt pulled another handful of fleece from the bag and began drafting again.

"Why do you have to do that before you spin?" a girl sitting closest to the wheel asked.

"You want to stretch the wool's fibers so it's easier to go through the wheel," he said, stretching the fibers for them to see. "We call it roving or batten once it's stretched. And after I've got a bunch of roving, I'll start to spin."

Kelly noticed most of the girls returned to their knitting, hats slowly forming on their circular needles. But they kept glancing up at Burt, watching the pile of fluffy roving grow in his lap. Once it did, Burt looked up at them with a smile.

"Okay, now I'm ready. Who's ever watched a spinner before?"

All the hands shot up in the air as each of the girls vied for Burt's attention, waving their hands as if they were in the classroom. Waiting to tell their stories.

"We went to the Renaissance Fair, and there was a whole bunch of them there," one girl said.

Others nodded and added their own stories of colonial demonstrations at school and the county and state fairs. Burt dutifully paid heed to each account and encouraged the girls to talk. Burt would have made a great teacher, Kelly decided.

"Okay . . . now that I've got a lapful of roving I can start spinning," Burt announced and pulled the wheel closer. "Take a look at the yarns you're knitting with. Hold them up and see how thick the strands of wool are. I'll bet each one of you has a different thickness."

The girls began to examine their yarns, holding up individual strands and comparing with each other's. "See, Burt's right," Kelly said, pointing around the table. "Yours is thicker than hers. I'll bet no two are the same."

"Does that happen when you spin the yarn?" a girl beside Kelly asked.

"Yes, it does," Burt answered. "And I'll show you how we do it. Spinners control the thickness of the yarn by how much roving they feed onto the wheel. Let me show you. You'll notice there's already yarn on the spinning wheel. See how it goes from the wheel over to the spindle, this funny-shaped thing. That's where it winds the yarn." He pointed to each part. "Now, we can control the thickness of the yarn by the amount of roving we let pass through our fingers onto the wheel. Watch."

Burt began the familiar movements, explaining as he went along. "First, we start the treadle going as we feed this roving onto the yarn that's already on the wheel." As Burt's feet began to work the treadle, the roving began to slide through Burt's fingers and onto the wheel, binding to the strand of yarn already there.

"See how the yarn is getting thicker now that I've added more to it," Burt observed. "If you want a thinner yarn you add less roving. If you want it thicker, then you add more."

Every girl around the table focused on Burt, seemingly fascinated. Kelly understood. She loved to watch the spinners, too. Burt, Mimi, anyone. She found it relaxing to watch. Even though Mimi and others had suggested Kelly might want to try it herself, she declined. There was no way she could get her feet coordinated with the wheel. She'd seen what happened when spinners let their fingers and feet go different speeds, and it wasn't pretty.

"That's cool," one of the girls decreed after a minute or so of watching.

"Yeah, it is," another agreed.

"Well, if any of you girls are interested, we were thinking of offering a kids' spinning class this winter," Burt announced. "On Sundays, like today."

Mimi appeared in the archway just then. "Well, it looks like you've captivated my junior hat class, Burt. Nobody's knitting anymore. Everyone's watching you spin."

"Guilty, Mimi." Kelly held up her hand. "I decided it was a good opportunity to show the girls how the wool got into those skeins you have on the shelves. "We're busted, girls. Better get back to those hats."

"Anyone need help?" Mimi offered, strolling around the table, eyeing the beginning projects.

A couple of hands shot up, and conversation started flowing around the table again as the girls picked up their knitting where they left off. Kelly decided this was as good a time as any for a coffee break. She walked over to Burt's corner and beckoned.

"Why don't we go have some coffee and let Mimi get these kids back on track?"

"Sounds like a good idea, Kelly," he said, rising from his wheel. "I could use some coffee before I start drafting again."

"You're a great teacher, Burt," Kelly said as they wound through the central yarn room toward the hallway that led to the café. "You really had the girls enthralled back there."

"Thank you, Kelly. I have to confess I love nothing more than working with a group of youngsters who're eager to learn."

"Well, I think you just planted some spinning seeds today. I wouldn't be surprised if several of those girls wanted to take classes." Kelly paused in the entrance to the café. Sunday morning busy. Jennifer and Julie, the other waitress, were loading their trays with plates of yummy breakfast dishes. "Wow, I always forget how crowded the café is on weekends."

"Mmmm, smells good," Burt said as they

headed toward the grill. "Makes me want to eat all over again."

"Don't start, Burt. If you weaken, so will I." She held out her mug to the grill cook. "Hey, Eduardo, could we get a refill, please? Then, I promise we won't bother you again."

"No bother, Kelly," Eduardo said with his usual grin. "Let me grab a pot. Jen and Julie are busy with customers."

"We noticed. Is that Pete busing tables?" Kelly pointed toward the dining room. "You must be shorthanded. Someone didn't show up for work, right?"

Eduardo poured a black stream into Kelly's mug, then Burt's. "You got it. Saturday-night curse. Late parties and everyone's hungover Sunday morning."

"Thanks, Eduardo," Burt said as he and Kelly maneuvered their way back toward the knitting shop. Jennifer spotted them and gave a hurried wave as she scurried through the dining room.

Kelly took a sip of the hot black nectar. "Ahhhh, I needed that," she said, eyes closed, tasting.

Burt chuckled. "I don't know how you can drink it right away as hot as it is."

"Practice. Learned how in college. My throat is probably cauterized by now." She took another sip as they wandered back into the shop, bins of yarns spilling over with tempting tactile creations. Kelly trailed her fingers over several skeins, and another thought came forward. "Have you read the newspaper today? Did you see where a young girl was found dead on the river trail? Sounds like it was on that section of trail near the golf course close to here."

Burt's smile disappeared. "Yeah, I saw it. That's a damn shame."

"Do you think it's related to those assaults that have been happening these last few months?"

"I don't know, Kelly. No one's ever been killed before. One woman was hit several times when she fought back against her attacker. But they still don't know if there's more than one guy who's attacking women."

"Have you talked to your old partner in the department yet?"

"First thing this morning. I left a message on his cell. I haven't heard back yet, because I'm sure they're still trying to sort through what they've got. But he'll give me a call when he can."

"Do you think it was a college student, Burt? Someone who hasn't been here these last few months and read about the stalker?"

Burt shrugged. "Who knows, Kelly? That's

certainly one possibility." He stood and sipped his coffee as he stared out the window.

Kelly glanced at her watch. "Well, I'd better get back to helping Mimi. Steve's working at his office all day, of course, so I'll be doing some account work at home. Give me a call whenever you hear something, okay?"

"Will do, Kelly."

Suddenly Kelly remembered something else she wanted to tell Burt. The newspaper's ugly headlines had swept the good news out of her head temporarily.

"Hey, Burt, has Megan given you guys a call yet?"

Burt look puzzled. "Megan? No, why?"

Kelly grinned. "Well, she will be. She and Marty gave us the good news Friday night. They're engaged. Isn't that great?"

Burt's face broke into an enormous grin. "That's fantastic news, Kelly! Boy, wait'll we tell Mimi. Do you want to do it after class?"

"Perfect. Mother Mimi will be ecstatic."

Kelly clicked out of the spreadsheet, then checked her watch. It was nearly six o'clock and Steve hadn't called yet. She'd left a message earlier that dinner was warming in the oven and beer was in the fridge, so she expected him to pull down the driveway any minute.

She glanced outside into the gathering dusk, then back to the blinking cursor on her computer screen. Might as well keep working. Kelly was about to open another spreadsheet when her cell phone rang. *At last.*

"Hey, you'd better get home soon. That Indian food is driving me crazy warming in the oven," Kelly said into the phone.

"Well, I'm afraid Mimi and I aren't very hungry tonight, but thanks anyway, Kelly," Burt's voice sounded. "I thought I'd give you a call because I heard from Dan."

"Oh, yeah, what have they learned? Or can you say?" Kelly logged off her computer and shut it down.

"Well, they've been able to establish identity of the young woman. Some of the hospital staff recognized her from last month. It's Holly Kaiser."

Kelly slowly rose from her chair, a chill settling over her. "Oh, no! That can't be. I just saw Holly the other day at the shop. She . . . she's been doing so well. What happened? What was she doing on the river trail?"

"I know, Kelly, I don't know what possessed her to go there, unless she was drunk or high again."

"Don't tell me she was on drugs again."

"They won't know until the medical examiner takes a look. They were able to identify Holly from the hospital records of her previous admission last month. She was unresponsive and unable to communicate then, so they fingerprinted her to see if she matched any missing persons. Little did they know, they'd be using those same prints to identify her body a few weeks later."

"I can't believe it! It's bad enough Holly got on drugs again. But then she wandered back to the same trail when that vicious attacker was waiting for his next victim. That's *horrible!*" Kelly walked to her living room and back as she talked.

"We don't know if Holly's death is connected to the assaults or not, Kelly. Police don't know how she died. Dan's not saying much yet, which tells me they're not sure. He did say there was a bump on the back of her head, but no mention of a head injury. He also said she wasn't sexually assaulted."

"So, what do you think happened, Burt?"

"I don't know, Kelly. And I'm not even going to speculate until I hear from Dan after he's seen the medical examiner's report."

"This is awful, simply awful. How's Mimi doing?"

"Not too good, Kelly. As you know, she lost her son to drugs years ago. And she'd become very close to Holly lately. She's in the bedroom crying now. It's hard."

"I'm so sorry, Burt. Tell Mimi she's in my thoughts."

"I will, Kelly. I'm sorry to be telling you this tonight, but you asked me to call."

"That's okay, Burt. I'm glad you did." She paused in front of the patio door, looking out into the darkening sky. Only last month Holly was standing on Kelly's patio. Stoned out of her mind, but alive.

Suddenly another image came into Kelly's mind. "Oh, no, Burt . . ." she breathed. "Who's going to tell Tommy?"

All Kelly heard was a long sigh on the other end of the phone.

FOUR

"Hey, good to see you," Kelly said to Lisa as she entered the knitting room. "I'm glad I decided to take a morning break now." She plopped her bag on the library table and settled into a chair.

"My therapy schedule keeps getting shifted around," Lisa said, barely looking up from the fuzzy orange red scarf she was working on her needles.

"Have you seen Mimi today? How's she doing?" Kelly asked.

"She seems okay. Quiet and subdued, but that's understandable. It sounds like she'd kind of adopted that girl. So, naturally Mimi's been grieving."

Kelly let out a sigh. "And I'm sure all this brings back sad memories of her son's death, too."

"Any news on how Holly died?"

"Not yet."

Kelly pulled Steve's winter hat from her

bag and shifted away from the sad topic. "How're your psychology classes going this semester?"

"They're getting harder. In fact, I'm only taking one class this semester because there's so much reading involved. And we have to write three big papers." She screwed up her face in displeasure.

"I know what you mean, Lisa. I used to hate writing those papers, too," Kelly commiserated as her fingers went through the familiar movements. Slip the needle under the stitch, wrap the yarn, slide the stitch. *Slip, wrap, slide.* Over and over. Steve's hat was halfway done. She'd definitely have it finished soon. In plenty of time for the winter cold.

"And the professor isn't half as interesting as Dr. Norcross."

"Well, that's about par for grad school, Lisa, you know that. You get winners and losers. Some professors can't teach their way out of a paper bag. They just stand up there and read from their notes. They might as well post everything online and save people the trouble of going to class."

Lisa snickered. "You're dead-on, Kelly. I had a deadly one like that last semester. I thought I was going to pull out my hair. The only thing that kept my sanity was Dr.

Norcross's class."

Lisa's mentor and advisor. Kelly was about to ask how the class was going when Jennifer sailed into the room.

"Wonderful. Two for the price of one. Now I can visit with both of you on break." Jennifer sank into a chair beside Kelly and withdrew the burgundy sweater she was now knitting.

"You guys busy this morning?" Kelly asked.

"Not that much, actually. Typical Monday-morning slow."

"Have either of you seen Megan or talked to her since we got together Friday night?" Lisa glanced up from her orange yarn.

Kelly shook her head. "I haven't seen her. What about you, Jen?"

"Nope. Which means she hasn't been in here because she always stops in the café for an Earl Grey to go."

"That's kind of unusual, isn't it? Megan always comes over here to get away from her crazy clients," Lisa added.

"Boy, I'm glad I don't work in IT. I've had to consult with this new client's IT guy so I could get all the data I needed for this developer's project. And I swear, it was like pulling teeth. He's positively anal."

Jennifer snickered. "I know the type.

93

They're usually sitting around the office on the desktop computers doing research and wondering why they don't have any clients. Clients aren't on the computer. They're outside. You've gotta go out and get 'em."

"Speaking of clients, how's that going?" Kelly asked.

"Not well, to be honest. The buyers who're looking are still browsing, and even if they were ready to buy, most of them nowadays wouldn't qualify. Like I said the other night, good jobs, good credit, and savings in the banks used to guarantee a loan. Not anymore."

"Does that mean I won't be about to refinance Aunt Helen's loan on the cottage? It's been over two years and the penalty clause is no longer in effect. I wanted to lower those payments."

Jennifer tilted her head to the side. "Actually, you're a different case, Kelly. You'll probably be able to get a loan because you've got what they call *significant assets.* You own all that land in Wyoming and the gas leases. And you've got savings in the bank on top of that. Most people have a job and some savings. Maybe a small retirement account, that's all. That used to be enough, but not anymore."

"So, you're saying I would get the loan,

then?" Kelly probed.

"Yeah, I think so. Do you want me to check with some of the lenders we work with? I can get a feel for what their responses would be and get back to you."

"Thanks, Jen, that would be great."

Just then a mini-hurricane blew into the shop. Megan charged into the main room with two over-the-shoulder bags. Cheeks flushed, jet-black curls rumpled, Megan looked frazzled.

"Hey, we were just wondering when we'd see you again," Lisa said, glancing up from her scarf. "No one's seen you."

"That's because I'm moving so fast, I don't show up on anyone's radar screen." Megan dropped both bags to the table and sank into a chair beside Lisa.

"What's up?" Jennifer asked, shifting her attention from the burgundy yarn.

"What *isn't* up?" Megan said, before taking a sip from her mug.

"Don't tell me you've started on wedding preparations already?"

Megan fixed Kelly with a look. "You don't want to know. I called my folks on Saturday to tell them the news, and my mother's gone completely nuts. She must have called me three times on Saturday and four times on Sunday." She rolled her eyes.

95

"That would be a 'yes' on the wedding preparations," Jennifer said with a smile.

"Your mom's getting excited, I guess," Lisa said. "That's understandable."

"Ohhhh, she's beyond excited. And she's beginning to drive me crazy. First, she wanted me to have the wedding back home in Minneapolis, but I told her 'no way.' I've been living in Colorado for six years, and this is my home now. Marty's a Colorado guy, and all our friends are here. Well, that just made her cry. She said all the aunts and uncles would want to come, and not everyone could fly out to Colorado. Of course, that made *me* feel awful and selfish, but I absolutely do not want to go back to Minnesota for the wedding. All those relatives can come out here or not come. Marty and I want to have our wedding in Colorado. It took me all day to get her calmed down."

"Wow, she sounds 'high-strung,' as Jayleen would say," Kelly joked.

"Ohhhh, yeah." Megan nodded vigorously. "You see, my sister Karen eloped with her boyfriend, so my mom didn't get to plan a wedding for her. So, she's really hyper about planning this one. And she must have spent Saturday night on the Web because she called me early Sunday morning with a

96

list of potential Colorado wedding 'venues,' as she called it." Megan closed her eyes and let out a sigh. "Woke us up, too."

Kelly and her friends laughed softly at Megan's descriptions. "What's on her list, Megan? Anything you can live with?" Lisa asked.

"Several, actually, but they're totally out of our price range. Like the Stanley Hotel in Estes Park, for example."

Jennifer laughed out loud. "The Stanley? It's gorgeous, but it's also way expensive and booked over a year in advance, too, from what I've heard."

"Yeah, my mom wasn't too pleased to hear that."

"Plus you could have snow up there in Estes. Didn't you guys say the wedding would be next fall? Then, we can plan on having snow. Anytime from September on, snow is possible in the high country," Kelly said.

"More like probable," Lisa added.

"I told her that when she first suggested it, but she didn't pay attention. Thank goodness the Stanley was already booked for nearly two years out. Whew."

"What else is on her list?"

"Ohhhh, let's see, places like the Brown Palace in Denver, the Broadmoor in Colorado Springs . . ."

Kelly had to join in the laughter that rippled around the table now. "Whoa, those places would cost an arm and a leg to rent. Is your family rich or something, Megan?"

"No, my dad's a college professor, and my mom's an office manager of a supply store. So I guess this is all just wishful thinking and dreaming on Mom's part."

"What's Marty say to all this?" Jennifer asked.

"Oh, he just ducks out of the room to laugh whenever my mom calls." Megan pulled a royal blue vest from her knitting bag and picked up her stitches. "I tell you, I had just begun this vest Saturday morning before my mom called, and look how much I've finished." She held up an almost finished vest. "This is how I kept my sanity on the phone with my mom."

"Wow, maybe that's why my knitting takes longer," Kelly mused. "I don't have any crazed relatives calling to nag me."

"Where would you and Marty like to have the ceremony?" Lisa asked. "You haven't said."

Megan's fingers picked up speed. "Actually, we'd love an outdoor ceremony if we could guarantee a beautiful fall day. But this is Colorado. There are no guarantees.

Weather changes in a heartbeat. But it would be gorgeous to be standing in some little valley surrounded by pine trees with the snow-capped mountains in the distance."

Kelly could picture that. She understood the call of the mountains. Gorgeous, captivating views. Kelly had been captivated herself. So much so, she'd actually bought mountain property to enjoy the views. Unfortunately, that property had a history of conflict attached to it, and Kelly willingly let it go. Now, she shied away when the mountains started singing their siren song.

She had gotten used to living in town now and was no longer sure she wanted to drive back and forth into the canyon every day and night. Especially on winding, twisting roads. Canyon living was beautiful, but driving could be treacherous, especially in the winter. Kelly had personal experience with that.

"Boy, that does sound pretty." Lisa looked off into the yarn room. "Maybe there are places in the canyons that you could rent for the ceremony. You know, then we could all come back into town for the reception."

"I don't know, that sounds like double the work," Megan said dubiously.

"You know, Megan, there are places that

schedule weddings and receptions near Rocky Mountain National Park," Jennifer offered. "I was at one several years ago. They had the ceremony down near the creek right by the water. Then the reception was held inside this main building that had a dining hall and outside decks and all that. It was really pretty."

Megan brightened. "Really? Where is it? What's it called?"

"Oh, I know which place you're talking about," Lisa broke in. "I went to a day meeting there. It's private, but it's right outside the entrance to the national park."

"Guys, that's still in Estes Park over seventy-five hundred feet up. Bad weather blows in fast there."

Megan dug in her bag. "Let me write that down anyway, so I can check with the park service."

Mimi walked into the room then, arms filled with yarns. Her somber gaze swept the table, landing on Megan, and her face lit up. "Megan! I'm so glad you came in. I heard the wonderful news, and I wanted to give you a big hug." Mimi dumped the yarns onto the table and hurried over to Megan.

They both embraced. "Oh, I'm so excited for you," Mimi said. "We all need some happy news around here." She squeezed Megan again. "I bet your family is ecstatic."

"Crazed is more like it," Megan said when they separated. "My mom is so excited she may not last a year till the ceremony."

Mimi laughed. "I'll bet. Have you two decided on the date yet? You mentioned a year from now."

"Yeah, we have some savings goals we're trying to meet first. Plus, it looks like we'll need all that time just to organize things."

"Well, I'll be more than happy to help you organize if you need me. After all, you did such a tremendous job with our wedding."

"Uh-oh, Megan," Kelly warned with a grin. "It's payback time. Remember how you ran Mimi and Burt ragged getting their wedding organized."

Everyone around the table laughed at that memory. Burt and Mimi were exhausted.

"Actually, I could use your help organizing this thing, Mimi. And I may have you try to calm my mother down. She's gone into hyper–wedding planner mode. My sister didn't have a wedding so it's all come down to me, I guess. I'm going to need some help with her. To keep her from driving me crazy."

"I understand," Mimi said, patting Megan's arm. "I'll be glad to talk to your mom and tell her everything that's available here in Fort Connor. Catering firms, musicians, hall rental, and all those things."

"Whoa, I didn't know you knew all that, Mimi," Lisa said.

"Oh, yes, I used to organize a lot of parties for the university when I was still married to my husband. So, I've got lots of contacts. Plus, several of my customers are in the business, too. Burt and I didn't use them because our ceremony was so small."

"Fantastic!" Megan exclaimed. "Mimi, you're a gold mine."

"Have you given any thought to what sorts of catering you'd like? Sit-down dinner, large buffet reception?"

"Matter of fact, no. We've just started thinking about the wedding and trying to settle on the exact date. We haven't even made lists yet," Megan admitted sheepishly.

"*What!* No lists? Megan, I don't believe it," Lisa exclaimed, hand to her breast. "You're going to have to start thinking about food, wines, liquor, reception halls, music. And lots more stuff."

Megan held up both hands. "I know, I know. Just thinking about it stresses me out. It's easier to plan other people's stuff. When it's yours, it's different."

"Don't forget a dress," Jennifer added

with a grin. "You'll have to choose a gown or something. Unless you two plan to get married in your softball jerseys and cleats."

Kelly laughed at the picture Jennifer created. "That would be kind of cute." She could almost picture Megan and Marty now, standing at home plate saying "I do."

Lisa rolled her eyes. "Only Kelly would think so. Speaking of dresses, are you going to have bridesmaids? Are we included?"

"Of course!" Megan declared. "I just wish I could have all three of you guys as maid of honor, but I'll have to choose my sister to keep my mom happy. But you guys will be my bridesmaids and you'll be in charge of keeping track of everything so I can enjoy the ceremony."

Kelly saluted. "Got it, Imperial Commander. We hear and obey."

"Oh, no, don't get her started."

"Just make sure you consult us when you decide to pick colors, okay?" Lisa said. "I went to a wedding once where all the bridesmaids were in charcoal gray, and it looked like a funeral."

"Okay, no gray, I swear," Megan promised with a nod.

"Why don't you come back tomorrow morning, Megan?" Mimi suggested. "I'll gather lots of magazines from my friends and we can start looking through everything and getting ideas. And we can make some notes."

"That would be great, Mimi," Megan said, visibly relaxing. "Thank you for helping me get organized. I've had so much IT work lately that I haven't had a chance to even think about the wedding except to listen to my mom."

Mimi reached out and patted Megan on the arm. One of Mother Mimi's maternal "pats." Meant to reassure. "And if you'd like information on jewelers, then Burt and I can help you with that, too. We've both lived in Fort Connor for years, and we know all the shops."

Megan closed her eyes and leaned her head back. "I know, I know . . . we have to choose a ring. But we have to save up for it. Marty wants to buy a big ring but he's still paying off his law school loans so he doesn't have that much saved. I told him I didn't need a big ring. I'd be happy with a small one or one of those other stones. I don't need a diamond to make me happy."

Mimi beamed at Megan. "You're the diamond in that relationship, Megan. And Marty knows it. You let him choose the ring. That'll be his surprise for you."

Kelly watched Megan blush at Mimi's

praise. Mimi was right on. Megan was a diamond.

Burt appeared in the archway then and gave Megan a smile. "Hey, can I have a congratulatory hug? Or, is it best wishes for the bride-to-be? I get them mixed up."

"Thank you, Burt," Megan said as she went to embrace him.

"I couldn't be happier if you were my own kids," Burt said, squeezing Megan before releasing her. "I've always thought of you girls like second daughters."

"Second and third and fourth . . ." Jennifer joked, counting heads around the table.

"You're a sweetheart, Burt. And so is Mimi. She's going to help me get organized. Can you believe I haven't made any lists? And it's *my* wedding."

Burt threw up his hands, feigning shock. "What? Megan has no lists? The same girl who made my life miserable a few months ago with daily lists? Well, I'll just have to make some up for you."

"Don't worry, Burt. I'm taking care of that detail," Mimi said. "I have a few minutes now, Megan, if you'd like to get started. Lisa and Kelly and Jennifer can jump in with suggestions."

Jennifer checked her watch. "Actually, Jennifer's break is way over, and she has to get back to the slow Monday café traffic. You guys can fill me in on what you come up with later."

Lisa shoved her knitting into its bag. "And I have to get to the university and study before class. See you guys."

Kelly decided this was a good time for a coffee refill and pushed back her chair. "Hey, Jen, I'll go with you. I need to fill my mug."

"I'll join you, Kelly," Burt said, accompanying them as they headed through the central yarn room toward the café.

Kelly waited by the counter as Jennifer refilled her mug, inhaling those enticing aromas of breakfast foods — eggs, bacon, sausage, pancakes. What was it about them that was so tempting? Aside from the fact they tasted so good.

"Thanks, Jen," Kelly said, accepting the mug. Jennifer refilled Burt's cup, then returned to checking customers. Kelly gave Burt a quizzical look. "What's up, Burt? I can tell you've got something to say."

Burt smiled and motioned her over to an empty table. "You and I are getting so we can read each other's body language, Kelly. We can't hide anything anymore."

Kelly settled into the chair across from Burt. "That's scary. I might like to get away with something sometime."

Burt took a sip of coffee, then spoke. "I heard from Dan this morning. The medical examiner has finished his work, and they've been able to establish Holly's cause of death."

"What was it? How was she killed?"

"There's no sign anyone killed her. She wasn't assaulted in any way. Just that lump on the back of her head. But the medical examiner found a large amount of opiates in her digestive system. They've ruled that an overdose of opiate narcotics is what killed Holly."

Kelly drew back, appalled. "Opiate narcotics? Good lord! Did she shoot up with something?"

"There were no signs of injection sites. Whatever Holly took, she ingested them, probably in pill form."

Kelly stared off into the café, where Julie was clearing a customer's plate and refilling his coffee cup. Kelly didn't even see it. All she could see was an image of pretty blonde Holly lying lifeless along the river trail.

"Why would Holly do that? She'd been off drugs for a month. She was taking classes again. What was she *thinking?*"

"I'm not sure she was, Kelly," Burt said, wagging his head sadly. "If someone's hooked on pills or drugs of any kind, it rules their lives. They don't think, period."

"How could she be so stupid? And what was she doing taking opiate narcotics? She was taking Ecstasy the night she showed up at my place. That's a hallucinogen like acid."

"Who knows? All sorts of pills are passed out and sold at those parties, Kelly. It can be a real pharmacological stew, I've been told."

"Did the examiner find out what she took exactly?"

"Sometimes all they can tell is what the main chemical ingredients are. Opiate narcotics are powerful painkillers, and they're carefully regulated and controlled because they're addictive. Doctors prescribe them in small amounts. Even so, they still wind up on the street. They're some of the most pervasive drugs out there."

"Which ones?"

"Vicodin is probably the most often abused, but Percocet is right behind it, along with OxyContin. They're called 'oxies' on the street."

Kelly stared at the design laminated into the table, unseeing. She'd never been able to understand how anyone could risk their body and their life by using illegal drugs just to get high. What would make Holly go back to that party scene and back onto the drugs when she was turning herself around?

Then Barbara's words came back to mind: *I've watched Holly try to change her dangerous habits before. Unfortunately, she always falls back into those old ways after a while.*

"Have the police contacted Tommy yet?"

Burt shook his head. "The police wouldn't even know to contact Tommy since he's not Holly's relative. Dan asked me if I knew of anyone who would be a responsible party that could authorize where her body should be taken. You know, a funeral home and all that. I told him Holly had no relatives in town anymore and had lost all contact with her father. No one knows where he is. And her mother is dead. I did give him Barbara's name and number. Maybe she will agree to do it. If not, Mimi and I will."

"Had you already spoken with Barbara?"

Burt sighed. "Yes, the night before. Right after I called you. I'm sure she's called Tommy by now."

Kelly stared off at a laughing couple at the corner table. Their whole lives in front of them. "This is going to break Tommy's heart."

FIVE

A slight breeze picked up, flipping Kelly's silky yarn scarf across her face as she stood with a small group of mourners at the cemetery gravesite. The normally bright Colorado sun was obscured by clouds this morning, making it chilly whenever the wind passed through the nearby trees.

The open grave was covered with a bright green tarp, but Kelly could still see the raw brown earth edging the tarp that indicated the ground had been freshly turned. Kelly shivered. Whether it was the wind or the bleak view of the waiting grave, waiting for the young girl who died much too early, it gave her a chill.

The minister's voice droned quietly as he read a passage from the Bible. Beside him stood Tommy and Barbara, both of their faces white and drawn. Patty stood next to Barbara and was holding tissues to her face, wiping away her tears.

Tommy's shoulders shook repeatedly with his obvious effort to quiet his sobs. Kelly, Mimi, and Burt stood across from them, and there were clusters of college students who hovered on the edges, looking uncomfortable. Behind them were four young men and a young woman who stood tall and straight. The insignias on their sleeves indicated they were all with the Fort Connor emergency medical team and ambulance service. Tommy's friends and colleagues.

The minister held up his hand and said a blessing, then invited everyone to bow their heads in silent prayer. Kelly fervently wished that some of the college students in attendance would let this experience be sufficient warning to keep them from following the same path Holly had.

"That's so sad," Lisa said, looking across the knitting table at Mimi, who was nursing a cup of Earl Grey tea.

Kelly took a sip of coffee. "Tragic, really. How could Holly throw away her life like that?"

Burt spoke up beside her. "I don't think any young person consciously thinks about it. I'm afraid too many of them have this belief that death happens to other people. It could never happen to them."

"And in answer to your question, Kelly, it sounds like Holly's problems started a long time ago when she was a child. It doesn't sound like she had much guidance or even affection at home, so the poor girl probably started looking for outside substitutes for affection," Lisa said, as her fingers worked the reddish-orange wool.

"Spoken like a psychology major," Kelly observed. "But you're right. Sounds like her home life was nonexistent."

"That's why she gravitated to Tommy. He became her guardian angel of sorts," Mimi said.

"So Barbara's house became a home for Holly," Burt added sadly. "Like a home away from home."

Steve's unfinished hat lay on the table, and Kelly returned to her stitches, picking up where she left off. "That was nice of Barbara and Tommy to take care of Holly's . . . uh, final expenses. You know, funeral service and all that."

"That's what family is for," Mimi said, leaning back in her chair. "Barbara and Tommy were the closest thing to family that Holly had. Once Holly was old enough to work and go to college, her father packed up and moved to Florida. Tommy said he never kept in touch with Holly."

"Poor girl, no wonder she felt abandoned. She really was," Burt said.

"I feel so sorry for Tommy. He looked devastated. He could barely hold himself together," Kelly said, looking up from the yarn. "Did you have a chance to speak to him after the service, Mimi?"

"No, I didn't even try. He looked like he'd fall apart if you tried to comfort him. Poor dear."

The front door's tinkling bell sounded, then loud anxious voices in the foyer. The voices came louder, moving through the central yarn room toward the knitting table.

"Tommy, *please!* Be sensible. You cannot stay away from your classes like that. You'll risk your scholarship," Barbara's voice came clearly.

"Mom, *stop!* I have to do this!"

Kelly and the others exchanged concerned looks. *What was Tommy up to?* Both mother and son paused in the archway. It was impossible to miss the anguished looks on both faces.

"Tommy, there is nothing more you can do for Holly. Please don't throw your future away," Barbara pleaded, her face already streaked with tears.

"Let me be, Mom," Tommy protested,

hands up between himself and his mother. "I've gotta do this. *Please,* let me be!"

Tommy turned away from Barbara and approached Mimi. "I wanted to thank you folks for coming to Holly's service this morning. I . . . I really appreciate it," he said, his face still puffy and his eyes red-rimmed.

Burt rose from his chair and came over to Tommy, wrapping a paternal arm around his shoulders. "Both Mimi and I know what it's like to lose a loved one."

Mimi stood and wrapped Tommy in a big hug. "You're family, Tommy, and we take care of each other. Please sit down next to Kelly and Burt, and let me bring you something warm to drink."

Tommy hesitated just a moment before he allowed himself to be guided into the chair between Kelly and Burt. "Some coffee would be good."

"I'll get it for you," Mimi offered, approaching Barbara, who was still hovering forlornly in the doorway. "Have you had anything to eat? I'll bring some of Pete's cinnamon rolls."

Without waiting for Tommy's answer, Mimi beckoned to Barbara as she headed toward the café.

"Some food sounds like a good idea," Burt

114

said, patting Tommy's arm. "You've rescued enough fainting people to know how easy it is to pass out on an empty stomach, especially in a stressful situation."

Tommy's face relaxed a little. "Yeah, you're right, Burt. I'll try to eat something."

"Is there anything we can do to help you, Tommy?" Kelly asked, wondering what had precipitated Tommy's argument with his mother.

Tommy's shoulders sagged and his head dropped as if some invisible weight had been placed upon his back. He clasped his hands between his knees. "I don't think anyone can help anymore. It's too late for Holly. I just want to find out who was the creep that gave her those narcotic pain pills that night. Holly had never used opiates before. She didn't know how to handle them."

Kelly wondered if what Tommy said was true. Had she taken opiates before and not told him? Holly's behavior had shown her to be reckless, so in Kelly's eyes all bets were off on Holly's truthfulness.

"How do you plan on doing that, Tommy?" Burt asked, his expression turning serious as he leaned toward Tommy, hands clasped between legs, mimicking Tommy's pose.

Tommy raised his head, his expression hardening. Kelly noticed the angry hunch of his shoulders now. "I'm going to start asking questions around campus. I'll crawl through the party scene until I find people who were at that party the other night. That's how I'll find out who was passing out pills. There's always someone at those parties who's selling stuff."

Kelly caught Burt's gaze, and they exchanged a look of dismay. That sounded like a really bad idea to Kelly.

"Tommy, that's not a good idea, and you know it," Burt advised quietly.

"Yes, it is, Burt. If I can get in with those kids, I'll be able to find out —"

"No, you *won't,* Tommy," Burt countered. "Those kids will clam up as soon as they see you. Most of them know you and Holly were together. And once they see you asking someone questions, the rest of them will head out the back door."

Tommy's expression turned anxious. "That's okay. I'll keep after 'em. I'll track 'em down at class, and —"

Kelly had to jump in. Tommy was clearly losing it. His grief over Holly's death was pushing him to irrational thinking.

"Whoa, Tommy. Do you realize how crazy that sounds? If you start showing up around

116

the university, following students to classes and stuff, that's the same as stalking. And if you try to get in someone's face and make them answer your questions, well . . . someone might charge you with harassment."

Tommy's eyes popped wide. "What? You can't be serious. I'm just trying to find the truth here."

"Kelly's right, Tommy. Right now, you're living on no sleep and no food. Take a look at yourself in the mirror. You're looking really ragged. If you headed over to the university and started hanging around students, asking questions, they'd probably call the campus police."

"You're exaggerating, Burt," he protested.

"No, he's not." Lisa spoke up from across the table. She let the knitted scarf drop to her lap. "I'm taking graduate psychology classes at the university now, so I'm over there every day. And there have been different occasions when the police had to escort someone off campus because they were becoming a public nuisance. Pestering students to buy some product or hand out brochures on some society or some such." She shook her head. "There are all sorts of folks out there who're not exactly playing with a full deck. You've probably been called

117

out to take some of them away yourself. And the last thing you want to do, Tommy, is to put yourself in their category. If you were charged with something like that, it would follow you. You might even lose your scholarship over it. Whatever little information you might learn wouldn't be worth the risk you'd be taking, believe me."

Kelly was impressed with Lisa's calm and cool line of reasoning that she presented to Tommy. It seemed to work. Kelly noticed the light of recognition go off in Tommy's eyes. Lisa had found exactly the right thing to say to penetrate the cloud of grief that had fogged Tommy's thinking. Lisa would make a great counselor one day.

Tommy's expression softened. "I hear you . . ." he said in a quiet voice. "But . . . but I've got to do something! For Holly's sake." His voice drifted off.

Burt placed his hand on Tommy's shoulder. "I know how you feel, Tommy. But the best thing you can do for Holly would be to go back to your medical school studies in Denver. Keep your promise to yourself to become a doctor. What better way to honor Holly than that?"

"I agree, Tommy," Lisa said. "You can do far more good by becoming a doctor and helping other young people like Holly. The forgotten ones. The ones who slip through the cracks."

Tommy sat up straighter. Lisa's words seemed to spark something inside him. Kelly could almost see it in his face.

"You're right, I know you are," Tommy admitted. "But I still hate to think that creep got away with handing out those pills that killed Holly. I'd just like to find out who it is."

"Why, Tommy? You want to go up and confront him or something?" Burt asked in a stern voice. "That's a worse idea than going over to the university."

"No, no, no . . ." Tommy backtracked, clearly startled by Burt's cop-like response. "I thought my buddies on the ambulance squad could go and have a talk with him. Nothing threatening, trust me. Just let him know that people die from stuff like that. We've done it before, and believe me, a real quiet talk changes some people's minds real fast. When we talk to kids, they listen."

Burt visibly relaxed. "That makes much more sense, Tommy. We've had guys on the force do the same thing on campuses."

The atmosphere of helping sparked an idea in Kelly's head, and in the spirit of the moment, she offered it. "Tommy, I'll be glad to help by asking around. I've got some girls on my softball team who're over at the university, and I can ask them to check into that party scene. And I'll report back to you what I find out, okay?"

A tiny smile started. "That's nice of you, Kelly. Thanks."

"And I'll ask around, too," Lisa offered. "I'm over in classes with students all the time."

Tommy's color started to return as his shoulders relaxed at last. "You guys are great. I really appreciate it. Why don't you start with Patty? She's still taking classes over there. And she still goes out to parties, too. She'll be a big help."

"Will do," Kelly promised, spotting Mimi coming toward the table with a big pot of coffee. Waitress Julie was right behind her, holding a large tray, laden with plates and several huge cinnamon rolls.

"It looks like everyone could use a pick-me-up about now, am I right?" Mimi asked, placing the coffeepot on the table.

"Right as rain, Mimi," Burt said with a smile. "I'd say Pete's cinnamon rolls are just what the doctor ordered."

Kelly glanced around the outdoor café on the university's main plaza. Located beside the student union, tables were scattered

120

around the plaza and were filled with students and university staff relaxing, studying, and clustered in meetings. September's balmy temperatures invited everyone outside into the mid-seventies warmth. Bright sunshine glinted off the glass-paned side of the campus student union.

Kelly sipped her coffee as she sat at the table. Patty sat across from her, her dark brown hair hanging straight across one shoulder, tied with a band. "Thanks for meeting me this afternoon, Patty. I know how hard it is to find time to juggle classes and work."

"I'm glad to do it, Kelly. Anything that'll help Tommy." She sipped her diet cola from a can. "I'm so glad you guys were able to talk him out of staying here in town and going to campus parties. That's crazy." She rolled her eyes. "Nobody would tell him anything. Most of them know Tommy, and they wouldn't admit anything even if they did see something."

"Yeah, both Burt and I figured Tommy was so strung out on grief, he'd stopped thinking rationally. So . . . we kind of shocked him into waking up. Burt and Lisa really helped. Lisa's a grad psych student over here, and she gave Tommy a verbal 'snap out of it.' "

"I'm glad you guys talked some sense into him. I wouldn't have been able to do it. Every time I looked at him yesterday, I burst into tears."

Kelly leaned over her plastic coffee cup. "I know we may be on a wild-goose chase, but at least we can tell Tommy we tried. If we learn anything, and his friends can go out and talk to the guy, who knows . . . maybe that'll help Tommy find some closure on what happened." Kelly shrugged.

Patty nodded solemnly. "Yeah, maybe so. I'll start asking around. I didn't want to admit this to Tommy, but I was actually at the same party that night. I saw Holly there, but she was only drinking vodka when I saw her."

That surprised Kelly. "You were at the party? Then you'll know who else was there. Don't worry, I won't tell Tommy."

Patty glanced up sheepishly. "Thanks, Kelly. I appreciate that. I used to do the party scene a lot heavier a couple of years ago, but, man . . . that will take a toll on you."

"Were you around Holly much that night?"

"Not really. I saw her in the kitchen talking to some of the new buddies she hangs with now. And like I said, she looked like she was just drinking. I got my drink and went back out to the living room." She ran her hand through her dark hair and flipped it off her shoulder.

"Where was the party?"

"Over on Washington Street, in one of those big old houses with a wraparound front porch. It's two houses from the corner of Mulberry. The guys that rent it have had lots of parties there, so there's always a huge turnout. And last Friday was great weather, as you know. Must have been in the eighties during the day so it was still warm at night. People were everywhere. In the front yard, backyard, all over the porch, and the house was packed."

"Do you remember some of the people?"

"Yeah, I do." She reached into her purse and pulled out a small notepad. "Let me start writing down names so I won't forget. That way, whenever I see someone on campus, I'll remember to ask them." She jotted down a couple of names. "I've got classes with these two, so I should see both of them tomorrow."

"That's great, Patty. You're bound to find somebody who was hanging around Holly." Kelly glanced at her watch. This afternoon had been consumed with nonbusiness activities. Well intentioned, but she needed to go back to work. "Well, I'd better get back to my own schedule. Gotta get some work done that'll pay the bills."

"I hear that," Patty said, gathering her backpack as she and Kelly rose from their chairs. "I have to go over to my job at the university catering service. We've got a big dinner to serve for some distinguished professors tonight."

Kelly handed Patty her business card. "Here's my card. My cell phone is there. Don't hesitate to call me. I work out of an office at home and am in my car a lot, so I can take calls anytime."

Patty studied the card as they walked across the plaza. Kelly noticed Patty was as tall as she was. "CPA, huh? So, you must be pretty good with all those numbers. I had to take an accounting course once, and it drove me crazy."

Kelly had to laugh. "Believe me, I feel the same way sometimes. Listen, I'm parked at a meter around the oval, so I'm going to cut across the plaza. I'm serious about calling me, Patty. Anytime."

"Will do, Kelly." Patty gave a wave as both women walked in opposite directions.

Six

"Carl, you are not paying attention," Kelly teased her dog. "You're looking the wrong way."

Kelly pointed across the yard where Brazen Squirrel was making a mad dash across the top of the chain-link fence, mouth filled with a ripe crab apple. Carl either read Kelly's mind or detected the movement, because he suddenly looked in Brazen's direction and took off running. Barking furiously, Carl charged into the fence, rattling the chain link. By that time, however, Brazen Squirrel was already out of Carl's reach.

Thwarted yet again, Carl stood on his hind legs, paws on fence, and barked doggy threats into the cottonwood trees above. Brazen perched contentedly on a branch, prized crab apple in his front paws, and smirked down at Carl.

Kelly wasn't entirely sure squirrels could

smirk, but if any of them could, it would definitely be Brazen. No matter how fast Carl ran or how fierce his bark, Brazen was always one step ahead of him to scamper to safety in the broad, leafy branches above. From the safety of his perch, Brazen chattered back at Carl, taunting him with a squirrelly shake of his tail before scampering to higher branches.

Kelly leaned against the open patio doorway, enjoying the morning sun's warmth. "Missed him again, Carl," she commiserated with her dog, who was pacing back and forth beside the fence, sniffing the ground for traces of essence of squirrel. "You've got to get quicker on the trigger, big guy."

The sound of her cell phone ringing on her desk inside the cottage got her attention, and Kelly pulled the screen door closed. Let autumn's warm weather and scents perfume the air.

"Kelly Flynn here," she answered in her usual fashion.

"Good morning, Kelly. Did I get you at a bad time?" a man's deep voice came across the line.

Kelly recognized the voice of Don Warner, her new accounting client in northern Colorado. Since Warner's development company was located in Brighton, Colorado, which was north of Denver, Kelly and Warner had been doing a lot of their consultations over the phone. She'd only traveled to his office twice.

"This is a good time to talk, Mr. Warner; how're you doing?"

"I'm doing quite well, Kelly, and you're going to have to start calling me Don. We keep a pretty relaxed tone over here."

"Okay, Don it is. How can I help you this morning? I'm almost finished with your August monthly reports, by the way."

"That's great, Kelly, but this isn't about reports. I thought you might like to come out here and take a look at our plans for this new industrial park we're planning outside Brighton. We've already broken ground."

"Why, thank you, Mr., uh . . . Don. I'd really like to see the development at this early stage."

"I kind of thought you would. I want to keep you in the loop on things as they're going along. That way, you're better able to understand how the expenses are moving around here. I've got a lot of projects simmering on the stove."

The idea of learning about a new building development from the ground stage up fascinated Kelly. Don Warner had developed projects all over northern Colorado. Shopping centers, office buildings, apartment complexes. She'd jump at the opportunity to see more of Warner's projects in person.

"I'm really anxious to see this new project. What time works for you?"

"I was thinking about Friday, day after tomorrow. How's that? Could you be out here early, say eight thirty? The contractors start at seven, so they'll be pushing dirt, digging foundations. Right now, we've got a lot of holes in the ground. But I want you to take a look at the scale model. It came out better than I thought. And it gives a good idea of the scope of the build-out."

"I look forward to seeing you, then. Friday morning at eight thirty. I'll bring my coffee," she joked.

Warner chuckled. "Don't worry. I know you like your coffee. We've always got a huge urn going plus plenty of fresh doughnuts."

Kelly groaned inwardly. Doughnuts and coffee. Everyone's early morning downfall. "See you Friday, Don." She'd need a lot of coffee to counter that sugar high.

"Hey, what are you two up to?" Kelly asked as she entered Lambspun's main room.

Mimi and Megan sat beside each other at the end of the library table. Open magazines

128

were spread all around them. They both looked up at Kelly at the same time.

"We're trying to get organized," Megan said, her face solemn. "And it's slow going."

"You mean the wedding? Hey, you've got a whole year. You should be fine," Kelly said as she dumped her bag on the table and pulled out a chair.

"*Ha!* That's what *you* think," Megan scoffed. "We've checked with a couple of hotels, and their banquet rooms are booked for next October already."

"Already? Wow." Kelly pulled out Steve's hat, so as not to dislodge the double-pointed needles clustered in a circle around the crown. She was in the finishing stages now.

"Fall is a busy time in a university town," Mimi said, before sipping from her teacup. "Everything from sports banquets to re-unions to regular business meetings keep all the larger rooms in town occupied. We may have to wiggle the dates."

Kelly picked up her stitches where she left off. This was the row where she was sup-posed to knit one stitch, then knit two together, then repeat that sequence around the row. Doing that for each row gradually tightened the circle at the crown smaller and smaller. Finally there would be only a small hole left, and she could easily gather those stitches together on a darning needle and pull the circle closed on the inside of the hat.

"How much wiggle room with dates do you have?" Kelly asked.

Megan sighed. "Not much, actually. We can shift from the last two weeks of September through the last week of October, but we'd be *really* risking bad weather after that. And Marty has a legal conference the second week of September. So, we've got a six-week window, more or less."

"Have you tried every hotel in town?" Kelly asked.

Both Mimi and Megan nodded in unison. "Yeah. All the bigger, nicer ones. I couldn't believe they were all booked."

"Don't worry, Megan," Mimi reassured. "There are other facilities available. Lots of churches and organizations rent out their large meeting rooms. We'll find something."

"I know, but I was hoping to have a . . . well, a pretty setting. Not some drab, gray conference room." She sounded a little forlorn.

"What about that idea of having the reception outside? September and October are usually gorgeous around here," Kelly offered.

"Except when a cold front blows in,"

Mimi teased.

"Or it snows," Megan added, a smile peeking out.

Kelly laughed softly. "Okay, you guys, you can make fun if you want. But I've been thinking about this. We've all been to outdoor events in the fall here, and even if the temperatures drop usually the sun is still out. They simply put heaters all around those big canopied tents. You could do that."

Mimi and Megan looked at each other.

"You know, we could do that, Megan," Mimi suggested, sounding hopeful.

"You think?" Megan stared at her, obviously unconvinced.

"Sure you could." Kelly picked up the ball and ran with it. "They've even got sides to those big tents, so if the wind started to blow or whatever, you just pull them down. Sure, it would be a gamble, but it would definitely be a pretty setting. You could put those tents up wherever you got permission. We could find out about local park space rental or restrictions. Find out which natural areas would allow weddings."

"I'm not sure they do, but there are plenty of private acreages that rent their open spaces," Mimi ventured.

Megan's expression changed, Kelly noticed. "Wow . . . now that would be what

I've always pictured. Someplace outdoors in nature. After all, we live in this gorgeous area."

"You could look at all sorts of locations, here in town near the foothills or up in Bellevue Canyon or Poudre Canyon. "That's natural wilderness area. I wonder if they allow stuff like that."

"I'm not so sure, Kelly. It's a protected area. They allow camping and picnics, but weddings? I think I know who to call, though. She works for the park service right here in town." Mimi scribbled on a sheet of paper beside the magazines.

Megan brightened. "Okay, now we're talking. Let's see what we can find out. Thanks for the suggestion, Kelly."

"Glad to help. What are you looking for in the magazines?" She indicated all the glossy colorful pages spread out. She spotted lots of photos of frothy white gowns. "Looks like wedding dresses, right?"

"Ohhhh, yeah. Mimi suggested I start looking at some of the gowns so I can decide which styles I like and which ones I don't." She flipped through a few pages. "But you know, they all start to look the same after a while. Lots of frothy, gauzy stuff. Ribbons and lace . . . that doesn't really appeal to me. I'm not the frothy type."

"A lot of girls aren't the frothy type, Megan, but they decide they want something very special for their wedding. You won't know what really appeals to you until you start trying on gowns."

"Yeah, I guess," Megan said dubiously, flipping through the pages.

Mimi glanced toward Kelly then back to Megan. "You know what you should do? You should take Lisa, Kelly, and Jennifer with you and go to some of those bridal shops. We've got a wonderful one here in Fort Connor. And there're two in Boulder, and another in Loveland. You could take a couple of weekends and start trying on gowns. It'll be fun. All of you together."

Megan looked up at Kelly. "What do you think, Kelly? Could we find a Saturday when all of us could check out these bridal shops?"

"Sure," Kelly said with a big smile. "That sounds like fun. We can start early and cover all four shops. We'll do lunch at someplace special."

"Yeah, and we'll have picnic stuff for dinner when we get back. That way it'll be easy. Cool." Megan grinned.

"Sounds like the super organizer is back," Mimi said with a laugh.

"I hate to bring this up, guys, but I *am* an

accountant, so I have to ask. Have you made a budget yet?" Kelly eyed Megan.

"We're working on that," Mimi said, holding up the piece of paper. "We've listed most of the expenses, but we're having to use estimates because we haven't called the vendors yet."

Megan scanned the list. "We've got caterer, florist, music, dress, wedding cake, hall rental, minister's fees."

"That sounds about right."

"Oh, yeah, photographer," Megan added, and Mimi dutifully scribbled it down.

"You really should start nailing down those expense categories," Kelly suggested. "Estimates can be way off, and you won't know where to start until you've decided how much you have to spend."

Megan wrinkled her nose. "Yeah, you're right. What do you think, Mimi? Should we start at the top of the list with catering and work our way down?"

"That sounds good to me. We can start calling right now, if you'd like. I've already written down all the companies Pete suggested."

Megan glanced at her watch. "Tomorrow would be better. I've got a conference call scheduled in an hour, so I'd better head back to work." She grabbed her bag. "Let me help you gather all these magazines, Mimi."

"That's not necessary, dear. I'm putting them in a special Megan pile in my office bookcase. You run along," she said with a smile.

"See you tonight, Kelly. We've got practice, remember?" Megan announced as she headed for the door.

"I'll be there," Kelly said with a wave. Once Megan was gone, Kelly glanced at Mimi. "You've having a great time, aren't you, Mimi?"

"You bet, Kelly. Helping Megan plan her wedding is helping ease the pain over losing Holly."

"I can understand that," Kelly said softly.

Mimi's smile returned. "Plus, I've never had a daughter, so I simply love having the chance to be substitute mother of the bride for Megan. I'm actually excited."

Kelly's cell phone jangled. "I could tell. Enjoy yourself, Mimi. You'll keep Megan on track." She flipped open her phone.

"Kelly? This is Patty. I had a moment before I head to another class, so I thought I'd tell you what I've heard so far."

"This is a great time, Patty." Kelly dropped her knitting and leaned over the table.

"So far, I've only talked to one girl who was at the party, but she spent most of her time in the house. I was outside a lot. She said she saw a couple of people offering pills around. One was a guy she didn't know, but the other one is someone I *do* know. Rachel Gebbard. She actually went to high school with Tommy and Holly and me. Tommy and Rachel used to date a lot before Tommy got really serious about Holly. Then he dropped Rachel."

"That's interesting."

"Yeah, well, Rachel has always been jealous of Holly and she bad-mouthed her whenever she got the chance. And . . . get this . . . the girl said Holly and Rachel got into an argument over Tommy. The girl was in the kitchen when it happened. She said Holly must have been drunk because she started talking trash to Rachel, and Rachel tried to hit her. But a guy pulled her back."

"Whoa, it sounds like there was bad blood between those two."

"Oh, yeah, for years. Rachel's never gotten over being dumped. And she still has a thing for Tommy."

"Wow, maybe the source of those pills wasn't some creepy pill pusher but a jilted ex-girlfriend."

"It's possible. I'll keep asking around to

see who else saw something. Gotta run now."

"Thanks, Patty. You're doing great. Keep me posted."

"Will do."

Kelly flipped off her phone and returned to knitting Steve's hat. Only a few more rows to go, and she would be able to close off the circle and finish. Knit one, knit two together. Knit one, knit two together. She almost wanted to say it out loud to keep herself on track.

Patty's phone call made Kelly wonder. Had this Rachel deliberately given Holly too many pills? Would Holly even take pills from Rachel? Kelly knitted another row, thinking about what Patty said. There was no way to know if Rachel gave pills to Holly or not. Would Holly simply swallow down whatever she'd been given? She certainly hadn't demonstrated good judgment at earlier parties. How many of those pain pills would it take to overdose? Kelly didn't have a clue.

"Well, hi there." Jennifer entered the room, dumping her large knitting bag on the table. She pulled out the chair beside Kelly. "I haven't seen you over here in the afternoon that much since you've gotten those new clients."

"Well, they're keeping me busy."

"How're you liking them? I mean, do you enjoy the work? I bet you do."

"Absolutely," Kelly affirmed with a nod. "It's intricate and challenging, and there are so many different parts to both their businesses that I'm still learning. I love that. I couldn't thank Curt enough for recommending me to both those guys."

"One's in real estate, right?"

"Yes, Houseman is a real estate investor and has properties all over Fort Connor, Loveland, Windsor, and Greeley. Warner is a builder and developer. Most of his projects are commercial, and they're scattered all over northern Colorado."

Jennifer pulled out the burgundy wool sweater she was knitting. "That will keep you challenged for a while."

"You bet. How're things going at the real estate office?"

"Everything's dead, basically. The only things moving are the foreclosure houses, but it's still hard for people who try to buy them. Hard to get loans. Nothing is easy anymore." Her fingers started working the wool.

"It's a good thing Pete's catering business picked up at the time real estate dried up last spring," Kelly said. "He's usually got at least two evenings a week scheduled, right?"

"At least. Sometimes we've got three to handle. It's all good, though. And yes, I am really grateful the catering picked up when it did. Otherwise, I'd be in trouble financially."

Kelly couldn't help it. Her mind was wired that way. Like with Megan and Mimi, she had to ask. "So, you're doing okay with your budget? I mean . . . you've got enough every month? Because if there's ever a problem, I can spot you some cash."

Jennifer looked over at Kelly and gave her a warm smile. "Thanks, Kelly, I'm doing all right. I'm paying my bills every month, and I've even started saving. I've gotten so responsible, I barely recognize myself."

Kelly laughed. "That's great to hear, Jen. I didn't know whether to worry or not. I didn't know if your trip back home this summer set you back."

"No, I actually found a super-cheap airfare online and my mom picked me up from the airport. I stayed with family the whole time I was there, so it didn't cost me much at all."

Kelly knitted without speaking, letting the quiet settle between them. Even though Jennifer hadn't said much about her trip home last summer, Kelly sensed it had been more than just a time to visit family. Something about the way Jennifer talked when she returned. When asked, Jennifer had simply said, "It was a good trip. We got to talk a lot."

Jennifer hadn't said anything else about the trip, other than she'd visited her parents and her sister who lived in the same suburb outside Indianapolis. Considering the traumatic experience Jennifer had gone through this past winter and how she had transformed her life in the months following, Kelly wasn't surprised her friend wanted to touch base with her family.

There was nothing specific that Kelly could point to that indicated the trip was a closure of some sort for Jennifer, but Kelly sensed it was. There wasn't any obvious change in Jennifer's demeanor. But ever since, when they were both sitting quietly and knitting, Kelly sensed a peacefulness about Jennifer that she'd never noticed before.

Kelly also noticed that Jennifer and Pete had started showing up together whenever the group of friends all gathered. The "gang," as they called themselves. They no longer arrived separately. Kelly often wondered whether Pete and Jennifer actually went out by themselves when they weren't working.

Deciding this nice quiet moment shouldn't be wasted, Kelly decided to ask. But first she'd have to work up to it. Jennifer was as quick as Kelly to pick up conversational ploys. Discarding one approach after another, Kelly fell back on what usually worked best for her: direct and forthright interrogation.

"I can't help but notice that you and Pete arrive together whenever the gang is gathering for pizza and movies."

Jennifer smiled over her knitting. "I wondered when you'd finally get around to asking questions. Frankly, I'm amazed at your patience. I didn't think you had it in you."

"Hey, if there's a compliment buried in there somewhere, I'll take it."

"Admit it, patience has never been your strong suit."

Kelly lifted her coffee mug. "Amen to that." She took a deep drink.

"So . . . the answer to your question is 'yes.' Pete has been picking me up, and we drive to Lisa's or Megan's or wherever the tribe is gathering."

"Well, it's definitely better for the environment to take one car. Not to mention the price of gas," Kelly joked.

Jennifer slanted a look Kelly's way. "Go

141

ahead, Kelly. I can tell you've got more questions."

"Okaaaay, now that you mention it." Kelly took another sip in preparation. "I simply wondered if you and Pete ever went out together for something other than catering or coming to join our communal get-togethers."

"As a matter of fact, we have," Jennifer admitted. "We've gone to dinner a few times, and we've also gone to the movies. We've even gone to the wine bar café you and Steve like so much. We really enjoyed it."

It was all Kelly could do to keep her mouth from dropping open, she was so surprised. She'd expected Jennifer to answer that she was "thinking" about going out with Pete. Well, it was obvious that she'd already thought about it.

"That's fantastic, Jen," Kelly enthused, knitting dropped to her lap. "I can't tell you how happy I am to hear that."

Jennifer gave her a smile. "I can tell."

"Have you told anyone else yet, like Lisa?"

"No, because no one has asked. I could tell all of you guys were dying to ask but everybody was holding back. Pete and I figured you'd be the one to break the ice."

Kelly held up her hand. "That's me. Kelly.

Icebreaker. One who charges in without asking. Whatever. You need people like me around. We do the jobs no one else will do."

"Yeah, yeah, yeah."

"Seriously, can I let it out? I mean, tell Lisa and Megan? That way it'll spread everywhere."

Jennifer held up her hand. "I give you permission. Blab away."

"Fantastic," Kelly repeated. "Tell me, did it feel funny at first for you two to be sitting at a restaurant waiting for someone else to serve you?"

Jennifer shot her a look. "Are you kidding? We loved it. Now it's my turn to ask questions. How's Steve doing?"

Kelly's lighthearted mood evaporated. "He's hanging in there. He's still working a double shift. At the architectural firm in south Denver during the day, then at night he drives over to northeast Denver to work for the commercial builder."

Jennifer glanced up, her concern obvious. "Boy, that's grueling. How's he holding up?"

Kelly shrugged. "During the week, I haven't a clue because he's been so busy he doesn't have time to call. If he's lucky, he'll make it up here on Saturday night. He's working at the builder's office all day Saturday."

"Poor guy."

"Yeah, I know. He's exhausted. When he does get here, he usually gobbles down some pizza and falls asleep in front of the television. Then, he's holed up in his Old Town office all day. I'm amazed I got him to go over to Lisa and Greg's last weekend." She took a deep drink of coffee. "When he's here, he's not really here, because he's either asleep or at the office. And the rest of the time, he's in Denver. So I don't really get to see him much at all anymore."

"That's hard," Jennifer said, watching Kelly.

"Tell me about it. And he's gotten so moody. Even when we have a chance to talk, he doesn't really say anything. He turns on the television and just disappears into a baseball game. And he's grouchy, too. Steve never used to complain about stuff before. Like when I was a couple of minutes late one night, he snapped at me. Wanted to know where I was. Sheeeesh." She shook her head.

"You two are going through a hard time right now. Steve may be the one who's financially stressed, but you're living with him, so you're having to deal with his problems, too. That's tough. Call me up whenever you need to vent, okay?"

"Thanks, Jen, I appreciate that. I haven't told anybody how I'm feeling, because . . . well, I feel kind of disloyal or something. I know Steve is hanging on by his fingernails, and I have to stand by and watch. But it hurts to watch all his dreams crumble. I wish he would let me help him, but he won't."

"If by help you mean money, you know Steve won't accept it. So don't even ask him."

"Everyone says the same thing." Kelly frowned. "I wish I could give it to him anonymously."

Jennifer laughed softly. "That only happens in the movies, Kelly. Not in real life. Steve would know it came from you."

Kelly sank back in her chair and sipped her coffee. A little movie magic would be in order right now. But someone had to believe in magic for it to happen. And right now, Steve wasn't in a magical mood.

SEVEN

Kelly spotted Burt getting out of his car across the knitting shop driveway. "Hey, Burt," she called out as she walked toward the patio garden behind the shop. Café tables were still occupied with customers even though it was late morning.

"Hi, Kelly. How are you?" Burt asked as he joined her on the stone path that wound through the garden to the café's back door.

"I'm doing great. I finished off my account work early this morning, so I'm giving myself an early break. Plus, I've run out of Pete's coffee. Time for a fill-up. Have you been doing errands?"

"Good guess, Kelly. Mimi had a long list. I've been racing around finishing the list so I could get back here. I'm teaching a beginner spinning class at noon and need to sit and draft a whole bunch of fleece to get ready."

"Well, let me get my coffee and I'll sit with

you. Watching you at the wheel or drafting fleece is guaranteed to relax me." She pulled open the door before Burt could get to it.

The aroma of bacon and eggs drifted on the air, teasing Kelly's nostrils. Breakfast food. Her big weakness. She waved her mug at Julie. She needed coffee so she wouldn't weaken and gobble down a second breakfast.

"Thanks, Julie. You saved me from inhaling a platter of bacon and eggs." Kelly watched the black stream pour into her cup.

"You know, bacon and eggs might be good to absorb some of that caffeine," Julie teased.

"What? And lose my edge?" Kelly retorted with a laugh. "It's the morning. Gotta have it."

Burt accepted a cup from Julie. "Did you even have breakfast this morning?"

"Yeah, a bagel and cream cheese." Kelly took a big sip and headed toward the hallway that led to the knitting shop. "How's Mimi doing with her caterer calls? I was sitting with Megan and Mimi yesterday and they've got a list as long as your leg."

Burt chuckled as he followed behind Kelly. "You're right about that. Mimi was worrying out loud about how expensive everything was nowadays. The last time she helped with a wedding was several years ago, so I think the prices were a big shock."

"Well, I gave them a nudge yesterday to come up with their budget first before they start making firm plans. Megan and Marty need to see how much they can afford to spend, then work from there."

"You're an optimist, Kelly. You know most people decide what they want to do first, then they figure out how to pay for it."

Kelly plopped her knitting bag on the library table while Burt pulled his spinning wheel from the corner. Kelly settled into a chair closer to him and retrieved Steve's hat from the bag. Nearly finished. Just a few more rows of reducing stitches and she could tie it off. If it was a hat for someone else, she'd make a fluffy pom-pom to sew on the top. But Steve was definitely not a pom-pom kind of guy.

Burt settled in his chair and pulled a large plastic trash bag of creamy white fleece beside him. He grabbed several handfuls and began drafting — slowly stretching the fibers so they could be spun properly and wouldn't bunch.

Kelly relaxed against her chair and watched Burt's movements for a couple of minutes before she picked up her knitting. "How's Barbara doing? Have you seen her since the funeral?"

"Yes, Mimi and I took a casserole over to her house last night. She's doing okay. Still worrying about Tommy as usual."

"Have you heard anything from him? I got an e-mail the day after the funeral thanking me again for being there. He also asked if Patty had learned anything about the party so far."

"I recall you said you were going to talk with Patty the other day. Did she offer to help?"

Kelly nodded. "Yeah, she was glad to help Tommy. And she was glad we had talked him out of trying to do the party circuit himself."

"That would have been a dumb move. Has Patty learned anything?"

"Yes, as a matter of fact. She started asking friends who were at the party. One of them told her an old girlfriend of Tommy's was there, and she and Holly got into an argument about Tommy. Sounds like it was kind of heated, too."

Burt looked up. "Did anyone make any threats?"

"Well, this other girl, Rachel, tried to hit Holly, apparently. But the girl also said that Rachel was passing out pills that night. So, we may have found the source for Holly's overdose."

"Have you e-mailed Tommy yet?" Burt's fingers continued working the fibers.

"Not yet." Kelly let out a sigh. "You see, Patty says Tommy and Rachel used to date before he got serious about Holly. Apparently this Rachel is still holding a grudge. So I don't know what to tell Tommy. Do I say one of his ex-girlfriends may be the source of Holly's pills? I don't know."

Burt drafted quietly for a moment. "I wouldn't say anything, Kelly. There's no proof this Rachel gave Holly the pills, so you don't want to upset Tommy. He might come charging up here again. It'd be better to simply say that you learned that some people were distributing pills, but you don't have names. After all, that's the way it usually goes. I guarantee you there were more than a couple of people handing out pills that night, especially if it was a large party."

"You know, I'm clueless about this stuff, Burt. I had some friends in college who did drugs, but that was years ago. Now they're passing around narcotic painkillers."

"Take it from me, it's a real grab bag out there." He grabbed another big handful of fleece. "You know, you might like to talk to one of our investigators. I'm thinking about a gal who has spent a lot of time in that campus drug scene. It can be a swamp. You might like to talk to her. She'll give you a quick education. Her name is Gloria Frobischer, and she works with the special drug task force that handles those situations. Tell her I suggested you call her. We worked on a couple of cases together a few years ago. She's a hardworking cop. You'll learn a lot from her." He stopped his drafting and pulled out a wallet from his back pocket. "Here's Dan's card. Call him first. He'll give you Gloria's number."

"Hey, thanks, Burt," Kelly said, taking the card. "I think I'll do that."

The familiar jangle of her cell phone sounded then, and Kelly dropped the card into her bag as she grabbed the phone. Recognizing her client Houseman's number flashing, Kelly rose from her chair.

"Business calling, Burt. I'll talk to you later." She headed through the central yarn room toward the front door and privacy.

"I can't believe it. Twice in two days," Jennifer said as she walked toward the library table. "Didn't I see you an hour or so ago in the café with Burt?"

"Yeah, I finished up client work earlier than scheduled so I came over to finish Steve's hat. And it's finally done." She pulled the last few stitches tightly together on the inside of the crown, then tied them off. "Ta-dah!" she announced, flourishing the completed gray tweed hat proudly.

"Looks good. That matches his scarf, right?" Jennifer pulled the burgundy sweater out of her knitting bag. It looked half finished.

"Yeah, I've been meaning to knit a matching hat since last winter but never got around to it. So, I'm getting an early start for this winter."

"Why don't you felt it? That wool would look good felted. And it'll make the hat even warmer."

"Really? I didn't know that."

"Yeah, felting tightens all the stitches together and shrinks the wool so it's nice and tight."

"Shrinks it?" Kelly looked in horror. "I can't risk that. It's the right size now."

"Don't worry. There are techniques to use that won't really shrink the size that much. Usually you put it into the washing machine with hot water. But there are other methods. Right now, it looks a little bit too big."

"You think so?" Kelly turned the hat over in her hands, examining it.

"Mimi's doing a fiber retreat next week, and she and Barbara are doing a couple of different felting techniques. You might enjoy it. Plus, it's up in the mountains at a lake resort. I've been there before, and it's gorgeous."

"Wow, that does sound nice. Where is it exactly?"

"It's called Golden Lake, and it's in the mountains between Boulder and Nederland. A little over an hour away. You ought to think about going. You'd enjoy it. It's Friday through noon Saturday, so you'd be back before Steve came home in the evening."

That was true. If it weren't for softball practice and games and evenings with her friends, Kelly would be rattling around the cottage all alone.

"Maybe I will. I'll check my schedule."

"They've got hot thermal pools carved out of the rocks, overlooking the lake," Jennifer tempted.

Kelly could picture that. Sliding into blissfully hot water and soaking while surrounded by gorgeous Colorado scenery. That was hard to resist.

"Wow, that does sound nice."

"Trust me, it is. I went there for a real estate workshop, and I swear, most of us spent every spare moment between meetings in the pools. You can even walk around in your thick fuzzy bathrobe and bathing suit."

"Okay. You sold me. That does sound really relaxing, and I could use some heavy-duty relaxation. I haven't taken any time off from work because Steve couldn't. I'd feel guilty if I went away for a weekend when he couldn't go."

"Well, Steve won't be here, so he won't care. You two can talk on the phone in the thermal pools."

Somehow the image of cell phones and thermal pools didn't match in Kelly's mind. She'd leave her phone in the bathrobe.

As if on cue, her cell phone rang on top of the library table. "Kelly Flynn here," she said, flipping it open.

"Hey, Kelly, this is Patty. I've talked to someone else who saw Holly at the party that night."

"Good. Did they see her taking pills from anyone?"

"No, this girl was hanging around with some others, but she did say she talked with Holly later that night in the front yard. The girl said she saw Holly get into a dark car and leave."

"Really? Did she see who was driving?"

"Nope. She just saw a dark car pull up.

Holly got in, and the car drove off. That's all."

"What do you think, Patty?"

"I don't know, Kelly. This summer Holly had been hanging around a lot with some people that I don't know real well. Someone said they're from Greeley. I didn't see them at the party, so maybe one of them came to pick her up."

"Maybe Holly called one of those Greeley friends since Tommy was busy studying in Denver. Any idea who they are?"

"No, but I'm still asking questions. I'll let you know what I find out. Listen, gotta run."

"Thanks, Patty. Talk to you later." Kelly flipped her phone closed and tossed it on the table.

"Okay, you have to explain that conversation. Who's Patty?" Jennifer asked.

"I met her at Barbara's class, remember? She grew up with Tommy and Holly. She was the one who said Barbara wasn't happy about Tommy dating Holly."

Jennifer nodded her head. "Ohhhh, yeah, now I recall your mentioning it that day at the table."

"Anyway, after the funeral Tommy told us he wanted to stay in Fort Connor and cruise around parties so he could find out who gave Holly an overdose. Burt and Lisa and

155

I convinced him that was a bad idea. Then I offered to ask questions to see what I could find out."

"*You're* going to start cruising campus parties?" Jennifer looked shocked.

"Not me," Kelly admitted with a smile. "Patty's doing the campus legwork. She's over there taking classes and goes out regularly. She knows lots of people. Anyway, she's asking questions and when she finds out something, she calls me, and I e-mail Tommy."

Jennifer eyed Kelly skeptically. "Why does Tommy want to know?"

"Well, Tommy wants to find out who gave the pills to Holly so his ambulance squad guys can go over and have a little chat with the person. Tell them that people are dying from those pills." She shrugged. "Tommy says they've done it before and sometimes it scares the person enough to make 'em stop selling."

"Do you realize how crazy that sounds, Kelly?"

Kelly laughed softly. "Yeah, now that I've tried to explain the situation, I have to admit it does sound weird. But Patty and I are simply trying to help Tommy so he won't leave med school and come charging up here."

Jennifer shook her head. "Trust me, Kelly. You do not want to get involved in that campus party scene. It's a swamp. I know, because I used to be in it years ago."

"Don't worry, I'm not going over. I'd stick out, and no one would talk to me."

"You got that right."

"Patty's got all the connections. Turns out she was at the same party Holly was that night."

"Why are we not surprised?"

"She didn't see much, other than Holly drinking. But some of her friends saw things. Just now, Patty said someone saw Holly leave the party and get into a dark car that night. No clue as to who was driving, though."

"Whoever it was probably gave her the pills," Jennifer said matter-of-factly as she returned to her knitting.

"Well, maybe not. Yesterday, a girl told Patty she saw Holly and this other girl, Rachel, get into a fight over Tommy. According to the girl, Holly taunted Rachel, and Rachel tried to hit her, but some guy intervened." Kelly took a sip of lukewarm coffee.

Jennifer rolled her eyes. "Boy, does that bring back memories. See why I called it a swamp."

"Yeah, it kind of sounds like that. According to Patty, this Rachel Gebbard and Holly had a past history. Tommy used to date Rachel before he got serious about Holly. He dumped Rachel, and now she's carrying a grudge. And the other day, Patty said someone saw Rachel passing out pills at the party."

"Rachel Gebbard, you said?"

"Yeah, do you know her?"

Jennifer sighed. "Yeah . . . I've waitressed with her on some campus catering jobs. She works over at the Grill every day. And I do remember running into her on the party circuit. I was leaving it and she was revving up, shall we say."

"So, you know her? Great. What's she like? Did you see her handing out stuff at parties?"

Jennifer gave Kelly a jaundiced look. "Who *wasn't* handing out stuff at parties? Believe me, when I say it's a swamp, I'm not kidding. And you don't want to wade into it. I had to get out because I was tired of watching kids throw up and freak out. It got way too weird."

"What's Rachel like? You said you worked with her."

Jennifer shrugged. "She was like scores of other quasi-students I've known over the

158

years. They stop going to college full-time and start working. And then they try to handle work and classes, which is tricky, but doable. But it takes discipline. And the majority of the kids I saw lacked discipline. They'd spend way more time partying than studying, then they'd flunk the classes and have to take them again. They always had really good excuses, though."

"Yeah, I've met quite a few like that over the years," Kelly admitted. "Motivation isn't their strong suit."

"That's about it."

Kelly's stomach growled, and she checked her watch. After twelve noon. No wonder she was hungry. An idea wiggled forward then. She toyed with it for a second, then threw it out to Jennifer.

"Hey, I'm hungry. Want to go to lunch? My treat," she offered, shoving Steve's completed hat into her bag along with the phone.

"I can't refuse an offer like that." Jennifer put away her knitting. "Should we go into the café or someplace else?"

Kelly shouldered her bag as she stood up. "I was thinking we might go over to the Grill and see what they have."

Jennifer shot Kelly a look. "What're you up to, Kelly?"

"I just thought I'd check out this Rachel girl. See if I can get a read off her." Kelly headed to the foyer.

"You're sleuthing, and you know it. What do you expect to see? Pill bottles falling out of her pockets or something?" Jennifer accused as she followed after Kelly.

"No, no, I simply thought I'd try to engage her in conversation, maybe. Go from there." Kelly pushed the wooden door open and stepped out into the gorgeous autumn day.

Temperatures were still balmy and in the seventies. During the night, however, temperatures were beginning to drop into the high thirties. That was enough to signal the sap in the trees to be ready. Once those freezing nights arrived, then the yearly ritual of changing leaves would begin. Kelly could smell the beginning of crispness in the air.

"Kelly, I've seen you engage your sleuthing targets in conversation, and it's not pretty. Face it, you're as subtle as a truck. It's a good thing I'm with you. Let me take the lead. Maybe she'll recognize me from catering. We'll go from there."

"I bow to your superior suggestion," Kelly said with a grin. "Let's take my car."

Kelly and Jennifer stepped into the brightly

painted café. Polished metal chairs and tables set off against red and yellow walls and posters of movie stars gave the café an almost vintage look. As if it were mimicking a diner decorated in 1950s style décor.

"Ohhhh, this is going to be deadly, I can tell," Jennifer said as they scanned for empty tables. "I can smell the French fries now, and I'm starving. I'd better order a salad before I weaken."

"Hey, those salads are working, girl," Kelly said approvingly. "I can tell you've lost weight. I told you running would help."

"Yeah, yeah, yeah. Let's grab that one." Jennifer pointed to a table. "I've already spotted Rachel. She's the one with the short brown ponytail. And it looks like she's working in that section."

Kelly picked out Rachel from the other waitresses as she followed Jennifer to the table. Glancing to the menu board behind the grill, Kelly saw one of her favorites. Philly cheesesteak. Her stomach growled louder. *Yes.*

Jennifer glanced at the menu. "Turkey salad, it is. Now, she'd better get over here before I weaken. I just saw a Philly cheesesteak on one of the tables."

Kelly rethought her original choice. It would be cruel of her to order one of those tempting sandwiches when Jennifer was trying to eat healthier. Kelly didn't even bother to open the menu. "Turkey salad sounds good," she said, ignoring her stomach's protest.

Rachel wandered their way, and Jennifer signaled her. "Remember, I'll start off. And you just stay mellow, okay?"

"Mellow," Kelly repeated, smiling. "Not sure I even know what that means, but I'll give it a shot."

"Hey, what can I get you two?" Rachel asked, notepad in hand.

"Two turkey salads, please," Kelly spoke up. "And I'll have black coffee."

"Make that two coffees," Jennifer said.

"Well, that was easy," Rachel said with a smile.

She had a nice smile, Kelly noticed. Jennifer was absolutely right. Rachel looked exactly like hundreds of other twentysomething young women who worked the cafés and shops and peopled the stores and classrooms and filled the university town of Fort Connor. Nothing exceptional, and certainly, nothing suspicious about her.

"Haven't you and I worked together before?" Jennifer offered with a friendly smile. "I waitress a lot of the catered jobs in town and around campus, and I think I

162

recognize you."

Rachel peered at Jennifer for a moment. "Yeah, come to think of it, you do look a little familiar. We probably have worked together. I waitress at the university for extra money all the time."

"Yeah, I still pick up a catering job over there every now and then, when I'm not working extra at my regular job. I'm over at Pete's Porch near the golf course on Lemay Avenue."

"Oh, yeah . . . I know where that is," Rachel said, eyes lighting up. "It's in the back of that knitting shop, right?"

"Yep. It's a great place to work. Plus the boss, Pete, does a lot of catering at night, too."

"Well, keep me in mind if he needs some extra help," Rachel said, flipping her order pad closed. "Can I get you two some water first?"

Kelly decided this was as good a time as any to jump in. "This may sound funny, but you look a little familiar, too," she said with a bright smile.

Rachel studied Kelly for a couple of seconds. "I don't think I remember working with you. Are you at the university, too?"

"No, no, I'm over at the knitting shop a lot, and I think I remember seeing you a few days ago. Didn't you go to that girl Holly Kaiser's funeral? There were a lot of college students there, and I thought I saw you." Kelly tried to sound as casual as possible. Jennifer was watching her closely.

Rachel's pleasant expression disappeared. Her face hardened. "I'm afraid you're wrong on that one. I know who Holly Kaiser is, but there's no way I'd go to her funeral. I grew up with her, and she was a conniving bitch."

Kelly blinked. She couldn't help it. Rachel's harsh comment on Holly's character was beyond blunt. "Wow . . . it sounds like you two go way back."

"Oh, yeah," Rachel said scornfully. "We went through high school together. She was a manipulating bitch then, too. If you got in her way, she'd bad-mouth you to anyone who'd listen."

Kelly noticed Jennifer looked as surprised as she did. Kelly couldn't resist following up. "Well, I didn't really know her, not really. But I know Barbara Macenroe at the shop and saw her son, Tommy, who was all broken up over Holly's death. He was her boyfriend apparently."

"Tommy was too good for her," Rachel said in a bitter tone. "I never could understand what he saw in her. Holly used to jerk him around like a puppet on a string."

Kelly feigned an amazed expression. "Really? Wow, it sounds like Holly had two different personalities."

Rachel's expression turned scornful. "Yeah. Around Tommy she was all sugary sweetness. But when Tommy wasn't there, she was cheating on him behind his back with another guy."

Kelly didn't have to feign shock this time. "Are you sure? All I've heard is how Tommy and Holly were sweethearts since high school."

Rachel's eyes narrowed. "Yeah, I'm sure. I saw her with some Greeley dude all summer. He and his friends come into Fort Connor regularly to party. Everybody knows about him. Even Tommy's old buddies from high school. Nobody wanted to tell Tommy, of course." Rachel glanced around the café. "Well, enough of the soap opera. I've gotta get back to customers. Your order won't take long."

"Sorry we delayed you, Rachel," Jennifer offered as Rachel turned to walk away.

"Whoa . . ." Kelly said, watching Rachel head to another customer's table. "I wasn't expecting that."

"Yeah, I could tell, but only because I've been briefed on this soap opera. You handled

165

it well, though, I have to admit. You've gotten to be an effective liar." Jennifer sent her a sly smile.

"Gee, thanks. I'm not sure that's a compliment."

"It's not. But it is a useful trait when you're out sleuthing around, right?"

EIGHT

Kelly guided her sporty red car around the curving canyon road. She was a lot more careful driving these winding mountain roads since her accident a year and a half ago. Of course, it wasn't winter now, so the roads that wound through Bellevue Canyon were clear and dry, not coated in ice. Even so, Kelly treated those curves with more respect.

At this higher altitude the nights had already dropped to freezing, so fall's colors were on display. The aspen trees were bright splashes of gold among the thick evergreens crowding the hillsides. Bushes that normally went unnoticed during spring and summer boldly proclaimed their presence, adorned now in pumpkin orange and scarlet red. Deep burgundy vines hugged the hillside and ran between rocks and into crevices. Color was everywhere.

Fort Connor was five thousand feet above

sea level, and Bellevue Canyon rose in a steady incline nearly two thousand feet above the city. Alpaca rancher Jayleen Swinson's ranch wasn't at the very top of the canyon, but it was close, so Kelly loved the opportunity to drive out there. Spring, summer, or fall, the mountain scenery was always gorgeous. Summer green or autumn gold and orange, the drive through the canyon was almost therapeutic. Kelly always started to relax the moment the road started to climb. Winter driving, however, was a different story.

"Some folks simply have to live up here in the mountains," Jayleen had once told her, and Kelly believed it. She'd thought she'd found the perfect place two years ago, but she'd been proven wrong. That ranch proved to have "bad juju," as Jayleen put it. Kelly dumped the property and hadn't regretted it.

Her cell phone rang on the seat beside her, and Kelly debated answering. Driving one-handed through the canyon was definitely trickier. She slowed down and reached for the phone. Patty's name flashed on the screen.

"Hey, Patty, thanks for returning my call," she said, guiding the car around a curve.

"No problem, Kelly. You said you'd

learned something?"

"Yeah, my friend Jennifer works at Pete's café at the back of Lambspun, and she said she'd waitressed with Rachel Gebbard before, so I got her to take me over to the Grill where Rachel worked. After what you said the other day, I wanted to check her out."

"Really?" Patty sounded surprised. "Well, uh, did you talk with her? What'd you think?"

"Yeah, Jennifer started because Rachel recognized her from the university catering jobs. So, I kind of jumped in and said she looked familiar, then I asked if she'd been at Holly's funeral last week. I'd remembered seeing several students there."

"You *didn't!*" Patty's voice sounded shocked. "Jeez, what'd she say?"

"Well, you were definitely right when you said she didn't care for Holly. She let us know exactly what she thought of her. And how Tommy shouldn't have wasted his time with her."

"See, I told you she hated Holly. She's always been jealous."

"Well, Rachel also went on to say something that surprised me. She said Holly was cheating on Tommy with this guy from Greeley. I wondered if you've heard anything about that when you've asked around."

"What! She's gotta be lying."

"Well, she sure sounded believable when she told us. She said she'd seen Holly at several parties, and she was with this new guy. Seems he and his friends come in from Greeley regularly to party here."

Patty paused. "Well, she was hanging with that different bunch lately, but I don't think Holly would cheat on Tommy."

"Well, I questioned Rachel, and she said even some of Tommy's old buddies from high school have seen her with this guy. Nobody wanted to tell Tommy, of course."

"Really?" Patty went quiet for a moment. "That makes me curious."

"That's why I called you. It made me curious, too, so I thought maybe you had heard something."

"Not really. Nothing specific, I mean. But, you know, some people did mention this guy. They just didn't go into detail. Now, I'm going to start asking other people what they know."

"I figured you would. And while you're at it, find out if anyone else saw Rachel selling pills. I want to tell Burt."

"Uhhhh, you better not. I . . . I asked my friend Colleen about it again, and it turns out she was talking about someone else. Not Rachel. She got them mixed up."

"So, she didn't see Rachel selling pills?"

"No, it was another girl in the kitchen who was talking to Rachel. Colleen doesn't know who the other girl is."

That sounded strange to Kelly. "How'd she get them mixed up? Do they look alike or something?"

"I don't know. Colleen drinks a lot, so she probably got confused. You know, fuzzy memory."

Kelly didn't have personal knowledge of that, but she'd seen enough people in a chemically impaired state and fuzzy memory was definitely part of the picture. Kelly couldn't help but remember Jennifer's warning about the party scene "swamp."

"You know, that makes me wonder if Colleen really saw an argument between Rachel and Holly or not. Maybe she was confused about that, too."

"I asked her again, and she swore she remembered them getting into a fight."

Kelly held the car steady around a curve as a large truck passed on the other side of the narrow road. "Okay, let me know if you learn anything else, Patty."

"Will do. Listen, I've got to run to another class. I'll talk to you later, Kelly." She

171

clicked off.

Kelly tossed her phone on the opposite seat again. Jayleen's ranch had come into view after that last curve, and Kelly slowed down to turn into the gravel driveway. She saw Jayleen's new silver-gray truck parked beside the barn. Alpaca grazed in the pastures, lifting their heads at the sound of tires crunching on gravel. The elegant creatures observed Kelly's arrival. Some returned to grazing while others wandered toward the fence bordering the corral and barnyard, curious.

Jayleen stepped out onto a porch that wrapped around the front and side of the log-beam mountain home. She waved as Kelly pulled her car to a stop beside the barn.

Kelly grabbed her shoulder bag briefcase as she left the car. "Hey, Jayleen. Have you got any coffee? I drained mine on the way up the canyon."

"You betcha, Kelly. I put a fresh pot on after you called me from the interstate," she said as she approached.

Kelly took the portfolio from her briefcase and handed it to Jayleen. "Here are your August statements. September is looking even better so far."

"Well, that's good news." Jayleen accepted

the long package. "Why don't you claim one of those rockers on the porch while I bring us some coffee."

Kelly looked over at the rockers, then the gorgeous mountain views across the pastures. "You know, that's exactly what I need right now."

Jayleen grinned. "Figured it might be. You've been out in Brighton all day?"

"Just about. Warner asked me to come in early this morning so I could go around with him to the building site for a new shopping center. He wanted me to get in on the ground floor so I'd know what was happening. That took all morning. Then he wanted me to have lunch with some of his partners, so it was after two before I left."

"Sounds like you're making yourself real indispensable, Kelly girl," Jayleen said as they walked toward the porch. "You're gonna have to get me up to speed with these new clients of yours. You go settle in and start relaxing, while I fetch the coffee."

Kelly didn't need further persuasion. She dropped her briefcase on the porch and chose a rocker. Nudging the chair into its gentle movements, Kelly kicked off her heels and settled back to enjoy the sight of snow-capped Rockies peeking over a forested ridge in the distance.

■ ■ ■ ■

Jayleen rested a ceramic mug on her denim-clad knee as she rocked beside Kelly. "I'm really proud of you, Kelly. You grabbed those two introductions Curt gave you and ran with them. Now, it sounds like you've got yourself two first-class clients. You won't be hurtin' for money anytime soon."

"Well, you're right about that," Kelly admitted with a smile. "I can never thank Curt enough for those recommendations, that's for sure."

"A recommendation will get you into the door, that's all. It was up to you to seal the deal with those businessmen. And once they saw the quality of your work, they were sold." Jayleen lifted her mug in salute. "Congratulations, Kelly. You done good."

Kelly returned the mug salute. "Thank you kindly, Miss Jayleen, ma'am."

Jayleen chuckled. "Sure beats bookkeeping, doesn't it?"

Kelly grinned. "Yep. It sure does. And speaking of bookkeeping, your accounts are looking really good. Income growing and expenses are in line. Congratulations on that. And I'm glad to see you got that new truck you were talking about. I'll bet you got the payment you wanted, too."

"Sure did. Car dealerships are hurtin' right now, so I felt like I was helping them out."

Kelly gazed at the distant peaks. September snows had already set the mountaintops glistening white. Snow always came early in the high country. The late afternoon sun set the peaks sparkling with an orange glow. Soon the setting sun would turn the orange to red.

The view from Jayleen's wide front porch looked out over a broad stretch of green that wasn't fenced pasture. This stretch of land was edged with evergreens and small brush. It was a perfect place for picnics, and Jayleen had invited Kelly and her friends several times. Like Curt, Jayleen was an enthusiastic host and enjoyed sharing the mountain scenery with others.

"This is such a pretty view. It drained every last bit of stress out of me," Kelly said with a laugh. "I'll have to come up here every time I go traipsing off to commercial sites in Brighton."

"Come up anytime, Kelly. I told Curt I'd be glad to have the party here, but he wants to have it at his ranch. Makes sense, too, since Marty is his nephew."

"What party?" Kelly stared blankly at Jayleen.

"Oops, I let the cat outta the bag." Jayleen slapped her leg. "Oh, well, Curt said he'd be calling all you folks today. So expect a message on your phone. He's planning to throw an engagement party for Marty and Megan in a couple weeks or so. He's gonna invite all the Colorado kin and Marty and Megan's friends. It's gonna be a steak cookout. So, you and Steve come hungry." Jayleen laughed then sipped her coffee.

"Hey, that's a great idea. We haven't had a barbeque since early August. I'll be sure to leave Carl at home."

Jayleen hooted. "Lord, lord, you'd better. I don't want him anywhere near that grill."

"I remember how mad you got years ago when he stole one of Curt's huge steaks you were grilling." Kelly cackled.

"Don't remind me. I was so mad I was about to wring off that puny excuse for a tail of his."

Kelly rocked for a minute. "I was kind of surprised at Marty and Megan's announcement, weren't you?"

"Not really," Jayleen said, leaning back in her rocker. "That's what young couples do when they're in love. After a while, they tie the knot." She sipped her coffee. "And

Megan and Marty seem to be a perfect match."

Kelly pondered that for a long moment. "Lisa and Greg are a perfect match for each other, but they never talk about getting married. And they've been together five years."

Jayleen shrugged. "People are different. Some just aren't the marrying kind. Some people don't like to be tied down. Some are scared off by their parents' bad marriages. Some of us have a bad track record at marriage, so we shy away."

Since Jayleen had opened the door on this topic, Kelly decided to follow up. Curt and Jayleen had been "seeing" each other for nearly a year now. They showed up together as a couple at get-togethers. They co-hosted barbeques at their respective ranches. They gave every indication of being a couple, except they both lived separately.

"Speaking of relationships, you and Curt seem to be getting along smoothly. Everybody was taking bets on when you two would get together." Kelly gave Jayleen a devilish smile.

Jayleen grinned. "Yeah, we could tell. You folks are as subtle as a pack of hounds who've picked up a scent."

Kelly laughed. "Everybody was really happy to see you together. You make a great couple."

"Well, let's just say we enjoy each other's company. We get along about as well as most couples. Nothing between men and women runs smoothly. There's always some choppy water. Trust me." Jayleen chuckled low in her throat.

That open conversational door beckoned invitingly. Kelly felt like she and Steve were definitely trying to row through some choppy water. And it wasn't easy.

"Is that why you two still live separately?"

"That and other reasons. I'm of the mind that it's good to have your own place. Everybody needs their own space. And some of us have gotten used to a lot of space over the years." Jayleen tipped back her mug.

"Well, whatever you two are doing, it seems to be working," Kelly said, looking out over the pastures. "You and Curt certainly look happy. Whether you're with each other or not."

Jayleen glanced over at Kelly. "I sense this rough patch Steve is going through right now is taking a toll on you, too."

"Ohhhh, yeah," Kelly said, still staring at the snowy peaks. "Talk about choppy water. Boy."

"Curt's told me what's going on. I know

it's hard, Kelly, but Steve's just going to have to weather this stormy period and find his footing again. You two will get through it. We know you will."

Kelly gave her a rueful smile. "If the choppy water doesn't swamp our boat, first. But right now, all I see are waves rising higher."

"You two will ride it out. This rough period is bound to turn around sometime next year."

"I sure hope so," Kelly said, staring at her ceramic mug.

Jayleen didn't say anything else, and both of them rocked quietly for a few minutes. The setting sun was turning the snowy peaks reddish gold. Kelly stared at the burnished color, letting anxious thoughts loose.

Finally Jayleen spoke. "How's Barbara doing? I haven't seen her since before that funeral. She's not been in the shop when I've stopped by."

"She's back to teaching her fiber classes. I've seen her in the classroom when I've dropped in to knit. She seems to be doing okay. Burt says she's still worrying about Tommy."

"Is he still grieving over his girlfriend?"

"Yeah, big time. But what had us all

concerned was Tommy wanted to stay in Fort Connor and try to find out who gave Holly those pills. They were some form of opiate narcotics, apparently. And Holly had never used those before. So, I promised Tommy I'd start asking around to see if any students remembered seeing Holly at the parties."

Jayleen shook her head. "Believe me, Kelly, you don't want to get into that mess."

Kelly gave her a twisted smile. "Exactly what Jennifer told me. That's why I asked a friend of Tommy's to check out the parties for me."

"I can tell you right now what you'll find out," Jayleen said, looking at Kelly sagely. "They're more pills at those parties than dogs have fleas."

Kelly had to laugh. "Well, that's kind of what she's found. And every time she learns something, it's all twisted around these different relationships. Or, it's not reliable because the person was drinking so much they couldn't remember correctly."

"Hate to say I told you so."

"I know. I was just hoping I could find something to tell Tommy that would give him some peace of mind."

"Well, I didn't know Tommy, but he sounds like a fine young man from what I've heard. He's simply going to have to accept the fact that his girlfriend was on a self-destructive path that leads only one way. Some people can turn themselves around in time and stay turned, like I did. Some can't."

"Yeah, I guess. It's so sad, though."

"It is, but it happens every day. Look around you at the counseling centers we've got going in town. That's why I had the retreat last summer here at the ranch. Trying to catch some young girls before they got on that dangerous path. But there're not enough of us to go around to reach everyone who needs help. Just look over at the Mission and the homeless shelter for some lost souls who've fallen through the cracks. Some of them have been on that path so long, they don't know any other way. I swear, some of them will sleep outside in the bushes along the river so they can nurse that bottle of whiskey rather than go into a clean bed at the Mission."

Jayleen's comment sparked an idea in Kelly. She toyed with it for a minute before throwing it out in the open. "Speaking of that, Jayleen, do you think you could do me a favor, for Tommy's sake? Could you ask your friends at the Mission who work with the street people to see if any of them were sleeping along the river trail that night? Maybe one of them saw something."

Jayleen furrowed her eyebrows for a minute. "Sure, Kelly, I'd be glad to. And I'll ask the counselors at AA if they've heard anything. They work with a lot of the guys who're trying to turn themselves around. What exactly do you want them to find out?"

"Just ask them to check if any of those guys saw a young girl wandering around the trail that night. If it's true what police say, then Holly may have walked on that trail for a while before she finally collapsed. At least, I'm guessing that's what happened."

"Do the cops think she walked from Old Town to where they found her? That's quite a ways."

"I thought the same thing, Jayleen. And Patty, the girl who was asking around campus for me, heard from someone that they saw Holly get into a dark car after the party that night. So, who knows what happened? Maybe the driver gave Holly the pills and let her out along the trail when he found she'd taken too many."

Jayleen wagged her head again. "I think you're right, Kelly. That driver is probably the one who gave her the pills. He could be a college student or maybe not."

"I told Burt what Patty had found out, and he passed it along to his old partner, Dan."

"All right, Kelly. I'll ask my friends tomorrow night when I go to the meeting. Let's see what they learn. Remember, though, these guys are pretty closemouthed. They don't want to get into any trouble. So even if they saw something, they might not admit it."

"I hear you, Jayleen. But at least I'll be able to tell Tommy something. Anything to help."

Kelly took the turn into the Lambspun driveway faster than usual. Her afternoon visit with Jayleen had lengthened when Jayleen invited her to share her famous chili. That was a dinner invitation Kelly couldn't refuse. However, when she returned to her car to drive home, Kelly was horrified to find two messages from Steve on the cell phone she'd left on the car seat.

Steve had come home unexpectedly so they could go out to dinner. He said he'd "wanted to surprise" her. Steve's first message sounded aggravated. His second message, downright angry. Kelly had driven as fast as Fort Connor's ever-vigilant police patrols allowed in an anxious effort to get home.

Unfortunately it was already past nine o'clock when she left Jayleen's canyon ranch, and canyon roads were treacherous at night so she couldn't risk hurrying too fast. Guilt prodded her every mile.

Kelly pulled her car to a sharp stop, grabbed her bag, and scrambled out. Racing to the front door, she burst inside, wondering what she'd find. Would Steve still be angry?

"Hey, I raced as fast as I could, but that canyon road is dark as pitch at night," she announced in an artificially cheerful voice. "You want to go out for pizza?"

Steve lay sprawled on the sofa, a bottle of his favorite ale in hand, watching television. Baseball players were on the field. Kelly recognized the Colorado Rockies uniform.

"Naw, I heated up a pizza from the freezer. I'm good," he said, briefly glancing up from the screen.

"We could still go out for a drink if you want," Kelly suggested, hoping to make up for her blunder of missing Steve's calls. She was feeling majorly guilty right now. Why did she leave her phone in her car? *Why?*

"Naw, that's okay," Steve declined, not even looking up this time. "I'm getting kind of sleepy anyway. I'm gonna turn in after this inning."

Kelly dropped her bag on a chair, kicked off her heels, and sank into an upholstered chair across the coffee table from Steve. Mentally, she was still kicking herself for screwing up. Steve had driven all the way back to Fort Connor early to go out with her, and she wasn't there. Not only wasn't she there, he couldn't even reach her because she'd left her cell phone in the car. She rarely did that.

Dumb move, Kelly. Dumb, dumb, her guilty conscience scolded.

"You going to your office in the morning or back to Denver?" she asked quietly. Steve, who was obviously engrossed in the game, was barely paying attention to her. Of course, the three empty ale bottles on the coffee table were probably the real cause of his inattention.

"I'll be working here in town. Fred forgot he had a business meeting scheduled tomorrow. Since he couldn't come into the office, he told me I didn't have to come in, either. He even paid me for the lost time, which was damn nice of him." He tipped the bottle. "When I couldn't reach you, I went over to my office. There was a mountain of mail waiting for me."

An invisible cloak of guilt settled over Kelly's shoulders. She could feel it. "I'm really sorry I didn't get your calls, Steve. If I'd known you might be calling, I wouldn't have left my phone in the car. But you said you wouldn't be coming back till Saturday night."

"Forget about it, Kelly. I'm pretty beat anyway. I'm practically falling asleep right now." He drained the bottle.

Kelly could almost see his eyelids drooping, so she decided she'd better throw out tomorrow's itinerary before Steve fell asleep. "Hey. Lisa, Jen, and I are going shopping with Megan tomorrow. She's starting to look at wedding dresses. We'll be back by late afternoon and thought we'd go over and watch the guys play ball at Moore Field. It's the Fall Classic. Will you be able to join us after you've finished at your office?"

The Fall Classic was one of Steve's favorite Colorado tournaments. Maybe that would capture his interest.

"I'll try. What time will you guys be there?" He set his empty bottle on the table beside the others.

Encouraged by this moderate response, Kelly continued. "The games start at six, so we plan to grab a cooler with some beer and get some chips and salsa and guacamole. They've got brats and hot dogs at the field."

"I'll . . . try," Steve mumbled, eyelids closing.

Kelly watched Steve's breathing slow down, nice and even. Soon, he was sound asleep. She sat for a couple of minutes, watching Steve sleep and watching the game before she got up and went to her bedroom to change into her sweats.

She might as well get a bottle of Fat Tire ale, watch the rest of the game, and keep sleeping Steve company. Meanwhile, that cloak of guilt weighed heavier and heavier on Kelly's shoulders. It didn't feel good at all.

NINE

"Wow, look at that," Kelly said as she and her friends stood beside the bridal shop window display.

"It's gorgeous," Lisa said, observing the ornate wedding gown behind the glass.

"I don't know, guys," Megan demurred, her expression skeptical. "That's a whole lot of beadwork. It must cost a fortune."

"Well, we won't find out unless we go inside," Jennifer suggested, gesturing toward the shop door.

"You'll probably find something here, Megan. This is a much bigger shop than those other two," Kelly said as she followed her friends into the shop. Sniffing a delicate floral scent when she entered, Kelly tried to identify it. "That smells good. Is it a flower?"

"Lilacs," Jennifer and Lisa chimed together.

The bridal shop foyer widened to a hallway that had two rooms opening on either side, one larger, the other smaller. A middle-aged woman in a pale pink suit rose from behind a mahogany secretary and walked toward them.

"Welcome, ladies," she said with a warm smile as she approached. "Which one of you is the bride?"

"The one with the dazed expression," Kelly volunteered, pointing to Megan, who was looking around the shop, eyes wide.

"How wonderful," the woman said, smiling maternally. "I'm Lucinda. What's your name, dear?"

"Megan."

"Well, Megan, I'm delighted you and your friends dropped by. I take it you're shopping for a bridal gown. We do have other accessories, as well as bridesmaids' gowns. Take your time browsing. I'm here to answer any questions." With that, Lucinda returned to her desk in the small room across the hall.

Kelly surveyed the shop's luxurious interior. The two rooms were decorated with antiques, either real or reproductions. After going through her cousin Martha's Wyoming ranch house, Kelly had learned a lot about fine furniture and antiques that she never knew before. She did notice, however, that there were only two gowns on display in the larger sitting room. Sofas and chairs and several ornate mirrors were scattered around the room.

"This shop is definitely more posh than the others," Lisa whispered as she strolled closer to one of the two gowns displayed on pedestals in the corner. "This dress is simpler, Megan. Look at the pretty lace over the shoulders, and the skirt is soft and gathered."

Megan cocked her head, observing the gown. "All that material looks like ruffles, and I don't like ruffles."

"Okay, no ruffles, no beads," Kelly announced as she walked over to the other gown. "Two out of three eliminated. What about this one?" She pointed to the sheath-style gown, which draped beautifully to the floor. Gauzy bits of lace served as straps. The entire shimmering fabric's surface was covered in embroidered designs. At least Kelly thought it was embroidery. She'd seen enough at the shop to recognize it. "This is simple and elegant, Megan."

"Oooo, that is gorgeous," Lisa said as she approached. "This is more your style, right?"

Megan slowly walked closer, surveying the gown as she approached. "I do like that style better. It's not poufy."

"With your great figure, it'll look fantastic on you." Jennifer stepped closer to the gown and touched the fabric. "Look at all that embroidery work. Beautiful."

Megan nodded. "Beautiful and expensive. All that embroidery has to be expensive."

Lisa gave Megan a stern look. "Megan, they're wedding gowns. They're supposed to have extra work on them. Either ruffles or embroidery or beads. Stuff like that. Get over it."

"It looks like you're going to have to choose a gown with stuff on it, Megan. Unless you get married in a bedsheet." Kelly joked.

"Don't give her ideas," Jennifer warned.

Lucinda strolled over to them. "It sounds like you've just started looking."

"You're right. We've been to two other shops, but I didn't like any of the gowns on display." Megan glanced around the room. "We were hoping you'd have more gowns we could see. The other shop didn't have many, either. Why is that?"

"Like other shops we used to carry several in the salon, but now we can actually show more gowns with digital videos."

Megan's eyes lit up. Familiar territory. "Really? What are some of the best websites we can go to?"

"Oh, there are several. All the designers have their gowns on display. But you can see those same gowns here." She walked over to a cabinet and opened the doors, revealing a large flat screen. "We have all their gowns on video, so our customers can see them without having to jump from website to website on their lunch hours." She clicked a remote control device and the screen came to life with bright images of brides and grooms and wedding parties, cakes, dancing couples, families together. Then — the image of a wedding gown appeared, with its name and number at the bottom of the screen. The model turned slowly so the back was revealed.

"Sit down and relax and watch." Lucinda gestured to the upholstered chairs. "If you see something you like, then make a note of the number. Don't worry if you miss it the first time. The video replays automatically."

"Oooo, look at that one," Lisa pointed to the gown on the screen. Strapless with a simple fitted bodice, the full skirt flared out gracefully to the floor.

"Pretty, but I recognize the designer's name," Jennifer remarked.

"I think that means expensive," Kelly said to Megan.

Yards of shiny material appeared next,

cascading down the back of a strapless gown and extending onto the floor.

"What's that fabric?" Kelly asked.

"Looks like taffeta," Lisa decreed.

"Boy, that's a long train," Jennifer commented.

"Cathedral. The longest," Megan said. "Next?"

Another strapless gown appeared, figure-hugging to the knees where it flared to the floor.

"Pretty."

"Yep, but it's covered in ruffles."

"They're small ruffles."

"Ruffles are ruffles," Megan intoned.

A simpler strapless style was next, which hugged the figure to below the waist where the skirt gradually fell fuller and fuller with a stylish drape in the center.

"Oooo, that's nice."

"Classic."

"No beads and no ruffles," Kelly offered.

Megan still shook her head. "Yeah, but look at that train in the back. Semi-cathedral or cathedral."

"What?" Kelly stared at her. "They've got classifications?"

"Yep. I've been studying."

"What do you expect? It's Megan," Lisa said as Jennifer laughed softly.

Another gown appeared with straps and V-neckline. The dress hugged the model's body tighter than the others until it poufed out at the knees to the floor.

"Vampy," Jennifer said. "Even Marty would be speechless."

"Riiiight," Megan joked while her friends laughed.

Another strapless gown, its long train gathered with lacy trim.

"Long train with imitation ruffles," Kelly announced.

A slinky satin gown covered in Chantilly lace came next.

"Do you have anything against lace?" Lisa asked skeptically.

"No, but it's so low I'd fall out of it."

A celebration of ruffles appeared next and laughter was the only commentary.

The screen flashed again showing another V-necked gown, but this skirt flared gracefully to the floor, a layer of white tulle draped over the underlying fabric. The model wore a large white-brimmed hat, which curved over her face.

"Well, ah declare. If it isn't Miz Scahlett," Kelly said to Jennifer with a grin.

"In the flesh."

"Like I could pull *that* off," Megan said with a snort.

"Now, y'all hush. I've just come in from Charleston, and I'm simply exhausted," Jennifer said in a magnolia-dipped accent. "Have a julep sent to my room, please. I must rest before all the festivities."

Soft laughter flowed around the room as several more gowns appeared only to be greeted with cries of "Beads!" or "Ruffles!" or "Froufrou!"

Then a simple unadorned white gown flashed on the screen. Spaghetti straps, soft tulle draping to the floor.

"*Voilà!*" Lisa cried, pointing to the screen. "You want simple? There's simple. It could be a prom dress it's so plain."

Megan peered at the image. "That's a lot of tulle."

Lisa closed her eyes and groaned as Kelly laughed.

Another strapless dress appeared, the slender skirt cascading to the floor in soft gathers.

"What about that one?" Jennifer gestured. "It's simple and there's no tulle."

Megan squinted at the screen. "It's got ruffles."

"Those aren't ruffles, they're *gathers!*" Lisa spouted, clearly out of patience.

Megan shook her head. "Ruffles, gathers. Same difference."

"Arrrrghhh!" Lisa cried.

Jennifer joined Kelly in laughing this time. Kelly sneaked a peek at Lucinda who was smiling broadly, obviously overhearing Megan's saga of the gowns.

"Look, it's back to the beginning again," Jennifer observed as the first gown reappeared on the screen.

"Megan, you're impossible," Lisa decreed, shaking her head. "You *will* have to get married in a bedsheet. You don't like anything!"

Everyone laughed, including Lisa as they jointly imagined Megan in her bedsheet at the church.

"Megan just hasn't found the perfect dress yet, right, Megan?" Lucinda said as she approached them.

"That's right," Megan said with an imperial sniff. "It's out there. I know it."

"You're right, Megan. And I have a feeling you'll find it, too. What's your time frame?"

"Time frame?" Megan looked at her blankly.

"When's the wedding?" Lucinda's smile widened.

"Ohhhh, we haven't nailed it down exactly." Megan gestured with her hand. "Sometime between the end of September and the middle of October next year."

"Well, you still have time yet. Six months out is as close as you can delay. Some of these bridal vendors need at least six months to deliver a gown."

"Okay, Megan. You've got your marching orders," Lisa said sternly. "A decision in six months. Or you really will be showing up in that bedsheet because there won't be any gowns available."

"Ohhhh, Megan won't have to resort to a bedsheet," Jennifer said with a wicked smile. "We'll just grab her before the ceremony and wrap her in yards of tulle and lace —"

"And ruffles," Kelly added. "Lots and lots of ruffles."

"That salmon salad was delicious," Jennifer said, polishing off the last tidbit of spinach on her plate.

"Wow, you went through that fast," Lisa said, poking through the arugula and sprouts for a garbanzo bean.

"I was starving. I don't know about you guys, but all that shopping wore me out. I feel like Miz Scarlett for real."

"How could it tire you out?" Kelly asked, forking the lone asparagus on her plate. "We were either in the car or in the shops."

"It was the stress," Jennifer said solemnly. "Ruffles, beads, trains too long, take off the tulle. Exhausting."

Kelly sipped her coffee as laughter bounced around the table again. She and her friends had stopped for lunch at a favorite café in Boulder, only an hour from Fort Connor.

"I can't help if I'm picky, guys." Megan shrugged. "I want what I want."

"That's okay, Megan." Jennifer held up her glass of iced tea. "You deserve to have your wedding exactly as you want. We'll be your forward guard. We'll run interference whenever you need it."

"One for all and all for one," Kelly declared as they all held up their glasses and cups. Just then, her cell phone rang. "Excuse me a sec." She dug out the data phone and flipped it open. Patty's name and number flashed on the screen. "Hey, what's up?"

"Hi, Kelly. I simply wanted to tell you what I found out at last night's party."

Last night was Friday night, Big Time Party Night on college campuses. Kelly stepped away from the table for privacy. "Oh, yeah. Did you hear anything interesting?"

"As a matter of fact, I did. I checked what you told me yesterday and learned that Holly really was cheating on Tommy. I talked with several of our old friends from

198

high school, and they confirmed it. This guy's name is Eddie something, and he is from Greeley. Apparently he and his buddies show up in Fort Connor every weekend to party, like you heard."

"So Rachel was telling the truth."

"Oh, yeah. And you'll never guess what else."

"Okay, you've got me. What else?"

"One of the guys said this Eddie sells pills regularly. Apparently he's got quite a little business going on."

Kelly's mind started racing. Maybe Eddie was the driver of the dark car that picked up Holly the night of the party. If he regularly sold pills, then he *must* have been the one to give Holly the opiate narcotics that killed her.

"Whoa, Patty, that's important information. I'm gonna tell Burt on Monday. Did you check with any others? Did anyone see Eddie selling pills at the party?"

"According to one of the guys, this Eddie is pretty careful when he comes into Fort Connor. He doesn't usually sell at parties because he doesn't want to take the chance he'll get on the cops' radar screen here. But he makes contacts and meets people, then sells to them later on."

"Clever."

"Yeah, it is," Patty continued. "You know, Kelly, I'm beginning to think Eddie was the one who picked up Holly that night and gave her the pills."

"I'm thinking the same thing, Patty."

"Maybe they went to another party in Old Town and she overdosed there. There were a couple more parties going on that night."

"You may be right, Patty. Who knows? Maybe Holly wandered away from that party and wound up on the river trail."

"Could be. Listen, I've gotta run. I'm working at the steakhouse tonight. I'll call you if I hear anything else."

"Take care, Patty. Talk to you later."

Kelly flipped off her phone and wound her way through the Mediterranean-style café toward the table with her friends. Meanwhile, she wondered how in the world she would pass this information along to Tommy. There was no way she would reveal Holly's cheating. Tommy had had enough grief already in his young life.

"Was that Steve?" Lisa asked when Kelly returned to the table.

"I wish. No, it was business," Kelly lied, deciding she didn't want to share the soap-opera tragedy with the rest of her friends. Jennifer knew, and that was enough.

"Will Steve be able to make it to the ball

field?" Megan asked after she drained her iced tea.

"I hope. But we won't know until we see him," Kelly said, then abruptly changed the subject. "Are we ready to attack the last Boulder bridal shop?"

A mixture of good-natured complaints greeted her suggestion.

"Okay, where's the guacamole? I know I put it in here," Lisa said as she pulled another beer bottle from the plastic cooler chest.

Kelly brandished a plastic container. "Found it." She placed it in the middle of the picnic table that sat near the duck pond in the middle of the city's largest ballpark. Four ball fields surrounded the lake like corners of a square.

Marty rushed up to the table. "Good. You brought chips and salsa." Marty reached across the table, snagged a chip, then scooped it full of salsa.

"Okay, we've got colas, water, iced tea," Megan counted off on her fingers. "No beer till after the game. We want you guys to win."

"Hey, we can win with beer," Greg said as he scooped a chip full of guacamole. "Lisa, did you bring tuna salad? We've gotta eat now before we start to warm up."

"It's in the green plastic tub," Lisa said, moving a plate of hot brats.

"Did you guys find a dress for Megan?" Marty asked, devilish grin starting. "I think I already know the answer."

"Of course not," Lisa retorted. "She didn't like *anything*."

Kelly brought out a container of green salad. "No ruffles, no beads, no lace, no trains —"

"Trains? You leaving Marty already? Now, there's the sensible Megan I know." Greg tossed a handful of chips into his mouth.

"No, I'm just picky about wedding gowns, that's all," Megan responded, separating a pile of paper plates. "No froufrou or fancy stuff. Like long *trains* on the back of the gown."

"I knew that," Greg quipped, dipping a chip into salsa.

"Sure you did," Lisa teased.

"That's my girl. No froufrou." Marty grinned then leaned over to give Megan a kiss.

"Hey, isn't that Steve?" Lisa pointed toward the parking lot.

Kelly looked up. Sure enough, Steve was walking across the field. "Well, how about that. He must have finished early. I wasn't sure if he would or not."

Steve waved at his former teammates, and several ran up to greet him. Kelly's heart tugged, watching Steve talk with his buddies. They wore their jerseys, and he was in jeans and a sweatshirt. No longer on the team.

"It doesn't seem right," Megan said quietly, voicing Kelly's thoughts. "Steve not playing, you know."

"Yeah, I know," Kelly admitted out loud. "I know he wants to. He's just not here enough."

"Okay, guys, lighten up," Marty advised. "Here he comes."

Kelly didn't wait. She walked over to Steve before he reached the table and gave him a welcome kiss. "I'm so glad you showed up. I was afraid you'd be swamped."

"Well, I am, but I'm also hungry, so I figured I'd eat dinner with you guys, then go back to work."

Half a loaf was better than none, Kelly recalled her aunt Helen saying more than once. "Hey, that'll work," she said cheerfully as they approached the table together to the welcome greetings of their friends.

TEN

"So, four bridal stores and seven hours later, we'd covered Fort Connor, Loveland, and Boulder," Kelly said to Lambspun shop assistant Connie. "Even with the lunch break in Boulder, we were shopped out by four o'clock."

"And Megan didn't see anything she liked?" middle-aged Connie asked, her surprise obvious.

Kelly took a deep sip from her refilled coffee mug before answering. "That's right."

"Wow, she must really be picky." Connie beckoned for a customer to approach the counter.

Kelly backed away, making room for the customer who had three skeins of tweed alpaca wool yarn in her hands. "She's not really being picky. Megan simply doesn't like all the fancy decorations that are on most of the gowns. You know, fluffy tulle, ruffles, beads, and long trains. She calls it 'froufrou.' "

Connie chuckled. "Well, that's Megan for you. Definitely a no-froufrou girl."

Kelly took another sip of coffee and headed for Mimi's office. Since she'd finished her account work, she had the rest of the afternoon for errands. Having completed Steve's winter hat, there were no unfinished knitting projects in her bag. A rare occurrence for her. She spotted Mimi in the classroom adjacent to the main knitting room.

"Hey, Mimi. Jennifer told me you've got a fiber retreat in the mountains coming up. Steve called and said he's not coming home this weekend because he's working a big project. Is it too late for me to join the retreat?"

"Of course not, Kelly," Mimi answered. "I'd love to have you. You haven't been on one of our retreats for a long time."

"Well, Jen made this one sound extra special. You're going to some lake resort in the mountains with heated thermal pools carved out of the rocks, I hear."

"That's right. And the lake is beautiful, surrounded by the mountains. Oh, and there's a spa there, too, if you want a massage."

"Oh, wow . . ." Kelly could almost feel

herself relaxing already. "Count me in. What day is it? I've got to put it on my day planner."

"This coming Friday. We're carpooling from here, and we're staying till Saturday noon. That way we'll have plenty of time for felting and relaxation."

"That sounds perfect. Where do I sign up?"

"Tell Connie at the front. She'll get you registered." Mimi eyed Kelly. "I was wondering when you'd want to try felting. I think you'll enjoy it, Kelly."

Kelly sipped her coffee. "It was Jen who gave me the idea. I've finished Steve's winter hat, and it's a little bit too big. She suggested it would look good felted. Plus it would be warmer that way. Warm is always a good thing for Colorado winters."

"You're right about that. And I agree with Jennifer. I've seen your hat, and that wool will felt up really well."

"As long as I don't shrink it too much," Kelly added with a laugh. Her cell phone rang then, and she gave Mimi a wave as she headed to a quiet corner of the knitting room.

"Hey, Kelly. Did I get you in the midst of your accounts?" Jayleen asked.

"Not at all. I finished up a few minutes

ago. I was about to do some errands. What's up?"

"Well, I think you'll want to make a detour to the Mission. There's someone here I'd like you to meet."

Kelly leaned against the library table as she sipped her coffee. "Did one of your counselor friends learn anything?"

"Oh, yeah. And we've got a guy sitting in the reading room right now. He's one of the regulars, I'm told. And apparently he saw a young woman on the trail that night."

Kelly's coffee mug stopped on its way to her lips. "You're kidding?"

"Sure as shootin'," Jayleen affirmed. "I figured you'd want to come out and talk to him. You'd better make it quick, too. Some of these guys aren't known for sitting still for long."

"I'll be right over," Kelly said, halfway to the door.

Kelly looked around the lobby of the Mission, searching for Jayleen. Several people were standing and talking in small groups in an adjacent room with chairs.

"May I help you?" asked a gray-haired woman behind the counter directly ahead.

"I'm looking for my friend, Jayleen Swinson. She asked me to come over. I think she's with —"

"I know where she is. Let me get her for you," the woman said in a cheerful voice as she picked up her desk phone. "Jerry?" she said after a moment. "Is Jayleen with you in the back? Someone's out front looking for her." The woman glanced up at Kelly. "Your name?"

"Kelly Flynn."

The woman repeated the name, then held on the line for a second. "Okay, thanks," she said, then hung up. "Jayleen will be right out. You can wait over there in the lobby."

Kelly wandered over to the waiting room. The large dining room that dominated most of the first floor of the building was empty. From what she'd heard from other volunteers, there were people in the kitchen already, cooking up tonight's dinner. The Mission served lunch and dinner to the homeless and out of work. She'd also heard that the number of people who showed up for free meals had increased. So had the demand at the local food bank for families.

"Kelly, come on back," Jayleen called, beckoning from a door at the rear of the lobby.

"How did your counselor friends find this guy?" Kelly whispered to Jayleen as they entered a corridor.

"My friend, Jerry, is director of the program that helps bring in the vagrants who're trying to put their lives back together. Jerry met with some of them yesterday, on Sunday, and straight out asked if anyone remembered seeing a young blonde girl wandering the river trail a couple of weeks ago. This morning, one of the guys came up to Jerry and admitted he'd seen someone that night. A young blonde girl."

"Wow, that's fantastic." Kelly glanced through the doors as they walked along the corridor.

"Here we are," Jayleen indicated. "Now, better hold back and let him tell his story. He's kind of skittish. He's one of the ones who's been out on his own for a while. Only this last year has he started wanting to make some changes, Jerry said." She opened a metal office door and motioned Kelly to enter.

A small man sat in a gray padded office chair beside a desk, holding a coffee mug. He could have been anywhere from forty to seventy years old, judging from the lines and wrinkles Kelly saw on his weather-beaten face. His hair was black and gray and shaggy and grew down his neck. A tall, slender, balding man stood beside him.

"Jerry, Malcolm," Jayleen said, nodding to

the tall balding man then to the seated one. "This is Kelly. She's a family friend of the young girl who died."

Kelly played along with Jayleen's exaggeration. "Thanks for inviting me."

"Hey, Kelly, I'm glad you could join us," Jerry said. "Malcolm here told us that he'd actually seen a young blonde girl on the trail one night. Do you want to tell Kelly the story you told me earlier, Malcolm?" Jerry sat in a desk chair beside the older man, who was dressed in a red-and-black-checked flannel shirt, faded work pants, and work boots. "Do you need a refill of coffee?" Jerry pointed to the ceramic mug in Malcolm's hand.

Malcolm glanced up at Kelly. She gave him her friendliest smile. Malcolm looked back at Jerry. "No, I'm okay. Did you find out what they're having for dinner tonight?"

A smile spread across Jerry's broad face. "I sure did. It's elk stew. One of our local hunters donated his share of a bull elk from last fall's hunting season. We've been parceling it out slowly because it's so good."

"Best thing you'll ever taste, next to prime beef," Jayleen decreed as she sank into a chair beside Jerry. She caught Kelly's eye and motioned to an empty chair.

"Damn right," Malcolm agreed, then

drained his coffee.

He glanced at Kelly again. "You that girl's sister or something?"

Kelly settled into the chair Jayleen indicated and quickly searched for something plausible to answer. "No, I'm just a close friend of the family. They're all broken up over Holly's death, and I'm trying to find out anything I can that might bring them some peace of mind."

"Holly. That's the girl's name?" Malcolm asked.

Kelly nodded, noticing Malcolm's watery blue eyes.

"Why don't you tell Kelly what you saw along the trail that night," Jerry suggested, leaning over, clasped hands between his knees.

Malcolm shrugged, then put his empty mug on a nearby office table. "Don't know if it'll be any help, but I'll tell you anyway." He crossed his arms and sank back into his chair. "It was Friday night before last. The Mission was filled with families, so some of us single men in line volunteered to sleep outside. Hell, we've been doing it for years. Plus, weather's still good. The cold hasn't settled in yet. So, I took my bedroll and headed down to a section of the trail that's kind of secluded and quiet. Lots of trees there beside the river, so you can bed down under the trees and nobody's the wiser."

"What part of the trail was that, Malcolm?" Jerry asked. "How close to the golf course were you?"

"Ohhhh, right next to it. During daylight you can see the golf course through the trees on that side of the trail."

"You slept on the river side, right?"

"Yep. I have some favorite spots beneath the trees. Nobody can see you from the trail, because of the leaves and brush. Anyway, I bedded down and went to sleep."

"About what time was that, Malcolm?" Jerry continued.

"Ohhhh, about ten o'clock or so. It was pretty warm that night so I went right to sleep."

"What woke you up?"

"It was that girl's voice," Malcolm said. "You get used to the sounds of traffic at night, but you're not used to other sounds. You know, high-pitched voices like that girl's."

"What'd she say?" Kelly couldn't help asking.

Malcolm shrugged again. "Couldn't tell. All it did was wake me up. That's when I looked over my shoulder and saw them."

That word jumped out at Kelly. "*Them?*

You mean she wasn't alone?"

"Nope. A man was with her. Looked like he was helping her walk down the trail. She wasn't too steady on her feet. I figured she was drunk. They were coming from the other end of the trail, near the crossroads."

Kelly recognized that as the crossroads of the avenue that ran beside the knitting shop and golf course and the large main east-west thoroughfare that ran through Fort Connor. The river trail ran underneath the intersection itself and came to a parking lot on the other side of the street.

"Could you see what the man looked like?" Kelly asked, leaning forward.

Malcolm shook his head. "Nope. He was wearing a dark jacket with the hood up. He was tall, that's all I noticed."

"You saw them walk along the trail and then what?" Jerry probed.

"The man walked the girl over to a rock and set her down on it. Then he walked back the way he came. Left the girl on the rock."

Kelly caught Jayleen's questioning gaze. "What'd the girl do? Did she call out or anything? Did she follow him?"

Malcolm shook his head. "She tried to. She got up off the rock and started walking a couple of steps then fell right down on

213

the ground. She lay real still, so I figured she was passed out. I rolled over and went back to sleep."

"The man didn't come back for her?"

Again, he shrugged. "If he did, I didn't see him."

"Was the girl still there in the morning when you woke up?" Jerry asked.

This time, Malcolm looked down and shifted in his seat. "Yeah, she was. Some guys were standin' over her, talkin' real loud. One of them saw me and asked who she was. I played dumb and said I'd never seen her before. I didn't want them to think I was involved. That's why I never said nothing to anybody until now. I don't want no trouble with the cops. No, sir!" He gave an emphatic shake of his head.

Kelly watched Malcolm. His apprehensive glance darted from Jerry to Jayleen to her. She couldn't tell if he was telling the truth or not, but Jerry and Jayleen seemed confident he was. And they both had a lot more experience with people who've been on the skids in life. Kelly bowed to their opinions.

Jerry reached over and gave a reassuring pat on Malcolm's back. "That's really good of you to come forward, Malcolm. Now maybe the police can find out who the guy was that left Holly on the trail that night."

Malcolm visibly flinched. "Damn. I hate talkin' to the cops. Can you stay with me, Jerry? I start to break out in a sweat when I see a uniform. They'll think I had something to do with her dying."

His comment made Kelly curious. "Were you still there when the ambulance came?"

Malcolm looked at her like she had two heads. "Hell, no! They'd have taken me in for questioning. We all skedaddled out of there. Joe went over to the Mission and told them a girl was lying passed out on the trail."

Jerry put his hand on Malcolm's shoulder. "Don't worry, Malcolm. I'll stay with you whenever someone comes to question you. I promise."

Malcolm looked at him with obvious relief. "Thanks, Jerry. Have you called them yet?"

"I'll call them now. I wanted to wait until Kelly had a chance to hear your story first. That way, she can let her family know if she thinks it'll help them." Jerry looked at Kelly, his doubt evident.

Kelly understood Jerry's reaction. She wasn't entirely sure if she should let Tommy or Barbara know about this. She'd let Burt decide. He could tell his old partner Dan and let him decide if Malcolm should be questioned or not.

"Thank you, Malcolm," Kelly said as she stood up. "I really appreciate your telling me this. At least I have something to help explain how Holly got down there on the trail."

"That took some guts, Malcolm," Jayleen added as she rose. "Gotta hand it to you."

Malcolm dropped his gaze to the floor and shrugged. "Well, you guys have always been straight with me. Thought I'd return the favor."

"You done good, Malcolm," Jerry said, clapping him on the shoulder.

Jayleen motioned Kelly to the door. "Talk to you later, Jerry. Bye, Malcolm. Enjoy the elk."

Kelly gave him a smile and a wave as she and Jayleen left. "You and Jerry acted like he was pretty reliable."

"He is, now that he's not hitting the bottle so much," Jayleen said as they walked down the corridor.

Kelly pushed through the door back into the lobby. "So, what do you think, Jayleen?" she asked in a lowered voice. "Should I tell Tommy or Barbara any of this or just tell Burt?"

"Just tell Burt. Let him decide. He'll tell his buddy on the force and let's see what happens. I wouldn't be surprised if they question old Malcolm."

"I think you're right. Thanks, Jayleen, for telling your friends. We'd never have found out about Malcolm without you."

Jayleen walked Kelly toward the lobby. "No problem at all, Kelly. Just part of giving back."

"So, what do you think, Burt? Will Dan want to question Malcolm?"

"Yeah, Kelly," Burt's voice came over her cell phone. "I think he will."

"Do you think I should e-mail this new information to Tommy?"

"I wouldn't if I were you, Kelly. Let the police do their job. Then they can tell Tommy what they found. It would be better if it came from them, anyway. More final. That should also help Tommy find some closure at last. And maybe some peace."

Even though Kelly's mind buzzed with other questions, she didn't voice them. "Tommy certainly deserves some peace," she agreed.

ELEVEN

Kelly held out her coffee mug for Jennifer to refill while she reread the first two paragraphs of the loan disclosure statement. "What do you think of these rates, Jen?"

Jennifer finished pouring the black stream into Kelly's mug, then glanced around the café with the practiced eye of an experienced waitress. "They're better than what other people are able to get right now, Kelly. That's because you've got higher scores and more assets. I have to tell you, I haven't seen rates this low since I've worked in this business. And that's been almost ten years."

"Well, that's a lucky break. It makes up for those nasty high rates I've been paying for over two years." She perused the columns of figures detailing the three available loans, rates, and terms. "Listen, would you be able to come with me to meet with this loan officer? I'd really appreciate your expertise."

"No problem. It's not like I'm tied up with clients or anything."

"Yeah, I've noticed you've been working through all of lunch nowadays." She looked around at the café's main dining area, filled with lunchtime customers. "Looks like Pete's business hasn't dropped off."

"Not the café, no, but the catering is slowing just a little. Boy, I hope it doesn't slow down too much. I'm depending on that."

"Well, remember my offer. If you need some quick cash, let me know." Kelly took a big drink of the hot, dark brew.

"I know what. I'll let you buy me lunch in Denver when we go."

Kelly peered at her. "We're going to Denver? When?"

"I just spoke with Mimi and she said we have to go, since Megan didn't find any gowns she liked in the other stores. Mimi insists Megan has to see everything that's out there. So, chalk up another Saturday."

Kelly closed her eyes and groaned. "How many stores are there?"

"Mimi mentioned at least seven or eight. Denver has a lot of suburbs," she added with a wicked grin.

Kelly flinched. "Oh, man . . . I don't think I can do that anytime soon. I think I'm developing an allergy to beads and lace, like

Megan."

Jennifer laughed out loud. "I'm sure you'd prefer jeans and a tee shirt."

"Hey, I suggested to Megan she and Marty could save a lot of time and trouble and money if they got married at the softball field. Wouldn't that be cute? Standing at home plate in their baseball jerseys and cleats."

"Only you would think that's cute," Jennifer said as she returned to her customers.

Kelly pushed away the remnants of her lunch salad and pulled the phone from her bag. She was about to call the loan officer's number at the top of the information sheet and make an appointment to start the refinancing process when the cell phone rang in her hand. Curt's name and number lit up.

"Hey, Curt, how're you doing?"

"I'm doing fine, Kelly girl. What're you up to?" Curt's deep voice rumbled over the line.

"Well, you'll be pleased to know that I'm looking over some loan information Jennifer got for me. I'm starting to refinance the cottage and get rid of that awful high-interest loan I've been paying for over two years."

"Good for you, Kelly," Curt enthused. "Like I said before, that will save you a bunch of money every month. Smart move."

"You bet it will. I've been waiting for that early penalty period to finish. I can't wait to dump that sleazy loan company."

"I'm surprised the same company is holding your paper. Most of those Denver bottom-feeders went out of business already."

"Oh, they did. My loan was sold early last year."

Curt's deep laugh rumbled. "That doesn't surprise me. Tell me, what do you have planned for that monthly amount? Are you gonna stick it in savings, I hope?"

"You read my mind, Curt. I figured I'd better put it away in case this economy gets even worse. Who knows? Maybe my new consulting clients will go bust. Maybe those construction and real estate loans will dry up."

"Not much likelihood of that, Kelly," Curt said with a nonchalant tone. "Those guys have access to private investment capital. They've both got proven track records."

"Good to know, Curt. Thanks for reassuring those little nagging worries that nibble at me every now and then."

"Glad to, Kelly. Now, let me get to why I called. You have Megan and Marty's engagement party on your calendar, I trust."

"You bet. Friday night next week. You need my help?"

"No, we're covered. Mimi and Burt offered to come early and help Jayleen and me get everything set up. Jayleen wanted me to call and ask if you could bring a salad or something instead of a dessert. She says we've got too many desserts."

Kelly had to laugh. To hear barrel-chested Colorado Cowboy Curt Stackhouse talk about potluck selections for next week's engagement party sounded so out of character. She decided to keep that observation to herself. Curt had been happily married to his first wife for over forty years. Kelly had no doubt Curt had a softer domestic side he didn't often show.

"I'll put it on my day planner, Curt," she said. "You two realize of course that this will be a store-bought salad, not homemade. I don't do homemade unless it's the holidays and I dig out Helen's gingersnap cookie recipe again."

"You shouldn't have reminded me of that, Kelly. Now we'll all be waiting for those cookies. Okay, I'll tell Jayleen someone else can bring a salad. I've got you down for Helen's gingersnap cookies."

"Curt, weren't you listening? I just said I don't do cookies except holidays."

"Well, this qualifies as a holiday, don't you think? Megan and Marty celebrating? I'll put you down for three dozen."

"Curt!"

"Talk to you later, Kelly." Curt's phone clicked off.

Darn it. He'd outtalked her. How'd that happen?

Kelly pulled her car away from the gas station and back into traffic. Her cell phone jangled on the seat beside her. Steve's name and number showed on the screen. She pulled into a parking space at a hardware store before answering.

"Hey, how're you doing?" she asked. "I haven't heard from you in a couple of days."

"Sorry. No time to breathe, let alone call. I finished at the firm early so I'm heading out to help Fred on another project. Thought I'd give you a quick call on the way over. How's everything going?"

Kelly paused before answering. She recognized Steve's distracted tone of voice. That was a tipoff he was only half-way listening. She heard it more and more these days. "Everything's okay. Busy at work."

Steve snorted. "Tell me about it."

Kelly didn't pause this time. And she didn't give Steve a perfunctory answer that would pass as conversation. Instead she told him what was on her mind. She couldn't help it.

"You know, Steve, I'm in the middle of refinancing the cottage now that I can get a lower interest rate. That means I'll have a lot of extra cash each month, which you could use. I wouldn't even miss it, and you need it. That way you could cut back on the second job hours and get some rest and —"

Steve cut her short, his voice sharp. "Kelly, I've told you I'm not discussing that. So don't even bring it up."

"But, *why?* You'd help me out if I needed —"

"That's enough, Kelly. Gotta go." His phone clicked off.

A wave of frustration washed over her, leaving her insides twisted in knots. "Dammit! Why won't he listen?"

She tossed the cell phone to the seat, then revved the car's engine, listening to its deep rumble before moving back into traffic. Her cell phone rang again, and Kelly grabbed for it as she drove. *At last. Steve's come to his senses.* "Glad you called. We need to talk," she said as she stopped at an intersection.

"I hope I'm not interrupting a conversation or anything," Burt's voice came over the line.

Kelly's frustration and aggravation whooshed out of her like air from a popped balloon. "Hey, Burt, what's up?"

"I thought you'd be interested to hear that Dan went over to the Mission this morning and questioned that guy Malcolm."

The calm logic lobe of Kelly's brain clicked into place. "Really? What'd Dan think?"

"Dan spoke to the staff counselors beforehand, so he had a pretty good read on this guy before he even spoke with him. Dan thinks this Malcolm is telling the truth."

Kelly gave a little sigh of relief. "Good. I thought so, too. So . . . will Dan be following up on anything, you think?"

She heard Burt's sigh on the other end of the phone. "To be honest, Kelly, there's not much more the department can do. There's no description of this guy. No license plate. No witnesses to identify him. So there's really nothing to go on."

"Well, Patty confirmed that Holly had been seeing this guy Eddie from Greeley lately. Maybe it was Eddie who picked her up from the party in a dark car. Maybe he gave Holly the narcotics. Maybe he dumped Holly on the trail when he saw her passing out." Kelly pulled to a stop at a red light.

"You know, Kelly, it doesn't really matter whether Eddie was the source of Holly's drugs or not. It could have been someone at the party, and he just picked her up. The fact is Holly is the one who overdosed. She took too many pills. No one forced her."

"But maybe he told her it would be all right," Kelly argued. "Holly would believe him, especially if she was drunk already. Patty said Holly was drinking vodka."

"There's no way to prove it, Kelly. You know that. It was still Holly's decision, even though her reasoning was probably impaired at the time."

Kelly exhaled an exasperated breath. "Yeah, I know, Burt. There's no way we can get around Holly taking those pills. She did it to herself. I saw the effects of her decisions firsthand last month when she wound up on my backyard patio."

"It's sad, I know, Kelly. But sometimes people get on a self-destructive path and stay on it. They may get off for a while, then they fall back again. They can't seem to stop themselves. I have to agree with Barbara. Holly has been on this risky behavioral path for years now, and it's finally taken its toll."

There was nothing Kelly could add to Burt's bleak-but-honest assessment. "I guess Dan will close Holly's case, right?"

"Probably. It will go down as an accidental death due to an overdose of opiate narcotics. Unfortunately, Holly isn't the first to be classified that way, and I'm afraid she won't be the last."

Kelly steered her car into the mall parking entrance. "So, will you tell Tommy, or do you think Dan will?"

"I'll tell Tommy about Holly being seen on the trail that night. I'll let Dan tell him the rest of the details when the case is closed. Tommy will be hurt, of course, but he'll understand eventually. And find some closure, I hope."

"Let's hope."

"Oh, before I forget. Dan told me he'd spoken with Officer Frobischer, who's on the drug task force. She said she'd be glad to speak with you anytime. Are you still interested, Kelly?"

Kelly grabbed her bag and opened the car door. "Sure thing. It's useful information. All these prescription drugs legally go into people's hands, then show up illegally at parties and on the street. That makes me curious."

"Okay, here's her cell number —"

"Do me a favor, Burt. I'm walking into the mall right now. Can you call me again and leave that number as a voice mail?"

"Ahhhh, cell phones. Can't do without them, can we?"

"I appreciate your taking the time to talk with me, Investigator Frobischer," Kelly said as she settled into her desk chair, cell phone to her ear. "Burt Parker said you're involved with the drug task force here in Fort Connor and could answer any questions I might have."

"Well, I'll be glad to answer any questions I *can,* Ms. Flynn," Frobischer's cool voice replied. "A lot of the task force's work is undercover, which we're not allowed to discuss."

"That's totally understandable. My questions are kind of general anyway. I was interested in the campus party scene and the drugs that are sold or passed out in those settings. We were all disturbed by the accidental overdose of the young woman, Holly Kaiser, a couple of weeks ago."

"Yes, that was tragic. Did you know her well?"

"No, I didn't. But I became interested in her case because she actually appeared in my backyard one night last month."

"Excuse me?"

"Yeah, I was surprised, to say the least, to see her standing there in the dark, totally

228

stoned out of her mind. I called the police, and they brought the ambulance and paramedics. Apparently she was using one of the hallucinogens that night, Ecstasy or LSD, they said."

"Sounds too familiar."

"They think she wandered away from a party in Old Town and found the river trail. My cottage is across the golf course, and I leave all the lights on when I'm out at night. She must have headed for the lights. Anyway, after she got out of the hospital, she started coming over to the knitting shop. She looked like she was changing her life. No parties, no drugs. So I was stunned to learn that she went back to the party scene and tried even more dangerous drugs."

"Some of them just can't keep away. The parties are what we call a guaranteed distribution system. The larger the party, the more drugs that are available. The users are drawn like moths to the flame."

"I figured that had to be it. Burt told me some of the drugs being passed out are Vicodin, Percocet, and OxyContin."

"That's correct. The Big Three."

"How do these college kids get a ready supply of these painkillers to sell? Supposedly they're carefully controlled and only available with a doctor's prescription. Do they steal them?"

"Most of the time, yes. And unfortunately, the controls in any system can be breached. Often, people will forge a doctor's prescription. Plus, they're motivated to be creative. They can get twenty dollars a pill when they sell them."

"Wow. I'd say that's plenty of motivation."

"That's why there's no shortage of people selling pills."

"Is there any kind of hierarchy or anything, like a network?"

"Actually, it's pretty much a free market. People like to buy their pills from someone they've built a relationship with. They trust them, so to speak."

"That's interesting. Which drug do people usually start with?"

"Usually it's Vicodin. After they've abused it for a while, it takes more and more to get the effect they want. Then they'll switch to Percocet. Then work their way up to Oxy-Contin."

"That could get expensive if they're paying twenty bucks per pill."

"Like I said, a free market. And there's never a shortage of market demand."

"What if someone isn't used to taking those opiate narcotics? How many would it take for them to overdose?"

"If they're not used to the drugs, then it would take about eight to ten pills to overdose. Of course, weight and size would affect that as well."

"That's a lot of pills."

"Yes, it is."

Kelly thought about that for a moment. "I can't imagine why someone would deliberately take that many pills. Especially if they weren't used to using something. It doesn't make sense to me."

Investigator Frobischer's voice came quietly, with a touch of world-weariness to it. "I'm afraid 'sense' has nothing to do with the campus drug scene, Ms. Flynn. Or any drug scene. People who're interested or even curious about the drugs often make stupid decisions. Sometimes it's peer pressure. Oftentimes it's more likely they've been drinking. Alcohol makes people less inhibited and more inclined to try something new, something different, something dangerous. Unfortunately, some of those decisions can have tragic consequences. As it did with Holly Kaiser."

"Bad decisions, tragic results," Kelly said sadly.

"I'm afraid so."

TWELVE

Barbara's SUV rumbled down the dirt road. Kelly sat in the back, watching the evergreens close in alongside the road leading to the mountain resort.

"Are we there yet?" one of Lambspun's regulars quipped from beside the rear window.

"That sounds like Jennifer whenever we're on a road trip," Kelly said, when the good-natured comments died down.

"It's only a mile further," Barbara announced from the driver's seat. "See, here are some of their staff cabins on the outskirts of the property."

The frame-and-screened-porch buildings looked like regular camp buildings to Kelly, rustic and wood-framed. Then, something else caught Kelly's eye. A glint of silver through the trees. Was that a lake? Kelly peered through the evergreen trees and glimpsed another silver streak. *Yessss! A lake,* she exulted inside.

The enclosure of evergreens gave way to bushes and shrubs and more cabins sprouting beside aspen trees. Across the road from the cabins, the land angled down to a rock-rimmed lake. It was larger than Kelly had thought it would be and much more beautiful. Surrounded by mountain ridges thick with evergreens, which were in turn surrounded by snow-capped peaks, the lake sat like a sparkling diamond in a green velvet jewel box.

"This is gorgeous," Kelly said, staring through the open car window. They drove beneath a sign that proclaimed GOLDEN LAKE RESORT. More buildings came into view. Larger than cabins, they sat separately. Each had a flagstone path leading to their entrances.

"That's the main lodge with the dining room. By the way, the food is delicious here," Barbara said, pointing to the largest building straight ahead. "Meeting rooms are there as well. And there are other cabins going up this road, too." She pointed to a road beside the lake before pulling into a gravel parking area. "Let's grab our stuff and head to the main lodge. Mimi and Burt have everything set up and waiting for us."

Kelly grabbed her bag and exited the car

with the other three women and Barbara. "Jennifer said there were hot pools sunken into the rocks. Where are they?"

Barbara lifted the SUV's back gate. "They're right up that same road with the cabins. See the cabins through the trees over there?" She pointed. "The pools are farther up that road where it's higher. And the view is even prettier, if you can believe it."

Kelly spied rustic cabin roofs peeking through the lodgepole pines. "Boy, I can't wait to start exploring. What's on the agenda?"

Barbara lifted a cardboard box from the back of the SUV. "We've scheduled the class first, so we'll have the rest of the day to relax and enjoy."

Kelly grabbed another box as did the other two women and followed Barbara up the flagstone path leading to the lodge. An inviting front porch wrapped around the front and side of the building.

Burt appeared on the front steps and waved to them. "Right on time, folks. Mimi's got everything all set up for us on the side porch. It's shaded and has a beautiful view."

"Better than what we're looking at right now?" Kelly called out.

"Just as pretty," Burt promised. "And

Lynette, our other student, is already here. She arrived a few minutes ago."

"Felting on the porch. That should be fun," the woman behind Kelly said.

"And don't forget the spa," added the woman bringing up the rear.

Ohhhh, yeah. Kelly hadn't forgotten the spa at all. She was counting on it.

"Okay, everyone. Let's take inventory of our supplies," Mimi directed as she stood at the head of a long worktable. Kelly and the three other women stood on both sides, and Barbara was stationed at the other end. The table itself was on a side wraparound porch that overlooked the cabins and trees dotting the hillside.

Burt hadn't exaggerated about the view. Gazing into the evergreens surrounding the lodge was "just as pretty" as gazing at the lake. Kelly couldn't wait to explore the grounds. Burt had teased that there were hiking trails. But first . . . the felting.

"Are we felting in these tubs?" one woman asked. "I thought you felted in a washing machine."

"Normally, you do felt by using a washing machine. But each project is different," Mimi replied. "There are only three things needed to felt. Heat, water, and agitation.

Most knitted items will shrink down one-third or one-half from their original size. But some don't need as much shrinkage as others. For instance, Kelly brought a knit hat that only needs to shrink maybe a half inch. That's not a lot, so she's better off using the small plastic tub and felting by hand with the sink plunger. That way she can control the shrinkage better."

Kelly waved the knitted hat. "This hat is for my boyfriend, so I don't want to screw it up."

"Let's take a look at everyone's project. Every item felts differently. Then we'll know whether you'll be using the washing machine or the laundry tub. Stacy, you first." Mimi gestured to the woman across the table from Kelly.

Stacy held up two large red wool mittens. "These are for my elementary-age nephews, so I'll have to shrink them down."

"That's right, Stacy, so you'll use the washer. Marianne, you knitted slippers and they're pretty big, too."

Marianne held up two enormous green wool slippers. "Jolly Green Giant size," she remarked.

Everyone laughed as the woman to the left of Kelly held up a long, tapered knit hat. Something about the woman looked

236

familiar to Kelly. Maybe she'd seen her around Lambspun before.

"And Lynette has the special ski hat. Felting will make it even warmer. And you'll want to check that washer vibration after fifteen minutes and see if the hat is down to the correct size. Or you can do as Kelly will be doing." Mimi picked up a rubber kitchen sink plunger. "She'll be shrinking her hat by creating agitation in the tub with the plunger."

"Okay, a washing machine agitation I understand," Kelly said. "So describe how I'm going to create the same agitation with that plunger. Going up and down won't be as strong a movement as the washer."

"That's exactly why we do certain items in the washtub with a plunger," Mimi replied. "They either don't require much shrinkage, like yours, or they're more delicate fibers. Some items are a combination of wool and silk."

"You can felt silk?" Marianne asked, astonished.

"Your knitted item needs to be at least seventy percent animal fibers, like wool. But it can have as much as thirty percent silk in it. No cotton or synthetics, though."

"Why?" Lynette asked.

"Plant fibers do not felt. Only animal

fibers will felt. They're completely different in texture. That's why I told all of you to bring knitted wool items to felt."

"No plant fibers? What about the silk?" Stacy asked.

"Silkworms, remember?" Mimi replied.

Stacy hit her forehead with her hand. "*Right!* Forgot about those little guys."

"Okay. Heat, water, and agitation," Marianne repeated. "Agitation in the washer with hot water, right?"

"Really hot. As hot as you can get it," Mimi said, lifting a bottle of shampoo. "And we use a very gentle, clear shampoo because shampoo is made for hair. And wool is *sheep* hair."

"Love it," Kelly said with a chuckle. "Do the washing machine folks keep checking the size as they go along?"

"You bet. Or you may wind up with something way too small. Once each item is finished, we rinse thoroughly in hot water and agitation to get all the soap out."

"Do we put them all in the dryer afterwards?" Stacy asked.

"Ohhhh, no." Mimi shook her head. "That would continue to shrink them with the dryer heat. After we rinse, we put each item on a clean, dry towel and pat them damp dry, then place the item on another clean dry towel to let it air-dry."

"Okay, then how do we get started?" Kelly prodded.

Mimi gestured to the other women. "I'll take two of you to the laundry room downstairs where they're allowing us to use two of their washing machines. So one of you can watch while the other items are agitating. It won't take long. Usually a half hour agitation will do it."

"So if a machine takes half an hour, then how long do I take with the tub and plunger method? Two hours? Good thing I play ball. My arms are strong."

Mimi laughed. "No, no. A half hour should be enough for you, too, Kelly. But make sure you check it after fifteen minutes and see where you are. You don't want to shrink Steve's hat." She winked.

"Got that right. Do we have a tape measure in all these boxes? I want to measure the hat now, so I can keep track."

Mimi pointed to a smaller box on the table. "There are several paper tape measures in there. Everyone take a tape and measure your knitted items right now. That way you'll have a starting point."

"Good idea," Lynette said, reaching for the box.

"And don't worry about hot water, Kelly.

Burt is heating a pot of water on the stove in the kitchen right now."

"Okay, then." Kelly picked up the plunger in one hand and the empty tub in the other and started weight-lifting movements. "I'd better wake up my muscles right now. Half an hour is longer than you think."

The heavy cotton chenille robe felt luxurious against Kelly's skin as she walked along the path that led to the sunken thermal pools. The forested hillside that contained the pools overlooked the lake, which was shimmering now in late afternoon reflected sunlight. Kelly pushed a pine branch out of the way as the path twisted through trees. It led to the middle pool, which hugged the cliff. Women's voices drifted out as the breeze caught phrases and words and tossed them into the trees or across the lake.

Kelly paused, enjoying the sound of the wind in the pines overhead, whistling in that distinctive sound it makes in the high country. There was a different sound at higher altitudes. The breeze spoke to you.

Turning a secluded bend in the pathway, Kelly came upon the pool. Literally cut out of the mountain, smooth rock lined the clear waters, sides and bottom. The stone-edged pool had a squashed circle shape and hugged the very edge of the mountainside.

"Oh, my gosh . . ." Kelly breathed, standing and staring at the lake. Trees were everywhere, so there was ample shade for those in the pool. A sunny pool was farther up the path. "This is gorgeous."

"It sure is," said one of the two women already relaxing in the pool. This woman was a stranger, obviously another visitor to the mountain lake resort, enjoying a getaway. The other woman was Lynette from Mimi's fiber retreat. Steve's felted hat was drying in the sunshine on the deck beside their classroom in the lodge with all the other felted projects.

"The water looks too inviting," Kelly said, slipping off the robe she wore over her bathing suit. "How hot is it?"

"Perfect," replied Lynette.

Kelly stepped carefully down the uneven, narrow stone steps into the water. Hot. Hot. Heavenly hot. She let out a long, loud sigh of pleasure.

"That's where I came in," the other woman said as she headed for the stone steps. "Enjoy, ladies."

Kelly picked a spot around the pool edge where she could relax in the water and look out on the lake at the same time. Two mountain jaybirds fussed in the branches above her head. Kelly stretched her arms out onto the rock-rimmed pool edge and leaned back . . . and relaxed. Really relaxed. She felt every muscle respond to the heated water, releasing tension she didn't even know she had.

"Feels good, doesn't it?" Lynette smiled across the pool at Kelly.

"Ohhhh, yeah," Kelly said. "I don't know why I never found this place before. My friend Jennifer at Lambspun told me about it. I'd never been here before today, but I'm definitely coming back."

"Me, too. If I can work it around my schedule."

Kelly had finally remembered where she'd seen Lynette. She was one of the paramedics who came to Holly's funeral. "You must really need some relaxation in your line of work. How many shifts are you scheduled on the ambulance crew? Four a week? Five a week?"

"I usually do four, since I'm trying to take a class at the university, too."

"Are a lot of paramedics taking classes?"

"Yes, several of us are. But it's hard to juggle more than one class, due to the length of the shifts."

Kelly was silent for a moment, letting the peaceful view and blissful water take over.

"That was so sad. What happened to Holly, I mean. But I bet you guys see a whole lot of those overdose cases."

Lynette's smile disappeared. "Way too many, I'm afraid. Some kids just keep pushing up against the edges of that cliff until they fall over. Some pull back in time. Others don't. Holly didn't."

"Well, I only hope Tommy comes to some sort of closure or peace of mind about it. I get regular e-mails from him asking if I've learned anything new." Kelly shook her head. "I've told him everything we've found out about the party that night. Well, almost everything. It turns out there are a lot of different relationships going on. Holly was involved with several groups of people. So nobody knows where she got the drugs from."

"That doesn't surprise me. Holly seemed to be deliberately pushing the limits these last few months. Ever since Tommy was accepted into med school in Denver. She was driving him crazy."

"Really?" Kelly had never heard that opinion expressed before.

"Yeah. He didn't let on to many people, but he and I worked together on several shifts, and he'd talk to me." Lynette ran her fingertips through the water, creating

243

ripples. "She'd call him up when he was in the middle of a shift, and they'd get into an argument."

"What about?"

Lynette shrugged. "The same old thing over and over. Holly would tell Tommy she needed him to pick her up from a party when she knew he was on duty. Tommy would get all frustrated and tell her he couldn't. Then Holly would start to cry. She'd tell him he didn't love her anymore, and he was going to forget her now that he was in Denver, and on and on and on. The same old garbage every time. It was making him crazy. Tommy told me he didn't know how he was going to be able to handle his medical studies and take care of Holly at the same time. He was at his wit's end." Lynette had a disgusted look on her face.

Kelly stared at Lynette. Here was someone else who corroborated Rachel's assessment of Holly's manipulative behavior. It showed that Lisa's earlier assessment of Holly was right on. "That's interesting. Tommy's description of Holly made it sound like she was a little lost lamb, and he was trying to protect her."

Lynette gave a rueful smile. "That's Tommy for you. I've seen him do that for the three years I've known him. But he couldn't lie to me. I was usually sitting next to him or in the ambulance with him whenever Holly called. So he told me the truth."

Kelly couldn't contain her curiosity. The water's relaxing effects were temporarily forgotten. "And what was the truth? Was Holly a lost lamb or a sly fox?"

"I'd say she was more fox than lamb. She was playing on Tommy's guilty conscience for not being at her beck and call like he had been before he went to med school."

"Any idea why Tommy had that guilty conscience? I mean, we all feel guilty about something, but it sounds like Tommy's was set on overload."

"Yeah, it was. He told me Holly tried to kill herself about two years ago. She took some sleeping pills and called him before she passed out."

"Whoa . . . that would definitely get Tommy's attention, wouldn't it?" Kelly caught Lynette's glance. "Do you think maybe Holly deliberately tried suicide? I mean, to make Tommy feel guilty?"

"Sounds like it to me. I'd never met Holly, so I don't know. But some people try a halfhearted suicide attempt as a call for help. You know, taking only a few pills then calling a friend or family member. The lucky ones get counseling. I don't know why

245

Tommy didn't insist Holly go to a therapist. He told other people when they needed it."

Kelly thought for a minute. "Maybe Tommy thought he could 'save' Holly. His mom Barbara said at the shop that Tommy had been 'taking care' of Holly for years. Feeling responsible for her, somehow."

Lynette nodded. "That's exactly it. A lot of people who're attracted to emergency medical teams and medical fields are what we call 'classic rescuers.' They want to save people, and in these jobs, you get good at it. The problem is some people get saved and some don't. I mean, we can pump someone's stomach if they've taken an overdose of pills. But if they don't start counseling to find out why they took those pills, a lot of them will do it again. And sometimes it's too late. We can't save them."

Kelly let Lynette's somber comments settle. She was right. It was exactly what Jayleen had once said. "That reminds me of what a friend from Fort Connor said. 'People have to save themselves.' "

"That's right."

Kelly let the hot water command her attention and relaxed. Still, it was only a few minutes before little thoughts started creeping from the back of her mind.

Tommy was definitely under a lot of pressure since he'd started medical school. Kelly knew friends who'd gone through that rigorous routine to become doctors. There was no such thing as spare time. No wonder Tommy had been losing patience with Holly and her demands. He didn't have time to be at her beck and call anymore. Add to that Holly's track record of perpetual drug abuse, and Tommy must have felt pushed to his limits.

Kelly decided to voice her thoughts out loud. Lynette was obviously Tommy's close friend and knew him better than anyone. "You know, it sounds like Tommy was finally starting to see through Holly's selfish manipulation. What do you think?"

Lynette glanced toward the lake. "Yeah, he was. That's why he drove up from Denver that Friday. He wanted to tell Holly in person that he wasn't going to be here for the weekends anymore. He had to study."

"How'd Holly take it?"

"Not good. Tommy said she blew up at him. Yelled and screamed and said if he really loved her, he'd stay in town."

"What'd Tommy say?"

Lynette looked down into the pool. "I don't know. He told me he just turned around and walked out the door, Holly still yelling."

"Wow . . . that must have been really hard for him to do."

Lynette ran her fingertips through the water again. "You have no idea. Tommy was all torn up inside afterwards. He called me on his cell as he was leaving Fort Connor. He was a basket case. I could tell he needed to vent or he wouldn't be able to concentrate on his studies. I was off duty that night, so I asked him over to my apartment for dinner. I live right outside town in Loveland."

Kelly watched Lynette's hand slow its movements in the water. She also noticed the expression on Lynette's face change. It softened, as did Lynette's voice.

"Tommy needed a sympathetic ear. He can't talk to his mom. She'd go into another rant about Holly. I was the only one he could open up to."

Kelly's instinct picked up something else. Something Lynette wasn't saying. "I'm so glad Tommy had you to turn to, Lynette," she said quietly. "He needs a close friend."

Lynette glanced at Kelly, then back at the water. "Yes, we . . . we've become really close."

Kelly saw her instincts confirmed in Lynette's brief glance. "Sounds like Tommy really needed to relax. Did he spend the night?"

This time, Lynette didn't look up, but a slight blush colored her face. "No . . . He . . . he left before midnight. He needed to get back to Denver so he could be at the study session early. But he's stayed with me several nights since Holly's death. He's been a wreck."

"Yeah, I could tell. We've all worried about him. It was clear he blamed himself for not being able to 'save' Holly."

"Ohhhh, yeah. Tommy's got major guilt about not staying in town with Holly that night. I've told him over and over he's not to blame. Holly chose to return to the party scene and take those drugs." Lynette stirred the water again. "Tommy knows that, and he's slowly coming to grips with it."

Kelly hoped the information coming out about Holly's recent party behavior and new relationship with drug-selling Eddie would help Tommy see things more clearly.

"I'm so glad you're there to talk sense to him, Lynette. You may be the only one who can. I hope you two continue your relationship."

A little smile quirked Lynette's mouth. "Thanks, Kelly. We care a lot for each other. Tommy's even asked me to move in with

249

him in Denver. I plan to next month."

Kelly gave Lynette an encouraging smile. "Now, *that* is good news. I'll keep it to myself."

Lynette smiled. "Please do. Tommy hasn't told his mom yet."

"Okaaaay, secret's safe with me."

Lynette pushed away from the pool's stone wall. "Well, I've got a massage scheduled." She started up the stone steps and donned her robe, then turned to Kelly with a smile. "Nice talking to you, Kelly."

"I enjoyed it, too. See you later." Lynette walked along the flagstone path and disappeared behind the pine branches.

Kelly slid down into the hot water, letting the heat relax her neck and shoulders. Lynette's revelations were good news. Tommy was slowly letting go of his past guilt-ridden relationship with Holly and moving toward a healthier one with Lynette. Someone who really cared about Tommy instead of using him.

She closed her eyes and let herself float in the hot water, bubbles bringing up heat from the submerged vents. A little thought wiggled from the back of her mind. Lynette said Tommy stayed at her apartment near Fort Connor until nearly midnight. What if after spending a wonderful evening with

Lynette, Tommy came back to his car and found a message from Holly on his cell phone? Another whining, guilt-inducing message demanding he pick her up from a party — as usual. What if that was one message too many for Tommy? He told Lynette he didn't know how he was going to handle his medical studies and Holly at the same time. What if he'd finally had enough?

Kelly's eyes popped open. She stared out into the pines without seeing, as another thought crept from the dark. What if Tommy had snapped? What if he'd decided to stop the guilt at last? A chill passed over Kelly despite the hot water surrounding her.

What if it was Tommy who picked up Holly from the party? The old vagrant, Malcolm, saw a man wearing a hooded jacket walk Holly down the river trail and leave her on a rock before walking away. What if that was Tommy? What if he was the one who gave Holly the opiate narcotics? As a paramedic, Tommy would know how to get those painkillers. And he'd know how many pills to give Holly. He'd know how fast they would put her to sleep. And how fast she would stop breathing and die. A painless way to die. She'd simply fall asleep and never wake up.

Was that what happened? Did Tommy

finally remove the burden of taking care of Holly once and for all? That thought played in Kelly's mind for only a few seconds before the contradicting thoughts pushed forward.

You can't be serious. Tommy's a straight arrow. He couldn't kill Holly, no matter how burdensome she had become. Tommy had spent years saving lives. He couldn't deliberately take a life.

Or, could he? Kelly mused as she leaned her arms on the rocks and stared out at the lake. Holly had already been taken in by authorities after overdosing on drugs and wandering the river trail. Everyone would assume Holly simply did it again. Her death would naturally be declared accidental. And there would be no witnesses. Even though Malcolm saw someone, he couldn't identify the man.

Was Tommy really the straight arrow he appeared to be? Grieving and mourning Holly's death at the funeral, asking Burt and Kelly to find out information for him. Was it real or a fake performance? Kelly didn't know. But she'd learned one thing over these last few years she'd been poking into murders and sleuthing. People were often not what they seemed.

THIRTEEN

Kelly settled a box of felting supplies — plastic tubs, plungers, shampoo — into the back of Barbara's SUV beside the other boxes filled with supplies from the fiber retreat. She took a moment to enjoy the view of the peaceful silvery lake. Maybe one of these days she could tempt Steve up here. He'd relax for sure in those thermal pools and the spa massage. Her muscles sighed inwardly, remembering yesterday's blissful relaxation and this morning's massage.

Lynette walked up to the SUV, carrying her backpack and wearing her newly felted ski hat.

"Your hat turned out well, Lynette. It looks good," Kelly said.

"Thanks, I'm really pleased with it. I saw yours all dried on the towel this morning. It only looks a little bit smaller than before. Did you get the size you wanted?"

"I think so." Kelly leaned against the SUV

and watched Burt approach. "I plunged and plunged for fifteen minutes, then stopped and measured, and it was right where I wanted it. Mimi suggested I only shrink it a half inch. I didn't want to take the chance it would shrink more."

"Hey, any more room in the back of Barbara's SUV?" Burt asked as he walked up to them, another box in his arms.

"Sure, there's always room for one more," Kelly said.

"Well, it's been great, guys. See you around Lambspun. I've gotta run back to Fort Connor. I'm on duty tonight."

Kelly waved. "Take care, Lynette."

"Drive safely," Burt added.

Kelly made way for Burt's box, wedging a space between two others. "Do you have a second before you and Mimi drive back?" Kelly asked. "There's something I wanted to tell you but we haven't had a good time to talk alone since we've been here."

Burt dusted off his hands. "Sure, Kelly. What's on your mind?"

Kelly motioned him away from the cars. "Let's head toward the lake. It'll look like we're having one last look. Which we are, actually."

Burt chuckled. "I can't wait to hear what's eating you."

She wandered down to the lake's edge, Burt alongside. The lake's surface was glassy smooth, not a ripple from oar or breeze. "I was in the hot pools yesterday afternoon with Lynette. She and Tommy have worked the ambulance shifts together for three years, and she revealed a lot of things about Tommy and Holly's relationship I'd never heard before."

"How did she know?"

"Apparently she and Tommy have become close friends, and she was sitting with him in the ambulance when those phone calls came in from Holly. You know, Holly begging Tommy to come pick her up from a party when she knew he was on duty. Lynette said Tommy and Holly would get into an argument each time. Holly would cry and tell Tommy he didn't love her anymore and he'd forget her. Stuff like that."

Burt looked over at Kelly. "Where're you going with this, Kelly?"

"Just hear me out, Burt. Lynette called Holly manipulative. And she's not the first person who's said that about Holly. The girl Rachel, who works at the Grill, told me Holly was manipulative, and she's known her for years. Granted, Rachel had an axe to grind about Holly, but Lynette has never met Holly. She's judging solely on her behavior with Tommy. Lisa even called Holly's behavior manipulative. And Barbara has inferred as much whenever she talks about Holly, and she's known Holly since she was a kid."

Burt stared at the lake. "Let's say they're all correct, and they may well be. What does it matter now? Holly's dead."

"Well, Lynette went on to say that Tommy told her Holly was driving him crazy. And he didn't know how he would handle his medical studies and Holly at the same time. Lynette said Tommy and Holly also had a big fight that Friday. He told Holly he wasn't going to spend weekends in Fort Connor anymore because he needed to study. Apparently Holly blew up and started yelling at him. So Tommy walked out on her."

Burt looked skeptical. "When did Tommy tell Lynette all this?"

"Right afterwards. He stopped at Lynette's Loveland apartment on the way out of town for dinner and . . . relaxation." Kelly let her words hang there, knowing Burt would pick up on their implication.

Burt paused, his face somber. "I see. Did he stay over?"

"I asked that, too, and Lynette said

Tommy left before midnight."

Burt turned to her, with a shocked expression. "Surely you're not suggesting that Tommy gave Holly those opiate narcotics, are you?"

Kelly shrugged. "All I know is those comments made me start thinking, Burt. Tommy was under a lot of pressure. What if Holly's constant demands made him snap? Tommy would have known how to get those pain pills. He could have picked her up from the party, given her the pills, then waited until she was sleepy, and dropped her off along the river trail."

"Kelly, you can't be serious," Burt said, clearly appalled by her suggestion. "I've known Tommy for four years. There's no finer young man out there. He's conscientious, kind, smart as a whip, and as honest as the day is long. There's no way he could harm anyone. Let alone the girl he'd loved for so long."

"But the girl he'd loved had turned into a demanding, manipulative burden who played on Tommy's guilty conscience."

"What guilty conscience? Tommy's never done anything wrong," Burt protested.

"Tommy told Lynette Holly tried to commit suicide a couple of years ago. She called Tommy after she'd taken too many sleeping pills. Ever since then, whenever Holly called, Tommy jumped. What if Tommy finally got tired of Holly's demands? He'd just spent the evening with a girl who cared for him, and it sounds like he cares about Lynette. What if Tommy decided to end the guilt trip once and for all?"

Burt frowned but didn't say anything for a minute. "I'll admit that is a disturbing thought, but I still think you're way out in left field with this one, Kelly. Tommy's not a killer."

"You may be right, Burt. I'm just speculating here. Can't help it. It's the way my mind works. One thing I've learned these last few years of sleuthing is that people are often not what they seem. I've met enough charming, manipulative liars to teach me that."

Burt shook his head. "I still don't think Tommy could do that."

"All I know is what I've seen and heard. Tommy has been under a huge amount of stress. People have commented on the heavy responsibility he felt for Holly, and how Holly was always calling Tommy to rescue her. What if he snapped under all the pressure? Anybody can snap, Burt. Including Tommy. Especially if he learned that Holly was cheating on him."

Burt stared out at the glassy lake for a long

moment. "I hear you, Kelly, and you're right. Any one of us can snap under pressure. Maybe I'm too close to the people involved to be impartial. I'll run all this by Dan and see what he thinks. He can decide if he wants to question Tommy or not."

"I'm sorry to tell you all this, Burt, but I thought it was important."

Burt let out a tired sigh. "You're right, Kelly. It is important. Let's see what Dan decides to do."

Kelly felt a little sad, like she'd brought news of the death of a loved one to a family. She didn't know what else to say, so she said nothing. Instead, she stood with Burt and stared out at the lake surrounded by green mountains. Soon winter would chase away fall's fragile beauty.

Kelly watched the black stream of molasses pour into the spicy dough mixture as she stirred it with a wooden spoon. She hadn't lost her touch with Aunt Helen's gingersnap cookie recipe. Even though she hadn't made them since last holiday season, they were turning out fine. At least the dough looked exactly right. Now, all she had to do was make sure each batch didn't overbake in the oven. She'd have to keep the timer with her constantly.

During the drive out of the mountains that afternoon, Kelly decided tonight was the perfect time to make the cookies for Megan and Marty's party. Nothing else was scheduled for this evening. Steve wasn't home this weekend, so Kelly was alone. She didn't feel like working on client accounts this evening, so she might as well do something else useful and make the cookies.

She'd called Steve on the drive home but had only gotten his voice mail. Hopefully, he'd call her later. They hadn't talked for days. Ever since that last conversation where he hung up on her. Kelly had left several messages, but Steve never returned them.

The dough formed into a big, sticky ball, and Kelly carefully lifted it out of the bowl and onto the plastic wrap she'd put on the counter. Wrapping the spicy-scented dough carefully, she put it into the fridge to chill. She'd roll the dough into balls and coat them with sugar while watching television tonight. Baking came after that. Aunt Helen's gingersnap cookies were an all-evening project.

Kelly grabbed her mug and her phone before settling into Helen's rocker. There were some other phone calls she needed to make. One of them had totally slipped her mind. She punched in Patty's number and listened to the rings.

"Hey, Kelly. How're you doing? I haven't heard from you for a while."

"I was out of town for one of Mimi's fiber retreats. We learned how to felt. It was a lot of fun, I have to admit."

"I've always wanted to learn how to do that. Maybe next time. Where'd you go?"

"Up into the mountains above Boulder to this pretty mountain lake resort. Golden Lake."

"Oooo, that sounds pretty."

"It was. Listen, I'd wanted to update you on what I've learned recently. I'd asked a friend of mine to check with the counselors at AA and over at the Mission to find out if any of the guys who sleep beside the river trail saw anything that night."

"You're kidding! Did . . . did one of them see something?"

"As a matter of fact, an old guy saw a man walking Holly down the trail."

Patty took in her breath. "Really?"

"Yeah, really. He said Holly wasn't too steady on her feet. The man set her down on a rock then turned and walked away. Apparently, Holly stood up and tried to walk back down the trail, then fell down on the ground. The old guy figured she was drunk, so he went back to sleep."

"Whoa . . . I don't believe it," Patty said softly. "We were right, Kelly. That man was *Eddie.* It had to be! *He's* the one who gave Holly the pills. Then the bastard dumped her on the trail!"

"You're probably right, Patty, but there's no way to prove it. No way to link Eddie to Holly. There're no witnesses who saw them together that night. So the police wouldn't have any reason to find Eddie, let alone question him."

"Damn. That is *so* wrong."

"My thoughts exactly."

FOURTEEN

"Kelly, thank goodness you dropped by. I can really use your help," Mimi said the moment Kelly stepped into the Lambspun main knitting room.

"Sure, Mimi, what do you need?" Kelly dropped her knitting bag onto the library table. No one else was there. In fact, the shop was practically empty.

"I won't be able to help Barbara with her felting class this morning because I'll be on the phone with a vendor. And Connie's busy with customers. Could you possibly step in again and help? It would only take an hour."

"My client accounts can wait another hour, Mimi. I'll be glad to help Barbara. Of course, I'm pretty new to the felting process myself, so I hope I'll be helpful."

Mimi gave a little wave. "Of course you will be, Kelly. You learned a lot at the workshop. I'm sorry to be asking you to help again, but this vendor has been having problems for several months now. Delaying shipments. Not sending everything we ordered. I need to find out what's happening. Maybe he's going out of business."

"When's the class?"

"About fifteen minutes from now. Barbara is setting up in the classroom."

"Tell her to prepare herself for her rookie helper again," Kelly teased as she dug her coffee mug from her bag.

Mimi laughed. "You'll do fine. You're a natural with students, Kelly. You explain clearly and patiently. Not every teacher can do that."

"Well, I guess that's one benefit of making so many mistakes. I've gotten good at correcting them," Kelly said, walking toward the central yarn room. "Tell Barbara I'll be right back. I have to have my morning coffee fix. Then I'll be ready for anything. Felters included."

She headed for the hallway leading to the café. The aroma of Eduardo's strong coffee had tickled her nose since she'd entered the shop. Spotting Jennifer pouring some of the black gold for one of the café's customers, Kelly waved to catch her attention.

"Save some for me," she said as she extended her mug.

Jennifer beckoned Kelly over to the

264

counter beside the grill. "We have a special pot for you, Kelly. Eduardo puts all the old grounds and shoelaces and stuff in there and keeps it boiling on the back of the stove. Don't you, Eduardo?"

"Absolutely," Eduardo agreed with a good-natured grin. "We even threw in some potato peelings this morning. Give it a little fiber."

Kelly pretended to flinch as Eduardo poured a dark stream into her mug. "Fiber in my coffee? Oh, no!"

Jennifer leaned against the counter. "I just had a call from Jayleen. Reminding me to make or bake some brownies. I figure I'll get Pete to make a double batch, and that'll take care of both our party donations."

Feeling a rare surge of virtue, Kelly gave her a smug smile. "Well, I've already made my Megan and Marty donation. Three dozen of Helen's gingersnap cookies, all wrapped in plastic and tin foil and sitting on my counter."

Jennifer's eyes popped wide. "You're kidding! You made Helen's gingersnaps? But it's not even close to the holidays. What got into you?"

"Boredom, that's all. I had yesterday evening free after coming home from the retreat, and I didn't feel like doing client work, so I made cookies."

"I'm impressed. And worried. Those cookies are deadly. I can resist brownies better than Helen's cookies. You eat one, then another, and before you know it . . . you've disappeared into cookie hell."

"That's why I'm taking then over to Curt's place tonight. He and Jayleen invited me to dinner, so I figured I'd get them out of the house and away from me. I saved a package for Steve the next time he comes home."

"How's he holding up?"

Kelly took a deep drink of the hot brew while she thought of what to say. She could answer honestly and say, "Not well." Or, "sleep deprived and short-tempered." Both would be accurate.

"He's surviving, that's the best way I can describe it. We hadn't talked in several days, but he finally called this morning. Fred, the guy he's working for at night, had a special project he was trusting to Steve. He worked till two in the morning. Steve said he was so exhausted he fell asleep in his car before driving to his friend's apartment." She shook her head. "If he doesn't find a minute to call me while he's driving from one job to the other, then I don't hear from him at all. It can be days before he returns my calls."

"And how're you doing?" Jennifer asked, concern evident in her voice.

Kelly shrugged. "I'm doing okay. I'm here in town and get to sleep in my own bed at night. My new clients are challenging, and I've got all my friends around. Not like Steve, who's virtually isolated in Denver except for quick mini-visits home. And he's barely awake while he's here."

Jennifer reached over and squeezed her arm. "Hang in there. Maybe you and Steve can have some quiet time together this weekend."

Kelly gave a wry smile. "We get quiet time whenever he's back. It's called sleeping." She pushed away from the counter. "I've gotta go. I promised Mimi I'd take her place helping Barbara with a felting class. Wish me luck."

"Luck," Jennifer said with a wave as Kelly headed down the hallway.

Barbara was busily arranging small wash tubs, bottles of liquid soap, and sink plungers on the table.

"Hey, Barbara. I've got my coffee, so I'm ready," Kelly said as she entered the room.

Barbara glanced up. "Glad you could help out, Kelly. We've got six people signed up, so it'll go much smoother with two instructors rather than one."

"Well, I'm not sure I qualify as an instructor, but I'm definitely an experienced problem solver." Kelly grinned. "That comes from making all those mistakes. What can I do to help set up?"

"I'm about finished setting up, but I've got to go down to the basement and bring up some fibers I want to show the students. Can you stay here and greet them and get them situated?"

"Sure. I can do that." Kelly decided she'd use this moment to probe a little. "By the way, how's Tommy doing?"

Barbara looked up, her expression changing. "I think he's doing well, but I haven't heard from him as much lately. Of course, that's understandable. What with his heavy class load and studies." She glanced at her watch. "I'd better get downstairs. See you in a few minutes."

Just as Barbara scurried from the classroom, Kelly noticed two middle-aged women enter from the other doorway. Next, two of the occasional Lambspun knitters wandered into the classroom. Kelly exchanged greetings with them and let them explore. Then two young woman appeared in the doorway. Both looked college-aged.

"Hey, are you here for the felting class?" Kelly asked as they approached.

"Yeah, and it looks like we found it," the tall slender blonde said. Her hair was held back by a scrunchy band. "Do we use those little tubs?" She pointed.

"You can if you have items that don't need to shrink much," Kelly said. "Most of the time, you'd use a washing machine."

The tall blonde extended her hand. "I'm Francie. And this is my roommate, Wanda. We both have been interested in coming over here ever since Lisa told me about the shop and all the classes you offer."

"You know Lisa? From the Sports Health facility, I'll bet."

Francie smiled broadly. "Yes, she and I have worked over there for about five years. You must be one of Lisa's friends."

Kelly shook her hand. "I'm Kelly, and it's nice to meet you. Our instructor Barbara is downstairs getting some more materials, so I'm helping out." Glancing at the other young woman, she asked, "Are you a physical therapist, Wanda?"

"No, I'm in grad school, studying chemistry. But I've been knitting for years and always wanted to try this, so here we are."

Kelly turned to the other four women in the room, who were either arranging their supplies or touching the yarns that filled the shelves lining the classroom. "Did you folks bring your knitted items to felt? Take a look around, and you'll see everything from slippers to hats to placemats."

Another woman held up her hand. "Placemat. I figured if I screwed it up, then I could simply throw it out. I'd hate to waste a perfectly good pair of knitted mittens."

"Ohhhh, now you made me nervous," Wanda said, reaching into her purse. She withdrew two royal-blue-and-white-striped mittens. "I was hoping these would felt up well so they'd be waterproof for skiing."

"I don't think we can guarantee full waterproofing, but you'll get close," Kelly said. "Of course, I'm not an expert, just a helper. What did you bring, Francie?"

Francie pulled out a large knit hat with peaked crown. "I thought this would look cool if the felting made the peak stand up straight. That way I'll look like Merlin when I zoom down the slopes."

One of the other women held up two oversized gray knit slippers. "That sounds exotic. I'm sticking with slippers. No one will see them except me, so if they're ugly, no one else will know."

Kelly laughed out loud. "Boy, you folks remind me of me talking about my knitting.

And yet all those things look pretty good."

Barbara strode into the room, hands full of supplies. "Well, we've got all our felters now. Excellent."

"That's right," Kelly said, gesturing around the room. "Let's start with names." When the women finished introducing themselves, Kelly added, "Wanda has the mittens and Francie brought the Merlin hat. Both are skiers."

"Oh, those should felt up fine," Barbara said, approaching the pair. She peered at Francie for a second. "You look familiar. Haven't we met?"

Francie smiled. "I was wondering if you'd recognize me, Barbara. I was your physical therapist at the Sports Health facility after you hurt your back. Someone ran into your car, didn't they?"

Barbara's smile vanished. "Yes, they did. Damn idiot was drinking and rear-ended me when I was at a stop light. Totally screwed up my back."

"Was your insurance company able to sue or get anything for medical expenses? I can't remember."

"Unfortunately, no. He was one of those uninsured motorists." She screwed up her face in a frown. "The bane of us responsible drivers."

"How's your back doing now? It's been over three years," Francie asked.

"Oh, thanks to you and Dr. Hensley, it's gotten stronger and stronger every year. I've been doing those exercises you gave me religiously."

"That's great to hear." Francie beamed. "Always like to hear good news about former patients."

"As someone who's had to rehab from various sports injuries over the years, I confess I swear by the PT exercises," Kelly offered. "One of my best friends is a therapist over at the Sports Health facility, too. I have to admit, having Lisa as my PT a couple of years ago nearly destroyed our friendship. She's brutal, I swear she is."

Francie cackled. "Ohhhh, yeah. We give her a hard time about that."

"What are these wash tubs and plungers for?" Wanda asked, pointing to the supplies on the table.

"Glad you asked, Wanda, it's a great way to start the class," Barbara announced. "Most of you will use washing machines to felt your knitted items. But we wanted to show you how to felt other ways. Things that don't need much shrinkage turn out better when you felt them by hand in the tub. And our helper today is an expert in that area.

She spent nearly half an hour plunging away, felting her boyfriend's knitted hat. And it came out beautifully. Did you bring it to show off, Kelly?"

Kelly withdrew Steve's newly felted hat from her bag and waved it proudly to appropriate praise.

"I can also attest that plunging away in that washtub is pretty darn tiring, not to mention boring as all get out. So, you folks may want to use the washing machine."

Kelly's cell phone rang in her jeans pocket, and she stepped away from the chattering felters into the central yarn room. Burt's number flashed on the screen.

"Hey, Burt, how's it going?"

"Not bad, Kelly. How'd that felting class go? Mimi told me you were filling in for her."

"It went fine, actually. I really enjoyed helping other beginners. I have a lot of beginner experience, you know."

Burt chuckled. "You're farther along than beginner, Kelly. Give yourself credit. I'm sure you did a great job." He cleared his throat. "By the way, I heard from Dan. I'd left him a message with your concerns about Tommy when we returned from the retreat, and I got a phone call this morning."

273

"What'd Dan say? Is he going to give Tommy a call?"

"Actually, he already has. He and Tommy met at a truck stop in Longmont between Denver and Fort Connor."

"Really? How did it go? What'd Dan say?"

"Dan said Tommy looked really nervous, so he explained about Malcolm's statement saying there was a man walking with Holly on the trail. Consequently, police wanted to check with anyone who might have been with Holly that night. Since Tommy was Holly's boyfriend, they were curious as to his whereabouts that night. He asked Tommy straight out if he'd been with Holly that Friday."

Kelly moved into the spinning alcove for more privacy. "And what did Tommy say? How did he react?"

"Dan said Tommy went white as a sheet, then blurted out everything that happened Friday. He told Dan about his argument with Holly and his walking out. He even admitted he'd been with Lynette until late that night before he drove back to Denver."

"Did Dan believe him?"

"Yeah, Dan told me he didn't pick up on any signs that Tommy was lying. Like I said, Kelly. Tommy's a real straight arrow. There's no way he could have deliberately harmed Holly."

"You're probably right, Burt. I was simply raising questions, that's all. I don't have any knowledge of Tommy's character. He certainly appears to be everything you say he is. I was curious, that's all. People under pressure do things they wouldn't normally do."

"Well, you can relax about Tommy. Matter of fact, I think I'll call him tonight and see how he's doing."

"Keep me posted, Burt."

"As always, Kelly."

Kelly took the turn into the Lambspun driveway on two wheels, her stomach in knots. She couldn't believe she'd screwed up again. She'd spent an enjoyable early evening at Curt's ranch house, complete with steak dinner and good conversation. Then she'd stopped by Mimi and Burt's to check if Burt had spoken with Tommy. Of course, Mimi brought out her delicious coffeecake, so Kelly's quick stop had lengthened considerably. Once again, she'd lost all track of time.

The problem was her cell phone was in her jacket pocket, hanging on a peg in Mimi's foyer, far from the family room. And as

275

the Fates would have it, Steve had — once again — found some free time and had driven back to Fort Connor. Once again, hoping to spend some time with Kelly. And once again, Kelly wasn't available.

How could she screw up again?

Kelly jerked her car to a stop, jumped out, and raced over to the cottage front door, bursting into the living room. Steve wasn't there. His truck was in the driveway, though. "Hey," she cried. "I'm back. Where *are* you?"

Steve stepped around the kitchen corner, a slice of pizza in his hand. "I'm here. Where were *you?*" He took another bite.

That now-familiar cloak of guilt dropped over Kelly's shoulders again. It felt heavier this time. "I was at Curt's ranch having dinner with them. Then I dropped by Mimi's and Burt's to talk about stuff," Kelly explained. "I wish you'd called earlier. Then I could have cancelled the stop at Mimi's."

Steve finished swallowing, then looked at her with an annoyed expression. "Or, you could have your phone with you. Where was it this time? In the car?"

Kelly noticed his tone of voice but ignored it as she walked toward the kitchen. "It was in my jacket, but that was hanging in Mimi's foyer so I couldn't hear it ringing. Like

276

I said, if you'd called earlier, I wouldn't have gone out. I'd be here. But I never figured you'd be coming back on a Monday night."

"There's no way for me to call earlier because these breaks just suddenly come up in the schedule. No way to know ahead of time. Turns out I finished the entire project early, and Fred told me to take the rest of tonight off." He took another bite of pizza.

Kelly watched him chew. His cool tone was bothering her. She'd been hearing more and more of it lately. And she didn't like it. She'd try apologizing again. See if that thawed him.

"Steve, I'm sorry I missed your call. But I just can't walk around with my cell phone in my hand all the time."

"Ever heard of pockets?" He tilted his cola can and drank deeply.

Kelly counted to ten. Then twenty. "Okaaaay, I promise I'll keep my phone in my pocket from now on. Providing I'm wearing something with pockets. But it never occurred to me that you'd come back on a Monday night. So naturally, I wasn't prepared for your call."

Steve didn't answer for a moment, simply finished off his pizza, then took another slice. "When did you finish dinner at Curt's?"

"About seven thirty. Then I went over to Mimi's and Burt's to talk about stuff. You must have called right after that."

"Yeah, around then. What sort of stuff? Something happening with the shop?"

Kelly shook her head. "Naw, I just wanted to see if Barbara's son Tommy had talked with Burt. I was curious how Tommy was doing after the police questioned him. They wanted to know his whereabouts the night Holly died."

Steve screwed up his face. "Police? Who's Holly? What are you talking about, Kelly?"

Kelly realized Steve didn't know anything about Holly's death except that she was the same girl who'd appeared in Kelly's backyard three weeks ago. Steve didn't know who Barbara or Tommy were, let alone their connection to Holly or to the people at Lambspun. And Steve certainly didn't know that Kelly had been sleuthing for details about Holly's last night alive.

"Holly was the girl they found dead on the trail a few weeks ago, remember? She was the same one who showed up on my patio. One of Mimi's teachers has a son, Tommy, who was Holly's boyfriend. Tommy's in med school in Denver and asked Burt and me if we would try to find out who gave Holly those pills. At the party, that is.

She was at a big party that night." Kelly stopped talking because the expression on Steve's face had gone from puzzled to annoyed once again.

Steve dropped the pizza slice to the counter. "I don't believe it. You were out sleuthing tonight when you could have been *here?* What in hell is the matter with you, Kelly?"

Kelly stepped back. *Whoa.* She wasn't expecting an angry reaction. "What do you mean? There's nothing the matter. Tommy is up to his neck with medical studies, and Burt and I are trying to help, that's all."

Steve stared at her, clearly getting angrier. "You're out helping other people when you could be here with *me.* Dammit, Kelly! I need your help, too!"

That did it. Steve's flash of anger sparked Kelly's own. "You won't *let* me help you!"

Steve's dark eyes flashed. He pushed away from the counter. "I told you I'm not going there, Kelly."

"But, *why?* Working those two jobs is grinding you down so far I don't even recognize you anymore," Kelly charged. "Hell, if you don't want to borrow money from me, then borrow it from Curt. That way you wouldn't have to work the second job. It's stupid."

Thunderclouds darkened Steve's face. "I don't wanta talk about it. I'm going to watch the game and sleep on the sofa," he said, storming out of the kitchen.

"*Fine!* Sleep on the sofa. It doesn't make what I said any less true," Kelly shot back, her pulse racing. Her Irish was up and that was always dangerous, as her dad would say.

She marched to the fridge and grabbed two bottles of their favorite ale and a foil-wrapped package. Stalking out to the living room, she placed one ale and the package on the coffee table. Steve had already sprawled on the sofa.

"I made Helen's gingersnaps for Megan and Marty's party, and I saved you some. Enjoy."

With that, she grabbed her laptop and stalked off to the bedroom, slamming the door behind her. Might as well spread some of that guilt around.

FIFTEEN

Kelly looked up at the burst of wind and energy that blew into Lambspun's main knitting room. "Hey, Megan, we haven't seen you around here during the day for a while. Have you and Mimi finished the wedding prep list already?"

Megan dumped her large knitting bag on the library table and fixed Kelly with an incredulous gaze. "You've got to be kidding. I'm only on wedding cakes, third on the list. It's hard finding time to balance work and interviewing vendors every day. I'm beat."

"Well, sit down and catch me up. We haven't had a chance to talk at practice or game nights lately." Kelly returned to the bright red yarn on her circular needles. "What's happening? Have you found a favorite bakery?"

Megan rolled her eyes and plopped into a chair on the other side of the table. "Oh, I've got plenty of favorites, but they're all so expensive. Mimi almost had a heart attack when she found out how much wedding cakes cost." She gave a dramatic shudder.

Kelly played along and pretended to flinch. "Okay, tell me. I'm ready."

"Some of the fancier cakes can cost six dollars per slice. Now, multiply that by the number of guests, and you get the picture."

This time Kelly didn't have to fake the flinch. The accountant in her took over. "*What!* I don't believe it."

"Believe it," Megan intoned, digging in her knitting bag. She withdrew a rose-pink half-finished sweater. "If you have two hundred guests, then the cake will cost over twelve hundred dollars. And we're gonna have at least two hundred guests. More, probably."

"What if some of us take a pledge not to eat cake, will they give you a discount?" Kelly teased, slipping a crimson wool stitch off her needle.

A smile peeked out finally. "I don't think it works that way, Kelly. Plus Marty has lots of nephews and nieces and cousins, so there will be bunches of kids there. And you know how much kids like cake."

Dollar signs flashed before Kelly's eyes. "Whoa, I see what you mean. By the way, have you come up with a preliminary budget yet? Sounds to me like you need to."

Megan kept her attention on her knitting. "We're working on it. We've come up with a list of things we really, really want for the wedding. You know, like food, drinks, music, flowers . . ."

"And a wedding dress, or were you planning on wearing that bedsheet?"

"Don't remind me. I cannot believe we have to go looking for wedding gowns again. And in Denver, next time. But Mimi insists. I swear, I can't face any more tulle or ruffles for a while."

"Don't take it out on the tulle," Jennifer countered as she hurried into the room and dumped her knitting bag. "It's not the tulle's fault you're on wedding prep overload." She pulled out the chair beside Kelly.

"I can't help it, guys. Lace and ruffles give me an itch. I'd much rather interview bakers and hotel managers." Megan's lightning quick fingers moved, stitches forming faster. Kelly had noticed long ago if Megan was upset or excited about something, she knitted even faster than usual.

"How's the banquet room search going?" Jennifer asked, pulling a burgundy-and-gold scarf from her bag. A match for her burgundy sweater, no doubt.

"Nowhere, I'm afraid. We're on the waiting list for the two largest hotels in town, but there are at least three or more people ahead of us. It doesn't look good. We may have to rent one of those church halls."

"That's not bad, Megan," Kelly offered, more red stitches forming on her needles.

"I know, I just wanted something really pretty, since we can't be outside."

"Why not? Are those park places reserved, too?"

"They've been reserved for months. That lodge near the river and the National Park entrance is booked out the ying-yang. We'd have to delay the wedding another year to snag that spot."

Kelly heard the familiar sound of her cell phone and quickly dropped her knitting. Digging out her phone, she pushed away from the table. "Excuse me, guys." Patty's name and number flashed on her phone screen.

"Hey, Patty, how're you doing?" she said as she walked into the central yarn room.

"I'm okay, I guess. Do you have a moment to talk? I have to work at the steakhouse in that shopping center near the shop, and I wondered if you were at Lambspun."

"Yeah, I'm here taking a knitting break. What's up?"

"Kind of hard to explain over the phone.

I'll meet you in Pete's café in half an hour, okay?"

"I'll be there," Kelly promised, wondering what was bothering Patty. She sounded different.

"Is that Patty, the covert college agent?" Jennifer asked as Kelly returned to the table.

"Yeah, the same Patty."

"Who's this?" Megan asked.

"She's one of Tommy's friends. Tommy is Barbara's son, remember?" Kelly explained, picking up her knitting where she left off.

"Ohhhh, yeah, now I remember. He's in medical school, and Holly was his girlfriend." Megan shook her head. "So sad to die that young."

Jennifer's fingers moved at their usual warp speed. "After Holly's death, Kelly and I went over to the Grill one afternoon to have lunch and interrogate one of the waitresses. Based on covert college agent Patty's observations."

Megan looked up with a puzzled expression. "Who were you interrogating? What in the world are you sleuthing, Kelly? I thought you said that girl died from an overdose."

"Nothing, really." Kelly tried to downplay Jennifer's description, even though it was accurate. "I'm just poking around into some stuff, that's all." She tried to affect a nonchalant tone.

Megan glanced from Kelly to Jennifer and back. "She's got that look, Jennifer. Ordinarily I'd be on her case trying to find out what she was up to, but I have got entirely too much aggravation in my life right now with all this wedding preparation. You'll have to ride herd on her."

"Excuse me?" Kelly said archly. "I do not need herding."

"Yeah, you do," Megan retorted, not even glancing up from her knitting.

"I'm on it," Jennifer promised. "If I need help, I'll call in Pete."

"Hey guys, I haven't done anything," Kelly protested. "I'm only talking to people, trying to help Tommy."

"Speaking of talking to people, I have *got* to find Mimi. She was going to check on florists." Megan dropped her knitting to the table and was out of the room in a flash.

"Who was that masked woman?" Jennifer joked, glancing in Megan's wake.

"I don't know, but she's in hyperdrive. Let's hope she saves some of that energy for practice tonight," Kelly said, picking up her knitting where she'd left off.

"What are you knitting?" Jennifer asked.

"I thought I'd knit another winter hat for myself and felt it. Now that I've learned how, I want to do it again."

She and Jennifer knitted quietly for a few minutes. Different thoughts darted about Kelly's mind, but one image lingered. She glanced over her shoulders to see if customers were browsing nearby. No one in sight.

"Steve and I had a fight last night," she said softly.

Jennifer glanced up. "What about?"

Kelly let out an aggravated breath. "He was all over my case because I missed one of his last-minute phone calls again because I didn't hear my phone ring. I was over at Mimi's and Burt's. If he would call earlier, there'd be no problem. But he swears he doesn't know until the last minute." She frowned. "It's so frustrating."

"Well, I'm sure it's frustrating for him, too. That's why he snapped at you. I'm assuming he snapped."

"Oh, he did more than snap. He went all sarcastic on me. When I told him I couldn't carry the phone around with me all the time, he asked if I'd heard of pockets."

Jennifer smiled as she continued knitting. "That's pretty funny."

Kelly snorted. "Not at the time. It was annoying as all get out and made me mad."

"So you snapped."

"No, I didn't, as a matter of fact. I simply

287

suggested he call earlier before I go out in the evening. I don't sit at home all alone at night, and he knows it." She exhaled a loud sigh. "Then he asked where I'd been, and I told him I was at Mimi's and Burt's talking about stuff. When he pushed, I told him I was checking things for Tommy since he was in med school. You know . . . the whole story."

"Oh, yeah. And I'm sure Steve understood, right?"

Kelly caught Jennifer's teasing tone. "Ohhhh, yeah. He was angry. He couldn't believe I was out sleuthing around, helping other people when *he* needed my help. That's exactly what he said." She let out an impatient breath, then took a deep drink of coffee.

Jennifer glanced up in concern. "Uh-oh."

"Uh-oh is right." Kelly set the mug on the table with a thump. "That's when I said he wouldn't *let* me help him. And that's when he *really* got mad. He refused to talk about it and stalked out of the kitchen."

"And you said . . . ?"

"I told him it was stupid to be exhausting himself working that second job when he could borrow money to get through this rough time. If he didn't want to take it from me, he could borrow it from Curt."

Kelly took another drink of coffee, trying to wash away the taste and memory of those angry words from last night. But they were stronger than caffeine. When she didn't say anything for a minute, Jennifer prodded.

"What happened then?"

Kelly shrugged. "He announced he was sleeping on the sofa. So I gave him a beer and the cookies I'd saved for him, then took my laptop into the bedroom. And that was that. He was already gone this morning when I got up."

Jennifer returned to her knitting. "Everything you said is true, Kelly. And Steve knows that. That's probably why he got so mad. You hit a nerve."

"Yeah, well, he hit some, too."

"Try not to dwell on it. It's only natural you two are going to have some friction. He's under a lot of pressure right now, and that puts pressure on you."

"Yeah, yeah, yeah. I'm getting tired of hearing that. I've bent over backwards trying to be understanding, and he jumps all over me. Frustrating doesn't begin to describe it." She glanced at her watch. "I'd better go over to the café. I told Patty I'd meet her there."

Jennifer checked her watch and shoved her knitting into her oversized bag. "I'd better check in at the office. There are a few more listings now, so I should check them out."

Kelly headed toward the central yarn room, Jennifer beside her. "Has Pete made those brownies for the party yet? I'd like to snitch one if I can."

"Too late. Brownies were made, wrapped, and left for Jayleen to pick up yesterday. I think Pete did them at night so none of us would be tempted. Marty probably would have left his law office early if he knew brownies were in the vicinity." Jennifer pulled her phone from her bag. "Take care, Kelly. Try not to let it get to you."

"That's why I wanted the brownies. Chocolate always helps with frustration."

Kelly headed down the hallway. Scanning the café when she entered, she selected a small side table in the alcove. It was quieter there.

Waving her empty mug at the waitress, Julie, Kelly settled into a straight-backed chair and returned to her knitting. Now that she'd learned how to felt, the irresistible urge to do it again took over. Since she'd become reasonably proficient knitting hats, it was a natural choice. She'd felted Steve's knitted hat and it came out really well. Now, she'd try it for herself.

Julie refilled her coffee, and Kelly picked up her stitches and knitted peacefully for a few moments until she spotted Patty approaching.

"Hey, sit down and relax." Kelly gestured to a chair. "You sound hurried."

Patty dropped her backpack and sank into the chair across from Kelly. "I've been running errands, but that's not what's bothering me." She leaned forward over her folded arms. "I heard something this morning that really bothered me, Kelly. And . . . and I don't know what to make of it. It's about Holly."

Kelly let her knitting drop to her lap. "What did you hear?"

"I spotted one of my friends I don't get to see too often. She went to school with Tommy and Holly and me. Anyway, it turns out she was at the same party that night. I don't remember seeing her there, but it was so crowded it was hard to find people. Anyway, Francesca wanted to know how Tommy was doing since she had been out of town for the funeral. I said not good. He was still trying to find some peace of mind about it all. Then I asked Francesca if she remembered seeing Holly at the party and if she noticed who Holly was talking to."

"Did she?"

"She said she saw Holly standing outside on the lawn when she arrived. Francesca joked with Holly, saying she was coming and Holly was going. Holly said she was 'pretty drunk' already. Francesca asked if Tommy was coming to pick her up." Patty's voice dropped dramatically. "And Holly told her Tommy was studying in Denver, but his mother was coming to pick her up. Then she laughed, kind of funny-like."

Kelly stared at Patty, totally surprised by the remark. "What was that again?"

"That's pretty much what I said, Kelly. So I asked Francesca if she actually saw Barbara pick up Holly. And she said she did. She recognized Barbara from her doctor's office. Apparently Barbara works for the same doctor Francesca goes to." Patty shook her head. "I thought she was mistaken, but Francesca said she even recognized Barbara's car. It's an old black Honda with a Broncos sticker on the back fender."

Kelly tried to picture capable, protective Barbara playing taxi service for drunken and maybe drugged-out Holly. Had Tommy asked her to be on chauffeur duty since he couldn't? What did she do with Holly? Did Barbara take Holly back to her apartment and drive away? The vagrant, Malcolm, said he saw a man with Holly that night on the river trail. Did Holly call her Greeley boyfriend, Eddie, to pick her up at her apartment? Is that how she wound up on the trail?

"Barbara's never said anything about picking up Holly that night."

"I know. That's what's so strange." Patty lowered her voice. "I mean, do you think Tommy asked his mom to pick up Holly and take her home? Maybe Holly wandered off again. I mean, she said she was drunk already. Maybe Barbara started arguing with Holly, and Holly left."

"Or wandered off when Barbara wasn't looking." Kelly picked up the imaginary thread. "Maybe Barbara felt guilty about letting Holly slip away. Holly must have called the guy from Greeley to pick her up. Remember, that guy sleeping beneath the trees saw a man with Holly that night."

Patty's eyes lit up. "You're right! That's gotta be what happened, don't you think?"

"I don't know, but Holly wound up on the trail later on with a guy, so she must have called him. Either she was at her own apartment or slipped away from Barbara."

"No wonder Barbara never admitted she picked up Holly that night."

"Or maybe she did," Kelly countered. "And maybe Tommy didn't want his mom to be questioned by the police."

Patty tapped her half-polished fingernail on the table. "My friend Francesca is pretty solid. So I believe her. Are you going to ask Barbara about it?"

"I'll mention it to Burt first and see what he says. He and Mimi have known Barbara for years. I'll let him talk to her. Someone should ask her about that night."

"Well, I'm not about to do it. Barbara can be pretty intimidating. If she likes you, she's all nice and smiley. If she doesn't, well, she can be pretty cold." Patty grabbed her backpack and rose from the chair. "Listen, I've got to get to my steakhouse job. Let me know what you learn, okay?"

"Will do, Patty. See you later."

Kelly watched Patty walk away, then stared out into the café again, pondering the various scenarios she and Patty had invented.

Had Barbara taken Holly to her house or to Holly's apartment? Had Barbara told Tommy she helped Holly that night? Or, did she keep quiet, afraid of being blamed by her son for Holly's death?

Kelly picked up her half-finished hat again. Meanwhile, puzzling questions buzzed inside Kelly's brain like pesky mosquitoes in summer. Where did Barbara take Holly? If she took her to her house, why didn't she keep an eye on Holly? Did they have an argument? Holly told Francesca she was already drunk. Did Barbara simply dump Holly at her apartment to sleep it off?

Slip, wrap, slide. Kelly's stitches formed rhythmically on the needle. One row, then another. Holly's boyfriend Eddie had to be the one who picked up Holly and gave her the pills. Did he panic when he saw Holly's reaction to the narcotics? Is that why he took her to the river trail? Maybe he simply dumped Holly there to sleep it off. Only Holly didn't wake up.

Kelly checked the width of the hat. She needed to knit at least another two inches or more. It was different to knit something you intended to felt. You had to intentionally make the item bigger than needed. She'd lucked out with Steve's hat. It had only been a little bit too large, so it didn't need to shrink much. But Kelly wanted to make this hat bigger and see how it felted.

Starting another row, Kelly noticed one of the buzzing insect thoughts was more persistent than the others. So she kept knitting, knowing it would eventually buzz close enough for her to capture.

Something about the pills. What was it?

Eddie must have given Holly the pills. If Holly had gotten the pills from someone at the party, then she would be showing signs of an overdose when Barbara picked her up. And Barbara would have definitely known something was wrong. Barbara was a nurse, after all. She would have taken Holly to the hospital. So, it had to be Eddie. And he dumped Holly on the trail when he saw her reaction.

Slip, wrap, slide. Kelly started another row. Something was missing. What was it? The annoying thought buzzed closer. What was it about that scenario that didn't fit? She knitted another row, then another. Finally the little thought buzzed close enough.

The pills. The detective said it would take at least eight or ten of those narcotic pain pills to cause death in someone who wasn't used to them. The respiratory system would keep slowing down until it eventually stopped, and the person died. Why would Eddie give Holly that many pills? Surely he didn't want her to overdose and die. Was he so drugged out himself he simply dumped a bunch of pills in her hand?

That didn't make sense to Kelly. Everything she'd heard about Eddie made him sound like he was into drugs for the money he could make selling, not the high.

Kelly knitted another row, then checked the width. Getting closer. She slid a finished stitch off the left needle onto the right one. And then another, letting the peacefulness settle over her. Ideas always came to her when she "knit on it."

Something was bothering her about the elaborate scenario she'd just created in her imagination. It didn't make sense that Eddie would deliberately or accidentally give Holly too many pills. But Eddie had to be the one who provided the pills, didn't he? After all, if Holly had gotten them from the party, Barbara would have noticed her reaction.

Slip, wrap, slide. Slip, wrap, slide. Slip the right needle into the stitch on the left needle, wrap the yarn around the needle, then slide the stitch from the left to the right needle. Slip, wrap, slide. Over and over as one row after another formed. Again and again. Then, from the back of Kelly's mind another little thought buzzed. This one hovered right in front of her eyes.

Maybe it was Barbara, not Eddie. Maybe Barbara gave Holly those pills. She would know how many to give so that Holly wouldn't wake up. Barbara's a nurse, after all.

Kelly stopped knitting and stared at her yarn. That last thought brought a chill with it. Surely her imagination must be working on overdrive. Barbara wouldn't kill Holly. She'd watched Holly grow up. Had provided a second home for Holly. She had no reason.

Yes, she did, another chilly thought insisted. *The best reason a mother could have. She needed to protect Tommy. Holly was a threat to Tommy and his future. She was manipulative and self-destructive. Barbara said so herself. Tommy would never become a doctor if Holly stayed in his life.*

Kelly let that sink in. Barbara had insinuated that, hadn't she? They all heard her pleas to Tommy not to "throw his life away," grieving over Holly. Was that possible? Was Barbara so afraid of Holly's hold on Tommy that she'd commit murder to set Tommy free?

That thought was colder than all the rest. Kelly made herself consider it. She couldn't assume anything. What if Barbara snapped? Kelly had wondered earlier if Tommy snapped. Constant pressure and manipulation from Holly proved too much. Well . . . the same thing could have happened to Barbara. Holly knew Tommy was studying in Denver, and yet she still had the nerve to call up and ask for a ride. Maybe that was the last straw for Barbara. Hadn't she said Holly was on a self-destructive path and would come to a bad end eventually? Maybe Barbara decided to have "eventually" come that Friday night.

Kelly picked up her knitting where she'd left off. Was that possible? Could Barbara cold-bloodedly give her son's girlfriend an overdose? She'd certainly know how much to give Holly. Barbara was a nurse . . . and . . .

Another thought buzzed forward. Barbara had a back problem. The girl who showed up at the felting class yesterday was Barbara's physical therapist. She asked how Barbara's back was doing. Barbara had gone to the orthopedic health center for treatment and therapy. No doubt Barbara's doctor prescribed medicine. Barbara said she'd recovered "thanks to Dr. Hensley" and PT exercises.

Kelly knitted another row. The thoughts buzzed faster as she began to picture Barbara picking up Holly from the party and giving her the pills. No doubt, Holly would take whatever pills Barbara told her to. After all, Barbara was a nurse. Did Barbara drive her around for a while until Holly got sleepy? Then, she took her out on the river trail and left Holly to fall asleep and die.

Another thought buzzed in front of Kelly's eyes. Vagrant Malcolm said he saw a "man" with Holly that night. A man wearing a dark hooded jacket. Could that have been Barbara? She's certainly a tall, big-boned woman. She could definitely be mistaken for a man, especially in the dark.

Another row, then another formed on Kelly's needles as the disturbing scenario unfolded inside her head. Holly would willingly trust Barbara. And by the time Barbara dumped Holly on the trail, Holly was probably so disoriented she didn't even know what was happening. Hadn't Malcolm said the young girl stood up and tried to walk then fell down and didn't move again?

Kelly tried to rein in her chaotic thoughts. They seemed to take on a "scripting" life of their own. Buzzing and buzzing. She glanced at her watch, then grabbed her cell phone and punched in Lisa's number. Client accounts were calling her. She had to push these racing thoughts aside so she could return to her cottage and client accounts. There was softball practice tonight, thankfully. No inner scenarios allowed on the field.

Lisa picked up after the third ring. "Hey, Kelly, what's up? Don't forget practice tonight."

"Already on my day planner. I have a quick question. If someone's been in a car accident and had lots of back problems, what sort of prescription medicines would doctors use?"

"Are you asking for someone, Kelly?"

"No, simply my own information. Ever since I had that meeting with the detective, I've been curious about certain drugs."

"Well, most of the docs over here prescribe one of the big three. Vicodin, Percocet, and, of course, OxyContin."

"Yeah, the detective said those are the same three narcotic painkillers that show up on the drug party scene. People get them illegally then sell them. Now I know why they're so common. That's what doctors are prescribing all the time."

"You got it. And some docs are more lenient than others about refilling prescriptions," Lisa said.

"No wonder so many wind up on the street."

"Hey, gotta get back to work. See you tonight." Her phone clicked off.

Kelly tossed her phone into her bag along with the nearly finished knitted hat. Lisa wasn't the only one who had to return to work.

Sixteen

Kelly stood on her back patio and watched Carl sniff around the yard while she finished up her first mug of morning coffee. Several client e-mails had kept her busy with account work and — more important — kept her mind from wandering off to conjure. She'd left a message on Burt's cell phone earlier this morning but hadn't heard from him yet. She needed to explain these suspicions to Burt and see what he said. Either she was off base, or she was on to something. Burt had good instincts.

Her cell phone jangled as it lay on the desk, and Kelly bolted through the open glass door to grab it before it went to voice mail. Burt's name and number flashed on the screen.

"Hey, Kelly, sorry I couldn't call before. I've been at a community meeting. What's up?"

"I wanted to run some things past you,

Burt. You're my barometer, you know. Do you have a few moments to talk?"

"Well, I'm about to pull into a shopping center, so let me park, then I'll give you my full attention."

Kelly poured more coffee into her mug then sat in her leather desk chair. Meanwhile, sounds of driving came over the phone. Then Burt returned. "All parked?" she asked.

"All settled. So shoot. What's on your mind?"

"Okay . . . this may sound a little crazy at first, but just hear me out, Burt, before you say anything. Patty came over yesterday and told me something that bothered both of us. A friend of hers who was at the party said she talked to Holly that night when she was standing outside. Holly told her she was waiting for Tommy's mother to pick her up and —"

"What was that?"

"That's what I said." Kelly took another deep breath. "This girl Francesca says she saw Barbara pick up Holly that night. She recognized Barbara from her doctor's office, and she recognized the car. A black Honda sedan with a Broncos sticker on the back." She paused for his reaction.

Burt didn't say anything at first. Then he

303

asked in a quiet voice, "Is this girl positive it was Barbara?"

"Patty said she asked Francesca the same thing. And Francesca swears it was Barbara. She grew up with Tommy and Patty and Holly, so she recognized Barbara when she saw her."

"I don't understand why Barbara didn't say anything about picking up Holly," Burt said in his quiet voice. Kelly recognized his thoughtful tone. Burt was having some of the same questions arise that she did.

"Neither do I, Burt. But Patty and I suspect that Barbara probably dropped Holly off at her apartment. Then Holly must have called that boyfriend Eddie she'd been seeing. Barbara probably felt guilty she didn't keep track of Holly that night. Francesca said Holly was already drunk. That's why Barbara didn't say anything. She didn't want Tommy to know she was involved."

"That might explain it. Since Holly was seen with a guy on the trail, it had to be that Eddie."

"That's what I figured, too. Then after Patty left, I started thinking about it, and something about that picture didn't make sense, Burt."

"What do you mean?"

"Like why would Eddie give Holly that

many pills? Investigator Frobischer said it would take about eight to ten pills to be a fatal overdose in someone who wasn't used to them. Eddie wouldn't deliberately give Holly an overdose. He *sold* pills. She was a customer. Plus, she was his girlfriend. Why would he do that?"

Burt paused. "Yeah, I see what you mean, Kelly. It doesn't make sense. Unless *he* was so high he wasn't paying attention."

"That didn't make sense either, Burt. And it kept bothering me, until something else popped up. Maybe someone else gave Holly a deliberate overdose of pain pills. Someone who knew how many pills were fatal."

"Who would do that?" Burt's tone was skeptical.

Kelly paused. "Barbara."

"*What!* That's crazy, Kelly!"

"Yeah, I know, but hear me out. We all knew how much Barbara resented Holly's selfish manipulation of Tommy. And Barbara made no secret of her feelings about Holly's behavior. I remember her saying that Holly was 'on a self-destructive path' that would lead to a bad end."

"That was simply a mother's concern, Kelly. You can't be seriously thinking Barbara would kill Holly. I mean . . . Holly was screwed up and self-destructive, but that's not a reason to kill someone."

"Maybe it was for an overly protective mother like Barbara," Kelly suggested. "Maybe she snapped. Holly knew Tommy was studying in Denver, yet she was calling him to drop everything and drive back to Fort Connor and take care of her. As usual. Maybe that was the last straw for Barbara."

Burt didn't say anything for a few seconds. "I still don't buy it, Kelly. I've known Barbara for years. She's a big, bossy gal who likes to tell people what to do, but she's not cruel. And leaving Holly to die along the trail was cruel."

"I agree, Burt. But I don't know Barbara as well as you do. Therefore I'm not influenced by past experiences with her. I simply look at her as she is now —"

"Wait a minute, Kelly. You've forgotten something important. That old vagrant along the trail saw a man with Holly that night. How do you explain that, Sherlock?"

Kelly couldn't help smiling. "As you pointed out earlier, Barbara's a big woman. Put her in a dark jacket with the hood up, and it would be easy to mistake her for a man, especially at night."

Burt didn't reply at first, then grumbled, "Okay, you're right on that point. But I still think you're mistaken about Barbara."

"Hey, don't get me wrong, Burt. I'm not trying to make Barbara guilty. I'm simply not ruling out any possibility and trying not to make assumptions. As I've said before, people are often not what they seem. And anyone is capable of murder if they have enough reason. You know that, Burt."

Burt sighed out loud. "Yeah, I know, Kelly. I know. So, what do you plan to do?"

"I think you and I should talk with Barbara. Just a friendly chat. Tell her what we learned and see how she responds. That will tell us a lot, watching her reaction. She probably doesn't think anyone knows she picked up Holly."

"Okay, I'll give her a call and see if she can swing by the shop this morning. I remember she has today off so she was planning to come in and choose some fibers for another class project. We can go into the back of the café and talk."

"Thanks, Burt. That would sound a lot more natural with your calling. By the way, I'm curious. Why didn't you quiz me on how Barbara got the narcotic pain pills? You questioned me on everything else."

"Because I already know. Barbara was taking OxyContin for her back injury years ago. She told Mimi and me that she didn't like to take the pills because they were addictive. So she never used all the pills."

"Want some coffee, Barbara?" Kelly asked as Julie poured a dark stream into her mug. The café was emptier than normal today, and no one was sitting in the back alcove.

Barbara waved her hand as she approached the corner table. "No, thanks. I'm good."

Burt took a sip from his mug. "Decided what you're going to teach for the winter classes yet?"

"Not yet, but I'm getting close," Barbara said, pushing up her university sweatshirt sleeves as she settled into the chair. "So, what's happening? Do you and Mimi want me to teach another class or something?"

Kelly settled into the chair beside Burt and watched him assume his "serious talking" pose. Hands folded, leaning forward over the table.

"Well, maybe so. But actually Kelly and I were curious about something. I'll let Kelly explain."

Kelly paused and chose her words carefully. Barbara had an I'm-busy-don't-waste-my-time expression on her face. "You know Tommy asked Burt and me to find out what we could about that college party scene Holly was involved in."

Barbara rolled her eyes. "Yes, and I appreciate what you and Burt are doing. It keeps Tommy from wasting his time and jeopardizing his studies by coming down here."

Kelly gave her a smile. "Well, I've been e-mailing Tommy everything I've learned, hoping that he'd find some sense of closure —"

"Thank you," Barbara repeated.

"But I learned something yesterday that bothers me and Burt, too." She gestured to him. "And we wanted to ask you about it."

Barbara stared at Kelly, a puzzled look replacing the impatience. "What is it?"

"One of the girls who was at the party said she saw you pick up Holly from the party that night. And Burt and I were wondering why you never mentioned it before. The girl said she recognized you from the doctor's office and also recognized your car." Kelly sipped from her coffee mug, watching Barbara's reaction.

It came swiftly. Total surprise. Barbara's eyes went wide and a startled expression appeared. Her mouth dropped open as well. She didn't say a word.

Burt's quiet voice came. "We were wondering why you never mentioned that. Did you tell Tommy?"

"No . . . I . . . I couldn't," Barbara stammered, her wide eyes looking anxious, as she glanced from Kelly to Burt.

Was that fear? Kelly wondered, watching capable take-charge Barbara stammer in obvious confusion. Clearly, Barbara didn't think anyone knew she'd picked up Holly that night. Burt and Kelly were right.

"We wondered what sort of condition Holly was in. We'd heard she was drinking heavily that evening," Burt continued, as if he had been leading the investigation. Kelly was grateful. Barbara trusted Burt, so maybe she'd tell him the truth.

Barbara's mouth twisted. "She was drunk, of course. Like she always was whenever she called."

"Were you afraid she'd call Tommy if you didn't pick her up from the party?"

Barbara gave Kelly a grateful look. "That's exactly right."

"Did you take Holly to her apartment?" Burt asked.

"Yes, and I told her to go upstairs and sleep it off." Barbara made an exasperated sound. "Of course, she promised she would. Obviously, she didn't. Otherwise, how would she have wound up on the river trail?"

"Did she call you again to tell you where she was?" Burt asked.

310

Barbara shook her head. "No, I didn't hear a word, and I was up for most of the night, too. I was so upset I couldn't get to sleep after that."

"Upset?" Burt prodded gently.

"Yes. Upset with Holly." Barbara's frown spread. "I couldn't believe she'd call me asking why she couldn't reach Tommy. She was obviously drunk. I told her he had his cell phone off because he was studying the whole weekend." She gave a disgusted snort. "Then she asked if I would come and get her. As if we were her personal taxi service. I told her to get a ride with one of her friends at the party. She said she asked Patty, but Patty didn't bring her car, and everyone else was still partying."

Kelly watched anger flash across Barbara's face. Clearly, Barbara resented Holly's demands. And the presumption that Tommy and his mother were both at her beck and call. Barbara made no pretense of her anger. "Why didn't you tell her no?" Kelly asked.

Barbara shot Kelly a sharp look. "Believe me, I wanted to. But . . ." She closed her eyes and exhaled a long breath. "I knew Holly would complain to Tommy that I had left her in some awful situation. I'm sure she'd embellish it, of course, and make me out to be a villain. And I'd promised Tommy to help Holly if she ever called when he wasn't available. So I had no choice."

"I think you did the right thing, Barbara. You'd promised to help Holly, and you did," Burt said. "You had no way of knowing Holly would leave her apartment later that night."

"I know, I know." Barbara stared off into the café. "But I still felt guilty, especially after I learned what happened. I was afraid to tell Tommy. He and I had argued over Holly so many times. I . . . I didn't want him to blame me for Holly wandering off that night."

Kelly searched Barbara's face for any hint of evasion and found none. Barbara seemed unapologetic about her annoyance with Holly and her reluctance to be a chauffeur that night. Barbara was as blunt and forthright as always. Her initial startled confusion was probably surprise.

"I don't think Tommy would blame you, Barbara," Kelly added. "But if you like, I won't even mention it in my e-mail to him."

Barbara gave her a grateful look. "I appreciate that, Kelly."

"I'll tell Patty not to mention it, either. She's e-mailing Tommy, too."

Barbara smiled. "Oh, I'm sure Patty

wouldn't tell Tommy. She's very considerate and wouldn't want Tommy to worry. She's grown up right beside Tommy and Holly. Almost like a little sister. I used to have her over for dinner whenever Holly came. They were all very close friends."

"Well, she's certainly a big help. She's been asking all her friends about the party that night. Checking if they saw who Holly was with, and all that. She'd call me with updates, and I'd e-mail them to Tommy."

"Patty is a sweet girl," Barbara continued, a maternal smile replacing her earlier frown. "She'd come over whenever I needed help with a project. Even cleaning out closets. Such a good-natured girl. I hoped that Tommy would become interested in Patty someday. I knew she had a huge crush on him. But Tommy only had eyes for Holly. Patty was a little sister to him." She shook her head. "What a shame."

Kelly listened, fascinated to learn this other side of Patty. Barbara had nothing but glowing praise for Patty, yet Patty had made some rather sharp observations about Barbara. Interesting.

"Well, let's hope that Tommy does find some peace of mind about this," Burt said. "He's a fine young man and will make a wonderful doctor someday."

The slight flush of maternal pride colored Barbara's face. "Well, keep him in your prayers, Burt. He's just begun that journey." She scraped her chair back and stood. "I'm going to check on those yarns now. Mimi will want a workshop description for the flyer this week before she sends it to the printer."

"I'll be there in a minute, Barbara," Burt said, leaning back in his chair. Barbara headed toward the hallway to the shop. Burt glanced at Kelly with a knowing smile. "Well, are you satisfied, Sherlock? I told you Barbara couldn't harm Holly."

"Yeah, you did, Burt, and you were right. Forgive me for raising the issue, but, hey . . . that's my job," she said with a sly smile. "I'm supposed to poke around in things other people don't want to. And ask bothersome questions. Someone has to do it."

Burt drained his coffee and rose. "Keep right on asking questions, Kelly. That's how you discover the truth. I'm afraid, however, we may never know the whole truth about Holly's death."

"Well, I think you and I came up with a reasonable explanation when we brainstormed earlier. Boyfriend Eddie is probably the source of the pills and provided transportation to the river trail. It seems to

314

fit, even though I've still got some questions."

Burt chuckled. "Kelly, you wouldn't be *you* if you didn't have questions. See you later." He sped down the hallway.

Kelly took a deep drink of coffee, letting some of those questions she mentioned rise to claim her attention. Boyfriend Eddie was still a question mark in her eyes. Maybe Burt was right. They might never know the truth about what happened that night — where Holly got the pills or how she wound up on the river trail. That thought didn't sit well. Kelly didn't like unsolved puzzles.

She checked her watch. There was enough time to finish her oversized hat. She'd already transferred all the stitches to the four double-point needles. She grabbed her knitting bag and headed toward the main room. Then her cell phone jangled in her jeans pocket. Steve's name and number flashed on the screen as she settled at the long table.

"Hey, how're you doing?" Kelly said cheerfully, hoping Steve was no longer annoyed.

"Okay. I got to go out with one of the firm's clients this morning. He's starting an entirely new development. Totally green building. Energy-saving materials and construction and all that. Plus, I saw the new solar arrays that are being developed. Man, they're way more powerful."

"Wow, that sounds great. You were doing some of that with the Wellesley site, weren't you?" It was good to hear Steve enthusiastic about something again. She hadn't heard that tone in his voice for months.

"Yeah, I could only do a little of it, though. Pricing was a problem. But that's more reasonable now, too. Listen, I got your message reminding me about Megan and Marty's party this weekend. Don't worry. I wouldn't miss it for the world. I'll be there."

"That's great. I'll tell everyone at the game tonight. There's going to be loads of people at the party. Marty has a large family, and it sounds like Curt's inviting all of them. Jayleen said they were getting writer's cramp from addressing invitations." She laughed softly.

"Sounds like fun." Steve paused. "Listen . . . I'm sorry I jumped at you the other night, Kelly. I . . . I was worn out, I guess."

"Apology accepted," Kelly said. "Maybe you can catch up on sleep while you're here this weekend. Looks like you really need it."

"I'll try. Listen, another call is coming in. Talk to you later." He clicked off. Gone as quickly as he'd appeared.

Kelly dug the nearly finished hat from her bag and picked up where she left off knitting onto the double-point needles. Decreasing stitches every row. Closing the crown circle slowly. She'd only finished one row when she heard Jennifer's voice come behind her.

"Hey, I'm glad you're here." Jennifer pulled out the chair beside Kelly. "Have you gotten any calls from Curt or Jayleen to help with the party this weekend?"

"No, I haven't. It sounds like they have everything well under control."

Jennifer took out the burgundy-and-gold scarf and began to knit. "Those two are way too efficient for words. The last thing I heard from Mimi was they're expecting over a hundred people. Can they fit that many in Curt's ranch house?"

"Megan told us at practice that Curt's ordered canopied tents for the yard. So we'll be sprawled all over." Kelly examined the slowly shrinking crown circle. "It should be beautiful weather this weekend."

"Steve's coming up, isn't he?"

Kelly nodded. "He just called and said he'd be here. He also apologized for jumping all over me the other night."

Jennifer looked up. "Oh, good. I'm glad he did."

"So am I. I told him he needed to catch up on his sleep this weekend."

"That will help." Jennifer checked the row she was knitting before starting the next. "Hey, I've been meaning to tell you something, but I was so busy yesterday it slipped my mind. I was still in the café yesterday when your covert college informant Patty came in to talk. I saw you two together, and I realized that I've met her before. I waitressed with her last year at some of those university functions."

"I'm not surprised," Kelly said, eyeing the shrinking crown circle. She was almost finished. "Patty works over there several nights, she says. It helps her pay for courses. She also works at the steakhouse in the shopping center across the street."

"Well, I simply wanted to tell you to be careful. I wouldn't believe everything Patty says, if I were you."

Kelly's attention left the yarn quickly. She peered at her friend. "What do you mean?"

"I've seen her steal from people's purses on two separate occasions and lie about it afterwards."

Kelly drew back. "What! Tell me what happened."

"I was working one of those university banquets with her and lots of other wait-

318

resses and staff. For the really big functions, they bring in extra staff to bus tables and set up. Most of those kids aren't too experienced and they leave their coats and purses draped over chairs or hanging on wall pegs in the storage rooms. I always lock my purse in the trunk of my car when I'm working the university. Too many strangers wander those hallways. Valuables can disappear in an instant."

"And you're sure you saw her stealing from someone's purse?" Kelly asked. That didn't sound like the Patty she'd been interacting with this past month. Nor did it square with the image Barbara painted of sweet-natured, good-girl Patty.

"Not just one person's purse. I saw her riffle several women's purses. She'd move to where a coat was thrown, she'd riffle the purse and take what she wanted, then move to the next one. She was very careful, too. Always looking over her shoulder. I was behind a divider, so she didn't see me."

"What did she take? Money, cell phones, PDAs?"

Jennifer nodded. "And pill bottles. I saw her hold up several pill bottles and read what was in them, then pocket them."

"Really?" Kelly caught Jennifer's gaze.

"Really. And I personally witnessed one of

the girls ask Patty if she saw anyone going through her purse that evening. And Patty got all wide-eyed and innocent and said she hadn't seen a thing."

"That's disturbing to hear," Kelly admitted. "Patty has been my chief source for campus and party information."

"And she may be entirely truthful in this situation. After all, she knows all the players. But I thought I should share that experience with you, so you'll be on your guard. In case you hear her say something strange. Just keep your ears open."

"Thanks, Jen. I appreciate it. I was telling Burt the other day I've learned that people are seldom what they seem. This is another example, I guess. Although, I confess, this surprises me. Patty always seemed so down-to-earth and stable."

"And she may very well be. Those actions may have been a bump along the road for her. Maybe Patty has straightened herself out. So I don't want to malign her as much as warn you in your dealings with her."

Kelly heard the sound of Jennifer's cell phone beep, and Jen dug into her bag. "I don't recognize this number. It must be business," she said, rising from her chair. "I'll be back."

Kelly didn't mind. In fact, she welcomed

a few moments of quiet. She needed to knit on what she'd just learned about Patty. "Sweet girl" Patty was a thief and a liar. That was a shock. She'd always appeared to be straightforward and open. Then again . . .

That morning's earlier conversation with Barbara returned to dance about Kelly's brain. Clearly, Patty wasn't everything she appeared to be. Or . . . maybe she exhibited different character traits to different people. Straightforward and helpful with Kelly. Sweet-natured and daughterly with Barbara. Sneaky and opportunistic with her fellow waiters and waitresses.

Kelly threaded a darning needle with the last strand of yarn, pushed it through the tiny crown opening, and gathered the last stitches. Then she pulled the circle tight, closing it. She looped a knot into the yarn and tied that off, then wove the yarn ends beneath the stitches. All the time, her mind going a mile a minute. Questions bouncing around her brain.

Shoving her finished hat and phone into her bag, Kelly headed for the foyer. She gave a goodbye wave to Jennifer on her way out the door. Kelly wanted answers to some of these new Patty questions that were bedeviling her now. But who could she ask? Not Patty's friend Francesca. She would immediately alert Patty that Kelly was asking questions. And she certainly couldn't ask Tommy. He would never understand why she'd be curious about his "little sister" Patty.

Only one person came to mind. The only person who could be counted on not to call either Tommy or Patty afterwards. Someone who had given Kelly helpful but harsh information earlier.

Kelly jumped into her sporty car and revved the engine. If she hurried, she could get to the Grill café before Rachel Gebbard finished her lunch shift.

SEVENTEEN

Kelly stepped inside the Grill café and quickly scanned the nearby tables. The café was nearly empty. Only two tables were occupied with customers. She spotted two waitresses and neither of them was Rachel. A lone grill cook was behind the counter, and it looked as if he was cleaning. The lunch shift was either over or winding down.

Disappointed, Kelly turned to leave when Rachel walked in from a back hallway. Sweater on and backpack over her shoulder, she looked to be headed to the university.

Kelly gave her a friendly smile and approached the door as if she was leaving. "Hey, how're you doing? Looks like you're headed to class."

"Yeah, I've got most of my classes in the afternoons so I can work mornings and lunch," Rachel said as she walked through the café door Kelly held open.

"You remember my friend Jennifer? She

works Pete's Porch in the mornings and works afternoons in real estate. Are you still working the university catering at nights?"

"Every chance I get." Rachel pulled out her car keys. "Tell Jennifer to keep me in mind for her boss's jobs, too. I can always use the money."

That gave Kelly an opening. "Will do. Hey, can I ask you a question? You said you grew up with Tommy Macenroe, Holly Kaiser, and Patty Warren. So you know them pretty well."

Rachel's expression turned wary. "Yeah. What's your question?"

"Tommy's mother told me at the shop that she's worried about Patty. She says Patty is acting kind of erratic lately. I wondered if you ever saw her taking drugs or pills at parties and stuff."

"Sometimes. Patty used to do a lot more a couple of years back, but not as much now." Rachel's mouth twisted into a half smile. "Now, she just sells stuff."

"Really? You've seen her selling pills?" Kelly made her eyes look as innocently wide as possible. "Where does she get them?"

Rachel shrugged. "Steals them mostly. At least that's what she told me. She's been doing it for years. I've seen her going through people's purses at parties when they're not looking. Backpacks, too. She does it at every party."

"Wow, that's really weird," Kelly continued. "Jennifer told me she'd worked with Patty at some university catering jobs and saw her stealing from people's purses in the kitchen."

"That's why I leave my stuff in my car. Too easy to get ripped off."

"You know, I asked Patty where she thought Holly got those pills, and she told me you probably sold them to her."

Rachel scowled. "Patty's a bitch and a liar. I've never sold pills."

Kelly continued, wide-eyed. "Now I don't know whether to trust anything she's told me. She said someone picked up Holly from the party that night. Someone in a dark car."

"Well, Patty should know. She was standing outside in the front yard talking with Holly. Patty always hangs out with Holly at parties. It's like they're joined at the hip."

"Did you see Holly leave? I wondered if maybe that Greeley guy came to pick her up."

Rachel shook her head. "Naw, I didn't notice. I was only in the front yard for a while with some friends, then went inside when they caught a ride with Patty back to their dorms."

Kelly let that sink in. Barbara said Holly told her that Patty didn't bring her car to the party. Clearly, that was a lie. What else had Patty lied about?

"So, Patty brought her car?"

"Sure, everyone does unless they live nearby," Rachel said, turning to leave. "Listen, I'd better get to class. Be careful around Patty."

"You know, someone said Patty had a big crush on Tommy. Is that true?" Kelly asked as Rachel started to walk away.

Rachel turned, a smirk appearing. "Big time. Ever since we were kids. That's why she hung around Holly, I think. So she could get close to Tommy. Bye."

Kelly walked to her own car as Rachel's comments raced about her head. Clearly Jennifer's observation was not a one-time thing. Rachel had known Patty for years, and she said Patty stole from people regularly and sold the pills at parties.

That meant Patty had a ready supply of pills to sell or use.

Kelly revved the car engine as ideas started bouncing inside her head. Patty always hung around Holly at parties. Rachel said she saw Patty outside with Holly before she left. Clearly, Patty wasn't there when

Barbara picked up Holly. Barbara would have mentioned it. Patty had also lied about having her car with her. Why would she tell Holly she didn't bring her car? Did she want Holly to drive home with someone else? *Why?* Patty evidently didn't mind driving other partygoers home.

Kelly pulled into the parking lot of a corporate coffeehouse chain. She needed caffeine — now.

Rachel's no-nonsense observations about Patty rang true to Kelly. Rachel had no reason to lie. Her comments were cutting but not spiteful. She'd grown up with all three — Tommy, Holly, and Patty. Rachel knew them well. Apparently, she also knew their secrets.

Kelly strode into the coffee shop and gave her order to the barista. Midafternoon and the shop was less crowded. She dug out her cell phone and punched in the Lambspun shop number. Rosa answered.

"Hey, Rosa, good to hear you. How's the second job going?"

"Okay, but a little tiring. It's hard being on your feet all those hours straight behind a counter. At least here, we can sit down and wind yarns when there are no customers."

"Boy, Rosa, I hope the downturn turns

back up soon. Steve's having a hard time, too."

"Yeah, I heard. It's everywhere."

"Hey, could you give me Barbara Macenroe's number please? I don't have it."

"Sure, hold on. Let me check the computer."

Kelly paid the barista and headed for the door, hot coffee in hand. She heard Rosa come back on the line.

"Here it is." Rosa rattled off the number while Kelly memorized it. One of the good things about being an accountant: she could remember numbers.

"Thanks, Rosa. Take care of yourself and the family. See you soon." She clicked off, then punched in Barbara's cell number. "Hey, Barbara, Kelly here. I wondered if you knew if Holly had a roommate or not."

"Yes, she did. Real studious girl, too. Holly always made jokes about Catherine studying all the time when Holly was out. Too bad Holly didn't spend more time studying."

"Do you happen to know her last name?"

"Sorry, I don't. Are you planning to talk with her, Kelly?"

"Yeah, there are some things about Holly's last night that bother me."

"Like what?"

"Like who took Holly over to the river trail. I figure she must have called someone after you dropped her off at the apartment. That person must have given her the pills. I'm thinking it was that guy Eddie."

"You may never know, Kelly. Holly had obviously gotten involved with a lot of druggies. Maybe it was this Eddie. Maybe it was another friend."

"I know. But every time I learn something new, it leads to something else. Sort of like dangling yarns. Start to pull one strand, and more stitches unravel. Like a sweater."

"I can understand. Let me know what you learn, Kelly."

"I promise. By the way, where did Holly live? Which apartment complex?"

"She lived in one of those condos on West Stuart near Overland Drive. I can't remember the exact address, but it was Unit B, right next to the sidewalk."

"Thanks, Barbara. Talk to you later."

Kelly tossed her bag into her car and slid into the seat. Instead of starting the car, however, she touched the screen of her newer data phone to access the Internet. Finding a common search engine site, she entered *Holly Kaiser, Fort Connor, CO* and clicked, hoping to find Holly's actual address.

Within an instant the screen filled with various Holly Kaisers. Kelly skimmed the list until she found the correct one. *Holly Kaiser. 2222 Bainbridge Drive, Fort Connor, CO 80526.*

Kelly checked her watch, then started the car. She'd wait outside in her car until Holly's roommate came home. Hopefully, the roommate would come home before softball practice, but if not, then Megan would have to understand.

Kelly drained her coffee and checked her watch again. She'd been waiting outside Holly's apartment building for over an hour. She should have brought her laptop computer with her. But then . . . she would be engrossed in accounts and forget to watch for Holly's roommate. Unit B was right on the sidewalk like Barbara said. The front door and stoop faced the street, which made it easier to observe.

She switched radio stations, listening to whatever music distracted her from the waiting. Rock, jazz, pop, country. Whatever worked.

A small gray car pulled up to the curb, close to the front stoop of Unit B. Parked directly across the street, Kelly watched a young woman with sandy brown hair open the car door. Reaching inside the backseat, she pulled out a large backpack and slung it over her shoulder, then walked toward the entrance of Unit B.

Okaaaay. Kelly exited her car and hastened across the street, hoping to reach the young woman before she closed the front door. She appeared to be in her mid-twenties or so, graduate-student age. And from the drag of that backpack on her shoulder, it looked like there were plenty of books inside.

"Excuse me," Kelly called out as she walked up the sidewalk leading to Unit B. "Are you Catherine?"

The young woman spun around, her face registering concern. "Yes. Who are you?"

"My name is Kelly Flynn, and I live in Fort Connor, near the Lambspun knitting shop off Lemay." Kelly gestured in the distance.

A puzzled expression crossed Catherine's face. "Yes, I know that shop. It's next to a golf course, right?"

Kelly nodded. "That's right. Several of us at the shop knew your former roommate, Holly Kaiser. One of the shop instructors is the mother of Tommy Macenroe, who was Holly's boyfriend."

Catherine nodded slowly. "Okay, I see.

You're wondering about Holly's stuff. I packed up her things in several boxes and left them in her room. I figured I'd hear from Tommy one of these days. He needs to pick them up, because I'll be moving to a smaller apartment in December."

Kelly used Catherine's assumption as an opening and approached closer, taking her cell phone from her pocket. "Thank you. I'll tell Tommy, and I'm sure he'll schedule a time to pick them up. What's your cell number?"

Catherine ran through her number while Kelly punched it into her directory. "Tell Tommy nighttime is better. I'm studying and in classes during the day. Like he is." A look of concern crossed her face. "How's Tommy doing, by the way? He really looked awful at the funeral."

"He's trying to come to grips with it all," Kelly answered truthfully. "Some of us promised him we'd try to find some answers to what happened to Holly and let him know. It'll help him find closure, I guess."

Catherine looked skeptical. "I don't know what answers you can find. Holly finally took too many pills. I'd been watching her do this to herself every weekend for months and tried to warn her." She shrugged. "But she didn't want to listen. Those party

332

friends of hers were a bad influence. Every time Holly promised Tommy to stay away from the drugs, someone would give her a pill to try, and . . . she was gone again." Catherine made a helpless gesture.

Kelly followed up on that, encouraging Catherine to say more. "It sounds like Holly was hanging out with the wrong crowd and making some really bad choices."

"Oh, yeah. I thought she'd finally turned around in August. She didn't go to as many parties and went to the knitting shop every day. She'd even started classes again. But then she and Tommy had that big fight. I came home right after Tommy left. Holly was fuming. I tried to calm her down, but she didn't want to listen. She got on the phone and found out where the parties were. I begged her not to go, but she just ignored me and walked out the door."

"By any chance were you still awake when Holly came home that night? Tommy's mother Barbara picked her up from the party. She said she dropped Holly here at the apartment late that night."

"Yeah, I was." Catherine shifted the backpack on her shoulder. "I was up late trying to write a paper. You know, drinking a lot of coffee, trying to finish."

Kelly held up her hand with a smile. "Hey,

been there. Still there, sometimes."

Catherine smiled. "Well, then you know. I was almost finished when I heard Holly's voice outside. I got up to look out the window and saw a car pulling away and Holly walking on the sidewalk. I was about to go open the door when a girl got out of a car across the street and came over to talk to Holly."

Kelly felt her pulse speed up. "Did you recognize the girl by any chance? Was she one of Holly's friends?"

"Ohhhh, yeah." Catherine nodded. "It was her buddy, Patty."

"You're sure it was her?"

"Absolutely. Patty was over here a lot. She and Holly would come over and go into Holly's room. Do more pills or whatever." Catherine shook her head sadly. "That's who Holly called after her fight with Tommy. Patty told her some friends would pick her up for the party."

Kelly tried to quiet her racing thoughts and reached for one from the back. "When you saw Patty later that night, do you remember if she was wearing a jacket or anything? Something kind of heavy?"

Catherine glanced to the side. "Uhhhh, let me think." She closed her eyes. "Yeah, she had on a black jacket. It was kind of bulky, I remember that. Why do you ask?"

Kelly tried to keep her sleuthing zeal in check. "I think someone saw Patty later that night, somewhere she shouldn't have been. I was just checking." She deliberately left her answer evasive.

"I see," Catherine said, peering at Kelly. "Listen, I've got to grab some dinner inside so I can go back to the library. Tell Tommy to give me a call whenever he wants to pick up those boxes."

"Will do," Kelly replied with a wave. "Thanks so much, Catherine. You've been a big help. We'll be in touch." Then she turned and sped across the street to her car. Maybe she could track down Burt before she had to leave for the softball field.

Kelly maneuvered her car through Fort Connor's rush-hour traffic while she held the cell phone to her ear. "So what do you think, Burt? I'd like to have a little chat with Patty tomorrow, wouldn't you?"

"Yeah, Kelly, I think that's a good idea. I have to admit you've dug up some interesting information. I'd like to hear what Patty has to say. Who knows? Maybe she took Holly somewhere else to meet Eddie. We don't know."

Kelly thought about that while she turned

335

onto the avenue bordering Lambspun. That idea didn't feel right. "Anything's possible, Burt. But I have a feeling Patty is the one who gave Holly those pills, then dumped her off on the river trail."

"Well, I'm free tomorrow morning, if you want to try and set up something."

"Okay. I'll give Patty a call and see if she can come over to the café."

"What'll you tell her?"

"That I found out some new information about Barbara. That ought to bring her."

"You know, Kelly, Patty sounds like an accomplished liar. You might not get anything out of her."

"Yeah, I know, Burt. But I figure we've got enough to interest Detective Dan. She may be able to stonewall me, but I sense Patty won't be able to hold up under police questioning. Not for long, at least."

Burt chuckled. "I think you underestimate yourself, Kelly. Let's see what happens. Talk to you tomorrow. Oh . . . is Steve going to make it up here for the engagement party this weekend?"

"He'll be here. He's not about to miss Curt's steaks and Jayleen's chili. I'll call you as soon as I speak with Patty. Take care."

Kelly tossed the phone to the nearby seat and used both hands to turn into the driveway behind Lambspun. If she remembered correctly, there was some leftover pizza and wilted salad in the fridge. Not too appetizing, but with less than an hour before softball practice across town, she didn't have much choice.

EIGHTEEN

"Jump in whenever you want, Burt," Kelly suggested as she watched Patty walk to the rear of the café. Kelly had already chosen a quiet table in the corner, away from the other morning breakfast customers.

"I'll follow your lead, Kelly. Let's see where it goes." Burt relaxed back into the café chair and sipped his coffee.

"Hey, Patty, glad you could make it," Kelly said, raising her mug.

"Hey, Kelly. Hi, Burt," Patty said, pulling out a chair.

Burt raised his cup. "Good to see you, Patty. Want some coffee?"

"Yeah, I could use it." Patty settled across the table and dropped her backpack to the floor. "I got up a little earlier to come over here before classes start."

Kelly signaled the waitress to bring coffee. "When's your first class?" she asked Patty as Julie poured a black stream into her cup.

"Ten fifteen this morning. It's an economics class, so I need to be awake." She accepted the full mug. "Thanks, this will help."

"You in the business school?" Burt asked.

Patty took a quick sip. "Trying to be. Those courses are hard, though. That's why I'm taking it slowly, so I'll have enough time to study."

Kelly folded her arms on the table and leaned forward slightly, talking position. "Studying is good. I've seen too many students drop out of university because they party hardier than they study."

Patty's mouth quirked into a smile. "I can relate to that." She glanced over her shoulder, then leaned forward, matching Kelly's position. "So what was it you learned about Barbara?"

"Well, Burt and I sat down with her a few days ago right over there at that table." Kelly pointed across the café alcove. "And I told her a student at the party saw her pick up Holly that night. And recognized Barbara from the doctor's office."

Patty's eyes went huge. "*Whoa!* What did Barbara say?"

"She was totally surprised that anyone saw her. Barbara said she hadn't admitted she'd picked up Holly that night because she was afraid Tommy would blame her for what happened. You know, blame her for not watching Holly closer or something."

"We were *right!*" Patty jabbed her finger in emphasis. "That's exactly what you and I thought."

Kelly nodded. "Yeah. And we were right about Barbara taking Holly to her home. She said she was fixing up the guest room when Holly slipped out the front door . . ."

Patty sat up straight. "What? She took Holly to the apartment, not her house."

Kelly leaned forward and looked Patty straight in the eyes. "How did you know that, Patty? Was it because you were waiting in your car across the street from the apartment? Waiting for Barbara to drive Holly home?"

Patty's mouth fell open as she stared at Kelly. "What . . . what . . . ? *No!* What're you talking about?"

"Someone saw you waiting for Holly that night. As soon as Barbara dropped her off, you came across the street and started talking with Holly. Then Holly got in your car, and you drove off together." Kelly let her voice drop lower as she continued to hold Patty's startled gaze.

Fear flashed through Patty's eyes briefly, and all color drained from her cheeks. "Wha— That's impossible . . . I wasn't there! I was still at the party."

Kelly shook her head. "No you weren't, Patty. We have a witness who saw you leave the party earlier that night. In fact, you took several people back to their dorms. Then you drove over to Holly's apartment, didn't you? You knew Barbara would be dropping off Holly. I'll bet you told Holly to call Barbara. You knew Barbara couldn't refuse. But you were the one waiting for Holly when she came home."

"I . . . I don't know what you're talking about," Patty protested, voice softer.

"You've been feeding me bogus information all this time, haven't you, Patty? I'll bet you don't even have a friend named Francesca. *You* were the source. You knew everything Holly did at parties because you hung around with her all the time. And you told me whatever you wanted me to know."

Patty didn't answer. She just stared at Kelly with a startled expression. Kelly leaned even closer, still holding her gaze. "You picked up Holly and took her to the river trail, didn't you? But first, you gave her those pills. Enough to put her to sleep forever. With Holly gone, Tommy would be free. Free for you to become Tommy's girlfriend."

Patty's gaze darted from Kelly to Burt and

back again. Burt sat not saying a word, simply watching Patty with his calm policeman's stare. "What are you talking about? Tommy and I are old friends, that's all."

"But that wasn't enough for you, Patty, was it? You've wanted to be Tommy's girl for years. Everyone told me so. That's what you've always wanted, isn't it, Patty? That's why you hung around Holly all the time, to keep track of Tommy and to keep control of Holly. Keep supplying her with whatever pills she wanted. Holly trusted you, didn't she? So she'd take whatever you gave her, right? Even an overdose of death."

"What . . . what are you saying? I couldn't hurt Holly! She was my friend."

"We know about your stealing the pills, Patty," Kelly continued in a cold voice. "We've got witnesses who've seen you steal pill bottles from scores of purses and backpacks. That's how you maintained a stash of pills to sell at parties and to give to Holly."

Panic darted through Patty's eyes this time. "That's not true! People gave me those pills, honest."

Kelly narrowed her gaze. "They saw you going through the purses, Patty. At the university catered dinners. At parties. I'll bet you even stole some of Barbara's Oxycontin when she was having back problems, didn't you?" It was a wild guess, but Kelly threw it out there.

The answer flashed across Patty's guilty face. "I-I —" she stammered.

Kelly didn't wait for Patty to find the words. She kept pushing. "It's time to stop lying, Patty. You gave Holly those pills then left her on the river trail to fall asleep and die, didn't you?"

Patty shook her head, both arms clutching herself. "No, it wasn't me . . . it was that guy, Eddie . . . remember?"

Kelly didn't miss a beat. "You were wearing a bulky, dark, hooded jacket that night, Patty. From a distance in the dark, that old vagrant could easily mistake you for a guy."

Shock registered on Patty's face. "How . . . how did you know . . . ?"

"What you were wearing?" Kelly completed the sentence. "Because I spoke with someone who watched you outside Holly's apartment that night. Someone who recognized you and told me what you were wearing. That same person also told me how you regularly came over to Holly's apartment with a pocketful of pill bottles. Stolen pill bottles, weren't they?"

Patty's lower lip began to tremble as her eyes started to glisten. "I . . . I didn't mean to. I didn't mean to give her that many.

343

But . . . but she *asked* me to! She wanted to get high."

"I don't believe you, Patty. I think you gave Holly too many pills on purpose. You knew Holly and Tommy had a big fight because she called you. You told her about that night's party. You even got someone to pick her up. And you recognized your chance to get rid of Holly and make it look like an accident. Tommy would be free at last. Free for you."

Patty shook her head, tears spilling out. "No . . . no . . ."

"The medical examiner found food in Holly's stomach. I'll bet you drove her to a fast-food drive-thru and bought her something. Did you crush up the pills and dump them into a cola or some hot chocolate? I'm betting on the hot chocolate. It was a chilly night."

Again, Patty stared back at Kelly with that fearful, startled expression, but she didn't say anything. Kelly decided to try a deliberate bluff. "You know, some of those late night fast-food drive-thrus have security cameras now. I'll bet some of those tapes show you in your car with Holly, ordering. The police will find that interesting, don't you think?"

Kelly watched desperation flicker in

Patty's eyes. She glanced to Burt, then back to Kelly again. No safe harbor available. "I . . . I . . ." was all she managed.

Burt spoke up finally. His voice quiet. "You know, Patty, my old partner Dan is still looking into Holly's death. I'll be calling Dan with this new information. He's going to want to question you —"

"But *why?* I didn't do anything wrong! I . . . I was only trying to help Holly," Patty protested again.

Patty was still refusing to admit the guilt Kelly could see in her eyes. Frustrated, Kelly searched for something, some information that would jolt Patty. Catch her by surprise and maybe put a crack in that stone wall of denial she was hiding behind.

Suddenly, Kelly knew. It jumped right in front of her eyes. Something she knew, but Patty didn't. And it wasn't a bluff. It was the truth.

"You know, Patty. All of your scheming and lying has been for nothing. You can't have Tommy. He's already got a new girlfriend. He's worked with her for years, and they've fallen in love. In fact, she's moving in with him."

Patty whipped her head around and stared at Kelly, clearly shocked by what she'd heard. "That . . . that can't be. Tommy loves *me!* He told me so!"

"Sorry, Patty. Tommy has already admitted it to Burt. And I've met the girl. Really nice girl, too. She's a paramedic."

Color flooded Patty's face now. *"No!* He can't! He's supposed to be with *me.* He told me he *loved* me! But . . . but he was with Holly, so . . . so . . ."

"He loved you like a *sister*," Kelly deliberately goaded.

"No! He really loved me! I *know* he did! But he was bound to Holly."

Kelly leaned her chin on her hand. "Tommy was at his new girl's house the night Holly died. I know because he told us so."

Patty's face started to crumble, and tears streamed down her cheeks. "No, no, he can't. He's supposed to love *me! Tommy belongs with me . . . he always has . . . even Barbara said so.* He loves *me . . .* he loves *me . . .* I did it for him . . . for Tommy . . . he belongs with me. . . ."

Burt leaned over and placed his hand on Patty's arm. "Dan is a very understanding man, Patty. You can explain everything to him." Burt pushed back his chair, clearly underscoring his statement.

Panic claimed Patty's face at the sound of the chair scraping against the wooden floor.

She clutched her hands to her chest. "No, I don't want to go! Please don't make me go!" she cried.

Nearby customers turned their heads at the disturbance. Burt placed his hand on Patty's shoulder in a reassuring fashion and leaned over to speak quietly. "Then the police will have to show up at your apartment or your workplace, Patty. Believe me, it would be better if you come down to the department with me now and give your statement. I promise I'll stay with you the entire time."

Patty looked up at Burt beseechingly. "Please, please! Don't leave me alone!"

Burt offered his hand for her to stand up. "I won't, Patty. I promise."

Patty stared at Burt's hand for several seconds, then allowed him to help her to her feet. "I'll miss my classes. Maybe . . . maybe I should wait."

"It's better to give a statement while it's fresh in your mind, Patty." Burt picked up Patty's backpack and took her elbow. "We'll go out Lambspun's front door. It's quieter," he suggested, guiding her toward the hallway.

Kelly watched Burt escort Patty out. All of Patty's lies had been stripped away. All the lies she'd told to Tommy and Kelly and

Barbara, to everyone. Even the lies Patty told herself. All of them were wiped away by the truth.

Tommy didn't love Patty. At least, not the way Patty wanted. Tommy loved someone else. "Little sister" love hadn't been enough for Patty. She'd wanted more. And her delusions led her on a deadly path. She'd found the perfect way to "get rid" of Holly. By leaving Holly on the river trail, Patty knew everyone would assume Holly was simply repeating her previous drug experience. This time with tragic, unintended results. An unfortunate accidental overdose.

Draining her coffee, Kelly rose from the table and walked toward the knitting shop slowly. She felt cold inside. She needed to surround herself with something warm and nurturing. Friends in the shop, Mimi's smiling face. Sit at the library table and strike up a conversation with someone who'd recently fallen down the rabbit hole like she did years ago.

She walked into the central yarn room and started touching everything in sight. Sinking her hands into bins of alpaca, merino wool, bamboo and silk, crisp ribbon yarns, and nubbly, bulky ones.

Her knitting bag was still on the library table. Was there any unfinished project stuffed in the bottom? She could relax for a while before returning to her cottage and client accounts. Steve wouldn't be driving back into town until tomorrow evening, Friday, for the party. Maybe they could go out Saturday night all by themselves. A night at the Jazz Bistro would be nice. She was tired of pizza dates. She wanted jazz and a good martini. That settled it. She'd make reservations for Saturday night.

The front door swung open and a frazzled-looking Megan appeared in the foyer. She had that look Kelly had seen before. The "wedding prep overload" look.

"Hey, how're you doing?" Kelly greeted her.

Megan hitched her shoulder bag over her shoulder as she approached and fixed Kelly with a warning look. "Don't even ask. I've been visiting caterers for the last four mornings. Do you have any idea how many things can be spread on a cracker?"

Kelly smiled as she beckoned her friend toward the café. "C'mon, let's get some coffee while you lecture me on canapés."

NINETEEN

Kelly selected from the variety of Colorado microbrews spread on Curt's kitchen counter. Finding her favorite ale, she grabbed two — one for her and one for Steve — then made her way back outside again.

Curt's ranch house and front yard were filled with Marty's and Megan's friends, relatives, and co-workers. There had to be nearly two hundred people there. Children of all ages ran and jumped and chased each other through the grass. The yard ran adjacent to a pasture that was empty of sheep at the time, so children gamboled there instead. The weather was late September perfect — warm and sunny with trees changing colors in the distance.

Kelly surveyed the crowd. Surely they weren't all coming to the wedding, were they? Megan and Marty would be in debt for years trying to pay for the festivities.

One year wouldn't be enough to save. Judging from what Megan had been telling her, Kelly figured Megan and Marty's budget was blown already.

She wandered toward the lawn chairs her friends had spread in a haphazard semicircle, handed Steve a beer, then settled into the chair beside him. Kelly savored the familiar ale's flavor. "I won't need to eat tomorrow," she said, leaning back. "That was one fantastic meal."

"Yeah, it's hard to beat Curt's steaks and Jayleen's chili," Lisa said as she sipped wine from a plastic glass.

Megan leaned her head back and closed her eyes. "Why did I have that second piece of carrot cake? *Why?*"

"I'm waiting for your blueberry pie," Steve said, then tipped back his beer.

Kelly glanced over at Steve. He was slouched in the lawn chair, looking more relaxed than she'd seen him in weeks. More important, he looked happy. He was clearly enjoying being in the midst of old friends, laughing and joking with Marty and Greg like before. Before his career went down the tubes.

Marty and Greg sauntered up, chocolate chip cookies in hand. "Boy, am I stuffed," Greg said as he plopped into a chair.

"Me, too," Marty said right before he took a huge bite of cookie.

"I can't believe Jayleen grilled a whole salmon for you, Greg," Kelly said.

"Ahhhh . . . delicious." Greg patted his stomach.

"Why are you two still eating?" Megan asked, staring at the cookies.

"Force of habit," Lisa answered. "They can't help themselves. Wait'll they turn forty. Then they'll start to cut back."

"*Never,*" Greg protested, then munched his cookie. "I'll just cycle more."

"Everyone's skinny in my family," Marty declared as he started on the next cookie.

"Stop bragging," Jennifer said as she and Pete sank into some chairs.

"Those steaks were too good," Pete said after tasting his beer. "No way could the café afford to buy steaks like that. Curt's are aged prime beef."

"Why don't you guys have a barbeque for your wedding? Maybe we could all do a potluck or something," Greg suggested, from behind his beer bottle.

"Ohhhh, don't even mention wedding food," Megan said, shaking her head. "If I never see another caterer again, it'll be too soon."

Pete chuckled. "Starting to get to you,

huh? Now you know why I don't do weddings anymore."

"Megan ran through the list of canapés the other day over coffee. It must have taken five minutes." Kelly lifted her bottle.

"What're canapés again?" Greg asked Lisa.

"All sorts of tasty things spread on crackers or toast points," Megan answered instead. "I swear, I must have seen hundreds of samples. I can't keep them all straight, let alone choose some."

"Stuff spread on a cracker? That won't do it for me, Megan. Nor the groom." Greg wagged his head.

"Careful, don't get her started," Marty warned. "She's got a short fuse on this."

Instead, Megan leaned over and sank her head in her hands. "This is driving me crazy. The caterers are all too expensive. The hotels and banquet halls are already booked by other people. And the only rooms that are left are too small." She looked up and gestured around the yard. "Look at all these people. Where are we going to put them? There's no place that can hold us all. At least, none that we can afford."

"Are you seriously going to invite everyone here?" Kelly asked.

Megan gestured helplessly. "How can we

not? Now that Curt's invited them to this engagement party, they'll all expect invitations to the wedding. How can we not invite them?"

"Easy. Just tell 'em, 'Dude, you're out!' " Greg jerked his thumb to the side.

Megan ignored him. "I don't know what we're going to do, guys. We're saving up for this, but we want to save for the down payment on a house, too. And we don't want to blow it all on a wedding."

"That's smart thinking," Jennifer said.

"You know, you don't have to have a big splashy reception, Megan," Lisa suggested. "Seriously. Why don't you scale down? Have it simpler. Greg can eat canapés and like it."

"I can?" Greg looked incredulous. Lisa gave him a swat.

"I think that's a good idea," Steve weighed in. "That way you'll be able to get a good deal on a house, especially in today's market."

"Yeah, and we're gonna buy one of yours," Marty announced. "There's one next to Greg and Lisa that we've been keeping an eye on."

"*What!* Who said you could be neighbors?" Greg protested.

Steve laughed softly. "Well, I'll guarantee

you get a good deal, guys."

"Fantastic!" Lisa said. "That's a great house. I've peeked in the windows."

"Jennifer took us in for a look around last week. It's got a different layout than Greg and Lisa's next door. And four bedrooms instead of three." Marty grinned. "We need separate offices."

"I can understand that," Kelly said. "Some of us like quiet." She noticed Burt approach their half circle. "Hey, Burt. Quite a spread, wasn't it?"

Burt patted his stomach. "You bet. I think I ate my ration of heart-attack food for the entire week."

"Heart-attack food? I don't even want to know what that is," Jennifer shuddered. "It's probably my normal diet."

"Mimi keeps me eating healthy." Burt grinned. "Kelly, you got a minute? I wanted to update you after my talk with Dan."

Kelly immediately set her beer aside and rose from the chair. "Sure. Let's go over where it's quieter."

"What've you been up to, Kelly?" Greg asked.

"Sleuthing again," Megan answered. "She's been poking around for a while now."

"Poking around in what?" Marty asked, eyebrow cocked.

Kelly decided to downplay her recent activities. "Oh, I was simply following up Tommy's concerns after Holly's death, that's all." She made a dismissive gesture.

"She did a lot more than that," Burt added. "Holly's death was thought to be accidental, but Kelly kept digging and asking questions until she found the person responsible for giving Holly those pills. And it appears she deliberately gave Holly an overdose of opiate painkillers."

Jennifer's eyes went wide. "Are you talking about who I think you are?"

Kelly nodded. "Yes, we are. Other people saw Patty stealing pill bottles, too. And regularly giving Holly pills."

"Wow . . ." Jennifer said softly.

"After Kelly got through questioning her, Patty was glad to talk with my old partner Dan." Burt smiled. "I swear, Kelly's a natural interrogator."

"She's a Rottweiler. I've seen her in action," Lisa decreed.

"I like her innocent routine best," Jennifer weighed in. "That works well, too."

Kelly shrugged, holding up both hands. "Hey, whatever works."

"What worked with this Patty girl?" Greg asked.

"Patty was a challenge. I'd learned that

she was a thief and an accomplished liar. So I had to sneak up on her."

Burt chuckled. "It was fascinating to watch. Kelly chatted her up for a while and waited for an opening, then she pounced. Grabbed hold and didn't let go."

"That's not a Rottweiler. That's a pit bull," Pete said.

"Hey, my uncle has a pit bull. He's a nice dog," Greg added.

"Kelly's nice, too," Lisa joked.

Kelly noticed Steve observing her as laughter rippled around the half circle. He hadn't said a word. Kelly decided to make her exit before someone asked her another question. She and Burt walked over to one of the few places in the yard that wasn't filled with people.

"So what's happening?" she asked. "Yesterday afternoon you said Patty admitted to Dan that she picked up Holly from the apartment, gave her the pills, then dropped her off on the river trail."

"That's right. She's got a court-appointed lawyer and will be brought before a judge on Monday. Meanwhile, she's been charged and is in custody now. There may be additional charges, too, because Dan got a search warrant for Patty's apartment. Patty's roommate let them in, and Dan found a whole stash of other people's pill bottles. All of them prescription painkillers, obviously stolen. Vicodin, Percocet, and Oxy-Contin, everything you'd find on the street. Plus, they also found a scale and plastic Baggies, which shows intent to distribute. All of that strengthens the case and leads to a longer sentence."

Kelly nodded. "That makes sense." She was about to say something else when her attention was drawn to Megan's frantic gesturing.

"Kelly, Burt, come over here!" Megan beckoned, clearly excited about something. Kelly noticed Jayleen had joined her friends.

"Looks like our presence is required," Burt said as they rejoined the group.

"You'll never guess what Jayleen has done!" Megan cried, face flushed. "She's offered to let Marty and me have our ceremony and reception at her ranch next year! In that gorgeous meadow! Isn't that *wonderful?*"

"Whoa! That's fantastic news!" Kelly enthused, giving her excited friend a hug. "Those views are gorgeous from that pasture."

"That is really generous of you, Jayleen," Burt said.

Jayleen gave a dismissive gesture and

smiled. "It's my pleasure, believe me. I'd been hearing from Curt about the hard luck these kids were having trying to nail down a pretty place for their wedding. So I decided I'd give Megan and Marty their wedding gift early. Besides, you know how I love to have folks over."

"Well, you're surely going to have a whole bunch coming for that occasion," Kelly said. "Judging from how many are here now, even your big pasture will be full."

Jayleen gave her trademark hearty laugh. "The more the merrier, Kelly."

"Pasture means animals. Does that mean we'll be stepping around alpaca piles while we're there?" Greg teased.

"Thanks for mentioning that, Greg. I'll put you on poop patrol," Jayleen said with a wicked grin. "You can be Head Pooper-Scooper."

Kelly stepped inside the darkened cottage and flipped on the lights. Steve followed after her and tossed his keys to the entry table beside the front door.

"I'm thirsty. Do you want some milk?" Kelly asked as she headed to the kitchen.

"No, I'm fine," Steve said, walking to the patio door. He slid open the glass. "Hey, Carl, c'mon in, big guy." Carl raced inside the cottage and immediately jumped around for pats and doggy rubs, which Steve provided — complete with doggy noises.

Kelly brought out a mug filled with milk and settled into the easy chair across from the sofa. Her favorite sitting spot. Carl raced up to Kelly for a head and ear scratch, and she obliged.

"That was so much fun," she said as Carl thrust his head onto her lap for more. More, more. There was never enough.

Steve sank into the sofa. "Yeah, it was. Marty and Megan make a perfect couple. They're made for each other."

"I know. Nobody but Marty could have gotten past Megan's shy barrier. He sneaked up on her." Kelly slipped off her shoes and put her feet on the coffee table between them.

Steve did the same. "It was fun to watch. I almost couldn't believe he had a strategy. He was such a total klutz, he made it look completely natural. Megan never saw him coming." Steve relaxed against the sofa cushions and took a turn stroking Carl's head.

Carl was clearly in doggy heaven. He had his beloved owner Kelly and his beloved Steve in the same room again. Consequently, Carl was ping-ponging back and forth between both "beloveds" in an orgy of doggy rubs and pats.

"Boy, I hope they put a lid on those wedding expenses," Kelly said in between sips. "It makes much more sense to save up money for a down payment on their first house. Especially now when prices have dropped."

"Oh, yeah," Steve agreed, rubbing an ecstatic Carl's belly. "I'll definitely give them a great deal. I'll even shave off some bare-bones costs."

"Can you afford that?" Kelly peered at him.

He smiled at her. "Not really, Ms. CPA. But I want to do it anyway. It can be my wedding present."

"That's nice of you, Steve. Financially crazy, but nice," she teased.

"Hey, I'm a nice guy."

He certainly was, Kelly agreed. That would be a very generous wedding present, given that Steve was holding on by his fingernails right now. Maybe by next year, though, the housing market would pick up. One could only hope.

Carl rested his chin on Steve's knee, and Steve continued to stroke his shiny black head. After another minute of quiet patting, Steve looked across at Kelly. "So, what do say, Kelly? Why don't *we* get married? We've been seeing each other longer than Megan and Marty."

Kelly was about to take another sip of milk, but Steve's question stopped the mug halfway to her lips. She stared at Steve, stunned by the question. It came out of nowhere.

"What?" she said after several seconds.

Steve leaned forward, elbows on his knees. "We could move into one of the vacant houses over there at the Wellesley site with Megan and Marty and Greg and Lisa. It would be fun. You know . . . getting together for movies and barbeques."

Kelly's head started buzzing with images. Marriage? Fun? Movies? Barbeques? *Marriage?* Thoughts tumbled over one another in total confusion. Speech deserted her. She kept staring at Steve, wide-eyed.

Steve peered at her. "Kelly?"

"Uhhhh . . ." was all she could manage.

Steve sat back. He studied Kelly's shocked expression, not saying anything.

Kelly realized she needed to say something. Steve was looking at her with an expression she'd never seen before. Disappointment.

"I . . . I don't know what to say," she stammered.

"I think you just did," Steve said in a flat tone. "Total shock."

"That's . . . that's because it was so . . . so sudden . . ."

He arched a brow. "*Sudden?* We've known each other over two years and been living together for over a year."

Feeling uncharacteristically clumsy, Kelly sought to explain her reaction again. "Not that kind of sudden. I . . . I mean out-of-the-blue sudden. . . ."

"Out of the blue," Steve repeated in a cool voice.

"I mean . . . you're fighting to keep your business afloat. And you're working two jobs in Denver. Not getting enough sleep . . ."

"You think this is a sleep-deprived suggestion?" he barbed.

Kelly realized she was digging herself deeper and didn't have a way out. Everything she said, all the justifications she pointed out couldn't erase her look of total astonishment when Steve asked if she wanted to marry him.

"No . . . no . . . I don't mean . . . Steve, you're hanging on by your fingernails! And you want to get *married?*" she cried, honesty overcoming moderation.

Steve studied her for another long minute. "I guess not." He rose from the sofa. Carl brushed against his hand for a pat, but Steve ignored him. "I think you and I need some time to think about our relationship."

Kelly stared at him, thought processes beginning to function once more. Brain cells coming back online. "What? What're you talking about?"

"I'm talking about us, Kelly. I thought we were building a future together. Apparently I was mistaken." Steve fixed her with a stranger's gaze.

This time, Kelly's mouth dropped open. But speech didn't desert her this time. "*What?* Steve! You're misinterpreting my reaction. I . . . I was just surprised, that's all!"

"I didn't misinterpret anything, Kelly. Your answer was written all over your face, and it was *no.*"

Steve turned and walked toward the front door, Carl tagging behind. Kelly jumped out of her chair and followed after him. "Steve, wait! Don't leave! Let me explain. . . ."

Steve opened the door, then leaned down to give Carl another pat. "Gotta go, big guy." He glanced up at Kelly. "You've explained enough, Kelly. I'm going to bunk in with Greg and Lisa."

"What? *Steve!* Wait a minute!"

But Steve had already closed the door behind him.

TWENTY

The shower spray hit Kelly right in the face. Hot, hot water. It felt good. Maybe the heat could warm up the cold feeling in her gut.

Kelly had tossed and turned the entire night in fitful, restless sleep. Images of Steve walking out the door and the expression on his face kept waking her up.

It was obvious that Steve had interpreted her shock and surprise at his sudden proposal as rejection. Rejection of the proposal — and rejection of *him.* But that was wrong. She wasn't rejecting Steve. Just the crazy idea of getting married in the midst of chaos.

Kelly lathered the shower beads over her body and let the water rinse them away. She knew she'd blundered badly when she didn't respond to him right away. But . . . she couldn't. She really had been shocked. And she couldn't hide it.

Steve's idea of getting married when he

was in the midst of a career meltdown and financial disaster made absolutely no sense to Kelly. It was *crazy*. And her reaction reflected only her opinion of the *idea* — not her feelings for Steve.

Kelly rinsed shampoo from her hair while other responses came to mind — more moderate responses. Less shock, more sympathy. Unfortunately, it was too late. Kelly's natural response to most things was direct, forthright, and honest — not moderate. That direct approach had always served her well, until last night.

Turning off the shower, Kelly stepped out and toweled dry. Her insides were still churning. She knew she had screwed up. Steve didn't want sympathy last night. He wanted affirmation, and he didn't get it. And it stung.

But why did he have to overreact and walk out? That was so extreme. Steve *knew* she loved him. How could he doubt her?

Kelly checked her watch and grabbed the blow-dryer. She wanted to grab some coffee before she headed off for Warner's retail development near Brighton. Warner had scheduled a Saturday meeting with his staff and wanted her there. She'd be up to her neck in business all day, and that was good.

There was no time to brood over what had

happened last night. Plus, it would give Steve some time to think and realize he'd overreacted. It was so out of character for him. Steve wasn't like that. Not at all. He'd come to his senses and call her. Surely he would.

However, no matter how hard Kelly's logical side tried to script a reasonable, sensible conclusion to her misunderstanding with Steve, the cold feeling in her gut didn't go away.

"Hey, Kelly. You have time to chat?" Megan beckoned from the café alcove.

Kelly noticed Megan sitting at a table with Lisa in the quieter section of the café. Since Steve had bunked in with Greg and Lisa last night, Kelly figured her friends were curious as to what was going on. She glanced at her watch. The interstate was fifteen minutes away.

"I've got five minutes, guys," she said as she approached their table. "I'm on the way to a client's Brighton development."

"On a Saturday?" Megan asked.

"Yeah, my new developer client called a staff meeting."

"Okay, we'll make it short," Lisa jumped in, her face registering her concern. "What in *hell* is going on with you and Steve? He showed up at our house last night right as we were getting into bed. And boy, was he in a black mood. He didn't want to talk at all, not to Greg or to me. He just asked for some blankets and a pillow and slept on the sofa. He was up and gone this morning before we woke up."

"Did you guys have an argument or something?" Megan asked, her pretty face pinched with worry.

"Not really. It was more of a . . . a difference of opinion." Kelly took a sip of the scalding hot brew.

"What! That's *crazy!*" Lisa exploded. "What could you two possibly disagree about?"

Kelly paused for a second. "Steve asked me if I wanted to get married. And instead of answering him, I just stared at him in total shock. I mean . . . it came out of nowhere."

Both Lisa and Megan took in their breaths and sat back.

"You said yes, right?" Megan asked.

"No, she didn't," Lisa said softly, worry claiming her face now.

"You're right, I didn't. I was so stunned by the idea that I couldn't answer at all. Not at first. Unfortunately, Steve took that as rejection. Of *him.*" She took another big

369

sip. "I wasn't rejecting him, just the idea. I mean, it's crazy! He's watching his entire career go down the tubes, and he's in the midst of financial chaos, and he wants to get *married?*" she said, incredulously.

"And what did Steve say to that?" Megan asked, chewing her nail.

"Don't ask," Lisa said in a flat tone. "I gather he didn't take it well."

"Ohhhh, no. Steve told me we needed some time to *think* about our relationship." Kelly took a big drink before adding the rest. "Then he said he thought we were building a future, but now he *guessed* he was wrong."

Megan made an anxious noise and kept chewing.

"Oh, brother," Lisa said, glancing to the side.

"I mean, I was stunned. He came out of nowhere with this idea . . . and I know I screwed up by not answering him right away, but . . . I was so shocked my brain wouldn't work and no words came out. I tried to explain, but he said my answer was written all over my face, and it was no. Then he walked out."

"Oh, no . . ." Megan's face puckered. She looked like she might cry any minute.

Lisa took a deep breath and placed both

hands flat on the table. "Okay, okay . . . Steve's under a lot of stress now, we all know that. And you know that suggestion was inspired by —"

"By his feelings of insecurity, yes. I know that, Ms. Psychologist. Steve was looking to me for affirmation and reassurance and . . . I dropped the ball." She sighed. "Unfortunately, there's no 'do over' here."

"Actually, I was going to say that Steve was inspired by Megan and Marty's engagement party. You know, happy and carefree. But I have to admit your answer is closer to the truth. Listen, Steve will calm down, I know he will," Lisa reassured her. "I've known him since grade school. He's an even-tempered guy —"

"Not anymore," Kelly interrupted. "I hadn't told you two, but Jennifer knows. Steve's been really short-tempered and snapping at me for weeks now. Last Monday he got positively snarky with me and blew up over a little thing." She stared out into the café. "Part of me believes Steve will come to his senses once he has some time to think. Then again . . . part of me isn't so sure. And that's got my gut all twisted in a knot."

Neither Lisa nor Megan said anything else. They simply watched her.

Kelly glanced at her watch. More than five minutes had passed. Deadlines pressed. "Thanks, guys. I really appreciate your letting me talk, but I've gotta go now. It's a long drive to Brighton." She pushed back her chair.

"Kelly . . . it's going to be all right," Lisa said in a quiet voice, looking into Kelly's eyes. "The stress is obviously getting to Steve, and it's affecting him. He . . . he just needs some space. Just give him some space . . . and be patient."

"Lisa's right. It'll be all right," Megan reassured, her eyes bright.

"Thanks, guys," Kelly said, then turned and walked toward the café's back door, giving a wave to busy Jennifer as she did.

Everything Lisa and Megan said made sense. But . . . they hadn't seen the look on Steve's face. She did. And every time she remembered, her gut twisted.

Kelly pulled her car into the parking area in front of her cottage. No sign of Steve's truck, she noticed. But then, it was only four o'clock in the afternoon. Too soon for Steve to be here . . . *if* he decided to come home.

She grabbed her briefcase and bag and headed for the front door. Maybe there was some leftover pizza in the fridge. Hunger had gnawed at her all the way home, but she hadn't stopped. Something kept urging her to drive. Drive.

Tossing her keys onto the nearby table, Kelly dropped her briefcase and bag into a chair and headed for the kitchen. She only took a few steps before she stopped.

Something was wrong. The living room looked different, somehow. She couldn't tell what it was, but it looked . . . off. She glanced around the cottage's small living room and dining area. Everything was in place. Carl was outside the patio door waiting to be let in to greet her.

Kelly decided she was probably tired from the long day and continued toward the bedroom to get out of her business suit and into some sweats. Then, scour the fridge for food. She was starving. . . .

Kelly walked into the bedroom, then stopped and stared. The bedroom closet door was wide-open. Her clothes were hanging on the right side, neat as usual, but Steve's clothes were gone. All gone. Shoe boxes from the top shelf were gone. Ties hanging on the rack. Gone. The cold feeling in her gut spread.

She stepped over to the dresser and opened the second drawer, even though she knew what she would see. Nothing. It was empty. Steve's clothes were gone. She checked the other drawers, robot-like, but they were empty, too. Scanning the room, Kelly saw where Steve had taken his mementos he'd had sitting on the dresser top. All gone.

Kelly wandered back to the living room and looked around again. Now she knew what had looked different when she first arrived. Books were missing from the bookshelves. Music players sitting on a shelf; stacks of CDs and DVDs . . . all gone. Steve had taken everything that was his . . . and left.

Her eye glimpsed a piece of white paper on the dining-room table. She recognized Steve's handwriting and felt her stomach clench. Picking it up, she read:

I think it would be a good idea for us to take some time away from each other. We need to think.

Kelly stared at the note and the empty shelves and felt tears press behind her eyes. Old fears crept from the back of her mind — where she thought she'd buried them. They were still there, waiting to whisper in her ear.

What's wrong with you, Kelly? Everyone you've ever loved leaves you. Either they die or they walk out.

Tears trickled down her cheeks, and she brushed them away with the back of her hand. Then the oldest fear of all slithered out of the bushes.

Even your mother left you. What's wrong with you? What's wrong . . . ?

Suddenly the front door banged open. Kelly spun around and saw Jennifer standing in the doorway, a stricken look on her face.

"Oh, Kelly . . . Lisa and Megan told me. I'm . . . I'm so sorry," Jennifer said as she approached, arms open. "I saw Steve drive away a few minutes ago."

Tears poured out now as Kelly ran to Jennifer and threw herself into her friend's embrace.

BRAIDED KNIT SCARF

This scarf pattern was created by Kim Manning of Denver, Colorado, who chooses to describe herself as a "devoted reader." Kim is much more than that. She's a very talented knitter as well as a hardworking part-time bookseller at the Barnes & Noble bookstore in Southwest Denver. Kim chose a soft acrylic yarn for this scarf because the soft texture allowed it to braid easily. She also mentioned she chose the available yarn called Caron Simply Soft Eco partly because 20% of it is made from recycled plastic bottles. She created a beautiful tricolor green scarf for me, and I love wearing it. Plus, it's good for the environment!

Level:
Beginner

Materials:
3 skeins of complementary colors (approximately 110 yards per skein)
US size 10 1/2 needles
stitch holders or large safety pins

Gauge:
4 stitches per inch

Instructions:
Color A: Cast on 10 stitches. Knit every row until the scarf measures 60″ or to desired length. Place on stitch holder or large safety pin.
Repeat for Colors B and C.
Braid the three knitted strips, adding stitches to the rows that need them to stay even. (Usually the middle row will need added stitches.) You'll lose about five inches with the braiding.
When you're satisfied with the lengths, bind off the ends. Tie the strips together about 1 1/2 inches from the end, using yarn from all three colors. Repeat tie at the other end. *(Kim adds that she prefers a tight braid that actually resembles intarsia.)*
Now you're finished, and you have a lovely warm scarf. And it was simple, too.

ALEX HAZARD'S "TRIPLE THREAT TRIPLE LAYER" CARROT CAKE

I met Alex when I was visiting my daughter Christine, who lives in Fairfax, Virginia. Alex's family and Christine's family are great friends. I was fascinated by Alex's descriptions of his recipes and "his restaurant." I have no doubt that Alex will create that restaurant one day. Once I heard about his carrot cake, I knew I had to include it in a Kelly Flynn mystery. Meanwhile, here's Alex in his own words:

"Alex Hazard is an eight-year-old junior chef. He has been cooking up the idea of owning a restaurant since he was three, when his brother had a painting of Monet's entered into an art show. Alex named his imaginary restaurant Monet's Garden. He is always adding new recipes to his menu, but the first recipe was for his Triple Layer Carrot Cake with coconut icing. He started cooking in his mind and, just last year, he had some cooking lessons from a great chef in Middleburg, Virginia. Now he is bringing his ideas and recipes to the kitchen, and usually they make it to our table."

Carrot Cake
1 1/2 cups flour
1 teaspoon baking soda
2 cups grated carrots (with cheese grater or food processor)
1 can crushed pineapple
3/4 cup vegetable oil
1 1/2 cups white sugar
3 large eggs
1 teaspoon cinnamon
1 teaspoon nutmeg
1/2 cup chopped pecans

Preheat oven to 375 degrees F. Grease and flour a Bundt cake pan.
Stir together the flour and baking soda. In a large, separate bowl, combine the carrots, drained pineapple, oil, sugar, eggs, cinnamon, and nutmeg. Add the flour mix to the carrot mixture and beat together on medium speed for two minutes. Fold in the nuts. Pour into the prepared pan. Bake for 45 minutes or until a skewer inserted in the middle of the cake comes out clean. Cool ten minutes in the pan, then flip the cake out of the pan and finish cooling on rack. Slice the cake in thirds and ice between the

layers and on top. Sprinkle the top with coconut.

Note from Alex: If you are out of time and need a quick and easy Triple Threat carrot cake to serve to your friends at the book club meeting, cook a boxed carrot cake mix in a Bundt pan and cool completely. Frost the cake with cream cheese frosting and sprinkle with nuts and coconut.

Icing
8 ounce package of cream cheese (softened)
3 tablespoons butter (softened)
1 1/2 cups confectioners' sugar
1 1/3 teaspoons orange zest
1 tablespoon fresh orange juice

Mix/beat until smooth.

ABOUT THE AUTHOR

Maggie Sefton was born and raised in Virginia, where she received her bachelor's degree in English literature and journalism. Maggie has worked in several careers over the years, from a CPA to a real estate broker in the Rocky Mountain West. However, none of those endeavors could compare with the satisfaction and challenge of creating worlds on paper. She is the mother of four grown daughters, currently scattered around the globe. Author of the nationally bestselling Knitting Mysteries, she resides in the Rocky Mountains of Colorado with two very demanding dogs. Please visit Maggie at her author website: www.maggie sefton.com.